JULIA

will "make your flesh creep. . . . Is Julia Lofting's husband coldly plotting to drive her insane? Is she unbalanced by the death of her child? Or is she truly being haunted by the ghost of a quite obscenely nasty little girl whose spirit appears to infest the Loftings' fashionable London house? You'll have to find out for yourself. . . ."   —*Cosmopolitan*

"Genuinely frightening . . . a taste for the depraved."
            —*Chicago Tribune*

"I haven't read anything that so terrifyingly evoked the presence of evil and supernatural threat since *The Exorcist. Julia* may be better."
            —*Buffalo Evening News*

"A crazy quilt of horror."   —*Milwaukee Journal*

"Definitely spooky . . . Julia is haunted and haunting in this clever, frightening, well-told tale."
            —*Publishers Weekly*

Julia

Peter Straub

PUBLISHED BY POCKET BOOKS NEW YORK

JULIA

Coward, McCann & Geoghegan edition published 1975

POCKET BOOK edition published October, 1976

This POCKET BOOK edition includes every word contained in
the original, higher-priced edition. It is printed from brand-
new plates made from completely reset, clear, easy-to-read type.
POCKET BOOK editions are published by
POCKET BOOKS,
a division of Simon & Schuster, Inc.,
A GULF+WESTERN COMPANY
630 Fifth Avenue,
New York, N.Y. 10020.
Trademarks registered in the United States
and other countries.

ISBN: 0-671-80751-X.
Library of Congress Catalog Card Number: 75-10464.

Printed in the U.S.A.

For Thomas and Alice Tessier

Contents

So a war begins. Into a peace-time life, comes an announcement, a threat. A bomb drops somewhere, potential traitors are whisked off quietly to prison. And for some time, days, months, a year perhaps, life has a peace-time quality. But when a war has been going on for a long time, life is all war, every event has the quality of war, nothing of peace remains. Events and the life in which they are embedded have the same quality. But since it is not possible that events are not part of the life they occur in—it is not possible that a bomb should explode into a texture of life foreign to it—all that means is that one has not understood, one has not been watching.

—DORIS LESSING, *The Four-Gated City*

Part One

The Haunting: Julia

1

The little blond girl, about nine or ten—Kate's age—
and enough like Kate to make Julia feel dizzy, ran floating up from nowhere along Ilchester Place and, wind-
milling her arms at the street corner, flew into the path
to Holland Park. Standing on the steps of the house with
the man from Markham and Reeves, Julia's first sensation was the sharp, familiar ache of loss, now so strong
as to make her feel that she might shock the man from
Markham and Reeves by being sick into the wilting
tulips; but the real-estate agent, who had clearly decided
that his customer was precipitous and eccentric to the
point of lunacy, might have done no more than mutter
something about the heat and pretend that nothing out
of the ordinary had occurred. That Julia had already
twice lost the keys to Number 25, that she had written a
deposit check for twenty thousand pounds on the first
day she had seen the house (the first house he had
shown her), that she was buying, as well, all the furniture from the previous owners, a retired carpet manu-
facturer and his wife already in Barbados, that she in-

11

tended to live alone in an eight-bedroom house—but he
had his own ideas on that point—had prepared him for
almost any conceivable vagary on her part. Conscious
of her haste and her oddness, and a little fearful of the
man's subtle contempt for her, Julia yet felt it possible
that the estate agent attributed some of this behavior to
her being merely another comically "rich American";
and so she felt, with a little flare of independence, only
the smallest qualm about obeying her second response
to the sight of the running blond girl, a feeling that she
must follow her. The impulse was overwhelmingly
strong. The man from Markham and Reeves was holding her by the elbow, very delicately, and beginning to
produce the third key from his waistcoat pocket—he
had tied a bright yellow ribbon through the hole at the
top of the key.

"Yellow for remembrance, Mrs. Lofting," he was saying, the edge of condescension clear in his voice. "Confess I pinched the idea from a pop song. May you—"

"Excuse me," Julia said, and went quickly down the
steps to the pavement.

She did not want to run until she was out of the
man's sight, and restrained herself until she too had
rounded the corner to the park and was shielded by the
wall. The girl looked remarkably like Kate. Of course
she could not be Kate. Kate was dead. But people sometimes caught sight of friends in a crowd or riding past in
a bus when those friends were in reality thousands of
miles away—but didn't that mean that the friends were
in danger or about to die? Julia ran a few awkward
steps into the children's play area and, already panting,
began to walk. Children were everywhere, in the sandboxes, racing around on the patchy grass, climbing the
trees she could see from her bedroom window. The
blond girl could be far into the park by now, Julia
realized, either on the long sward of green to the right
or on one of the paths up ahead, or over toward the
Orangery. The child might not even have taken the path
into the play area but run straight up the long lane to
Holland House. Surely Holland House *was* that way?

Up there past the peacocks? Julia did not feel sure enough of the park's geography to pursue her phantom —who in any case was just an ordinary little girl on her way to meet friends in Holland Park. Julia, who was still unthinkingly walking up the path past the sand-boxes, stopped. Chasing after the child had been un-reasonable, perhaps hysterical: typical of her. I really am losing my grip, she thought, and said "Damn" so loudly that a stout man with a brushy gingery mustache stared at her.

She turned about, embarrassed, and looked up across the back walls of gardens to the upper row of windows in her new house. The house was monstrously expen-sive: she could not allow Magnus to know that she had purchased it, that she had signed every paper put in front of her. For a moment the thought of Magnus—the idea of Magnus, enormous with rage—drove everything else from her head, and she felt a second of terror. She might have been unreasonable, even unbalanced—he would be quick to say it—but about Magnus, reason was not possible. The long, restrained lines of the house, which she had thought beautiful the moment she had seen it, helped her to quiet her feelings.

Holding one hand to her chest, Julia walked back down the path to the corner of Ilchester Place. She re-membered the man from Markham and Reeves only when she saw him leaning against the front door, his expression one between confusion and boredom. *He* had written her off when, telephoning her bank from his office, he had learned how much money she kept in a checking account.

She expected the man to say something, but he ap-peared to be past courteous formulas. He merely straightened his shoulders and offered the key, holding it by the flagrant yellow ribbon. Now he did not look so much bored as weary. And in any case, what could Julia say? She could not explain her sudden action by telling him that she had wanted to look again at a girl who reminded her of her dead daughter: he did not know anything about Kate or about Julia. She did the best she could.

"I'm so sorry," she said, looking up into his gray, rather compressed-looking face. "I wanted to check on something around the back before you left."

He looked at her oddly: to examine the back, of course, she would have gone through the house rather than around the corner.

"Not a lot of children on this street, Mrs. Lofting," the man said. "They play in the park of course but you'll find that Ilchester Place is a quiet sort of neighborhood, as I've told you." Was this, too, more tired sarcasm? But the man had noticed the girl, and was making an effort to be courteous. He had looked straight through her weak excuse.

"Thank you," she said, taking the key and putting it in one of the short pockets of her dress. "You've been very patient with me."

"Not at all." The man looked at his wristwatch, then for a moment at his car, and then at the Rover, where suitcases were piled up on the backseat, crowded in with some potted plants, two short stacks of books tied with string, and a box of floppy dolls she had had since childhood. These were the only things she had taken besides her clothing, and they were all from the room she had been using since leaving the hospital. The books were an indulgence, but they were hers, not Magnus'.

"No, you needn't, please," Julia quickly said. "I couldn't dream of asking you, after . . . everything."

"In that case," he said, palpably relieved, and began to go down the steps, "I have some things to attend to at the office, so if you'll excuse me, I'll be leaving you to your new house." He glanced up at the long, warm brick exterior. "It *is* a beautiful house. You should be quite happy here. And of course you have our number, should anything arise. Am I correct in thinking that you do not know Kensington thoroughly?"

She nodded.

"Then you have before you all the pleasures of investigation. Where was it you were living before? Before today? Hampstead, wasn't it?"

"Yes."

"You should find this part of Kensington very sympathetic."

He turned away to walk toward his car. When he had opened the door he faced her again and called across the pavement and lawn. "Do ring us if you have any problems, Mrs. Lofting. By the by, I think you might have some spare keys made for you at one of the shops in the High Street. Well, good day then, Mrs. Lofting."

"Bye." She waved from the steps of the house as the man drove away. When his car was out of sight, Julia went down to the Rover and looked back up at her house—now truly her house. Like all the other houses on the short, elegant length of Ilchester Place, it was neo-Georgian, brick, secure. There she would be safe from Magnus. The house had spoken to her need for quiet and for restful seclusion the moment she had seen it: almost as if it had in fact spoken to her. Buying it had been as much a compulsion as following the little Kate-like girl had been. She *could* live in it, apart from Magnus: in time she could telephone him or write a note, after he had got used to the idea of her bolting. She had spent the previous night in a Knightsbridge hotel, afraid that every step meant the approach of Magnus, his face red with false sympathy, with the effort of trying to contain his violence. Magnus could be terrifying: it was the other side of his impressiveness, that huge male authority. No, she would let Magnus be for a while. Her note had explained all that could be explained.

Now the suitcases and the rest of her things had to be got into the house somehow. She pushed the button beside the door handle and, when it resisted her, pushed it again harder. The car was locked. Julia pulled a key from her pocket, but it was the house key on its taunting yellow ribbon. She bent over to look through the window and saw the rest of her keys dangling from the car's ignition. *Helpless.* She felt the oncoming of tears.

For a moment she experienced an intense gratitude that Magnus was not beside her. "Julia, you are completely incapable." "I wonder if you ever do anything right." Or a short, brutal condemnation: "Typical." A barrister, Magnus had an arsenal of techniques for suggesting that other people, especially his wife, were weak in the head.

"Oh, thank God," she said aloud; she had noticed that the window on the passenger side of the Rover was rolled down, although that door too was locked. "Typical" as that might be, Julia took it as a good omen for the first day she was to live in her new house. Perhaps Magnus really might be kept from finding her—for a week or two, at least.

As if the two were related, the thought of Magnus recalled the girl again, and Julia, opening the other door by reaching in through the window and pressing down on the inner handle, thought of trying to find her inside Holland Park. She fought down the image of herself and the girl, sitting together on a bench, talking. Beneath this lay another image, an image of horror and despair, and Julia, sensing it coming to her consciousness as it had during the weeks in hospital, deliberately made her mind empty. She would think about the luggage and the plants; one of the pots had broken, shearing away a section of clay nearly seven inches long and exposing granular black soil webbed with thin white roots. Julia had, she realized, bought the house on Ilchester Place the same way she had taken Magnus for her husband, in a rush.

But she had spent *her* money on *her* house: it was the first utterly free thing she had done since she had married Magnus eleven years before. Then, in 1963, she had been twenty-five, a rather more than pretty young woman with striking reddish hair and a soft, unlined, contented face: "the face of a girl at an Impressionists' picnic," her father had said. She had gone through her private school and Smith College, it seemed to her now, in a sort of trance, at a great distance from herself. Little but her courses and a few professors had moved or touched her. She had lost her virginity to a boy from Columbia, a tall, intense Jewish student of English. Most of his courtship had consisted of anecdotes about Lionel Trilling and the sex lives of famous poets; they had seen a great many French movies together.

Afterward there were other boys, but none of them came any closer to the inner Julia than the Columbia student; she slept with none of them. When she graduated from Smith, she took a job with Time-Life, in the clipping library at *Sports Illustrated,* but quit a year later when she overheard another young woman, one she had thought of as a friend, describe her as a "fucking heiress." Quitting was a relief: she knew that she was incompetent at the job, and had lasted a year because the head of her department, a married man named Robert Tillinghast, was fond of her. She liked him, but not enough to remove her clothes in his company, which was clearly what he had in mind. For six months, then, she lived in her parents' home, reading novels and watching television, feeling more and more afraid of any world beyond the front door or the Smith campus; then she ran into a Smith friend in a restaurant and heard that the publishing company she worked for was looking for a young woman to do editorial work; in a week she had another job. Here, she enjoyed an almost mechanical, rootless pleasure in the work, editing academic books in the firm's college department; she was fond of saying that she learned things from each new book. She took an apartment in the West Seventies. She seemed to be settling into a dazed, busy, thoughtless life: taking the bus to work (on principle, she rarely rode in taxis), doing her correspondence, working with manuscripts, eating with one man or another, she often thought that she was merely watching herself perform, as though life had not yet truly begun. Then one morning she woke up in her bed beside Robert Tillinghast, and decided, panicked, to leave New York and go to England. "I'm moving horizontally since I'm not able to

move vertically," she told her friends. Robert Tillinghast drove her to the airport and said, Good God, he
wondered what would become of her. "I guess I do
too."

In London, she first took a room on Drury Lane, and
six months later, after she had found a job with a pub-
lisher of·art books, moved to a two-room flat in Camden Town. "You're living in a kennel," her father had
blustered when he flew across to inspect her new life.
"Where the hell are the want ads?" He found her a self-
contained, large-windowed flat with two bedrooms
("You need a room to work in!") in Hampstead, three
times the cost of her place in Camden Town. One night
several months after she had moved in, she met Magnus
Lofting at a party given by a married couple who both
worked for the art-book publishers.

They were Hugh and Sonia Mitchell-Mitchie, both
Julia's age; Hugh, who wore denims and T-shirts and
the golden curl of an earring in one ear, was the head
of the art department. Sonia, like Julia, did editorial
work. In manner, both were bright and inconsequential;
Julia, who liked them while she was a little unsettled by
them—both seemed to spend an abnormal amount of
time discussing their love affairs—had not known that
their idea of a party was to spend two hours drinking as
rapidly as possible and the rest of the night playing
parlor games.

When the others began to play, Julia faded backward
in the room, hoping to go unnoticed: she was made
insecure by all games. Sonia began to taunt her; in a
moment, twenty people were staring at her. Julia felt
cruelly exposed.

"Don't be a bully, Sonia," a man said. "I'll talk to
your friend."

Julia turned to the source of this authoritative voice,
and saw a big rocky-faced man in a pinstriped suit; he
was years older than anyone else at the party. The hair
above his ears was already going gray. "Sit down next
to me," the man ordered.

"You saved my life," she said.

"Just sit down," Magnus ordered.

She gladly sat.

Ten years later, she could not remember the conversation they had had, but she knew that, immediately, there had been something impressive about him: he was purely male, with a suggestion in every gesture that he could take her as easily as he could light a cigarette. With the instincts of someone who had grown up surrounded by prosperous people, she recognized that he was successful at whatever it was he did; he seemed to understand her utterly, or to be utterly indifferent to anything he did not understand. In a chilling way, he was fascinating. They spent the rest of the evening talking to one another, and while Hugh and Sonia and the rest of the party were beginning another game, one in which a "murderer" assassinated his "victims" by winking at them, Magnus said quietly to her, "I think I'll be going. Shall I give you a lift? How did you get here?"

"I took a bus," she confessed.

"Too late for a bus now." He stood up. He was a head taller than she and too big to be merely burly. When he raised a hand, she flinched; but he carried it to the back of his head and smoothed down his hair. "I'll take you home unless you live somewhere unreasonable. Blackheath or Guildford are out of my range."

"I live in Hampstead," she said.

"Grace abounds. So do I."

They walked to his car, a black Mercedes, parked on the Fulham Road; she learned that he was a barrister, and that he had once lived next door to Sonia Mitchell-Mitchie, who had become a kind of adopted niece. He asked few questions of her, but Julia found herself talking compulsively. For some reason—a reason she was not to understand for years—she even mentioned Robert Tillinghast when describing why she had left New York.

It was only when she knew that she was going to leave Magnus that she recognized that she had married him—had fallen in love with him—in large measure because he reminded her of her father. And they were

both prodigal, casual adulterers. Julia saw very early
that Magnus had other women: he was brutally offhand
about them. On the ride back to Hampstead, he had
said that he wanted a drink, and drove to a club behind
Shepherd's Market, where he signed her name in a guest-
book and led her into a dark, half-filled room in which
elegance was still a few paces in advance of shabbiness.
The waitresses wore long pastel gowns revealing outsize, separated breasts. A third of the men were drunk;
only two women, besides Julia and the hostesses, were
in the club. One of the drunks put his arm about Julia
as soon as she entered the room. Magnus pushed the
man away without looking at him. He ordered drinks
and began to look aggressively about the room as if he
were looking for another man to knock down. Both of
the other women, Julia saw, were looking at him. She
felt pleasantly excited, stimulated, sipping at her drink.

"Do you gamble?" Magnus asked her.

She shook her head.

"You won't mind if I do?"

"No," she said. "I suddenly feel very awake."

Julia followed him through a door at the end of the
lounge and continued, following his broad back, to a
grilled-in counter where Magnus took money from his
wallet and bought chips. She watched as he placed five
fifty-pound notes on the counter, and, after hesitating
a second, a sixth. He seemed to get a surprisingly small
amount of chips for all this money.

Together, they skirted various gaming tables and went
up to a roulette wheel. Magnus placed four of his chips
on the red. Breathless, Julia watched the ball spinning
across the ratchets. It landed, clattering, on red. Magnus left his chips where they were, and the ball landed
again on red. Then he moved everything he had won to
black; again he won. How much money did those chips
represent? Five hundred pounds? More? As she watched
Magnus glowering down at the stack of chips, she felt
exhilarated, slightly disoriented: he must have loathed
the party, she realized. The next time the wheel spun,

he lost some of his chips, but his face remained immobile.

"Your turn, Charmaine," he ordered. He shoved a stack of chips toward her. With desperation, Julia realized that they were worth at least two hundred pounds.

"I can't," she said. "I'd lose your money."

"Don't be cowardly," he said. "Bet any way you please."

She pushed the chips onto the red, since that was what Magnus had first won with. This time the ball clattered down onto the black. She looked up at him, stricken.

"Doesn't matter," he said. "Put more on it." He slid chips toward her.

She did as he said, and lost again. She stepped away from the table.

Magnus continued to gamble, seemingly indifferent to her. She stood beside him, watching chips pile up before him. Winning seemed not to affect him in any way; he simply stolidly stood there, scowling at the table, moving piles of red and white chips back and forth. Several times men approached and spoke to him, but Magnus replied with short, curt sentences and turned away from them.

After half an hour, a thin black-haired woman Julia remembered seeing in the lounge came up and kissed Magnus. "Darling," she said, "you haven't been here in ages. You might lose all your old friends." Saying the last two words, she looked tauntingly at Julia. Julia felt at once undressed.

Magnus whispered a few words to the black-haired woman, and then turned back to the table. When he cashed in his chips, Julia saw that he had won nearly a thousand pounds.

In the car she said, "Was that woman your mistress?" It was the first time she had heard him laugh.

When he left her at her door he asked for her telephone number and, after she had given it, brought two fifty-pound notes from his jacket pocket and put them in her hand. "I'll ring you Wednesday," he said, and moved out the door before she could protest. Julia put the money in a drawer, intending to give it back when she next saw him; two months later, when she found the two notes again, it was too late to return it. Eventually, she gave one note to Oxfam and the other to Amnesty International.

At work the next Monday, she learned two things about Magnus: he had been Sonia Mitchell-Mitchie's first lover, and Julia had been expected to sleep with him. "Magnus always does that, picking up some girl at a party and then taking her home and ravishing her," Sonia said to Julia. "Weren't you ravished?"

"He barely touched me," Julia protested.

"He must have been off his feed," Sonia said.

In the following weeks, Magnus came to occupy more and more of her time; but he made love to her only when she had begun to wonder if he ever would. He was certainly the biggest man she had ever gone to bed with. By that time, two months after the Mitchell-Mitchie party, he had become a reference point in her life. She tended to judge other men by Magnus' standard, or by trying to guess if Magnus would like them. Certainly no other man was as exciting as Magnus Lofting: he had an absolute assurance a younger man could not possess, still trying to consolidate both his manhood and his career.

Yet it was only after he had described his childhood to her that Julia, already in love, knew that she must marry him. He and his sister—"poor Lily," a year older than he—had been raised by monumentally distant parents. Entirely absorbed into themselves, entirely indifferent to the opinions or sensibilities of others, the Loftings had traveled much, leaving the children at home with a succession of tutors: before she drew Magnus out on the subject of his childhood—he was seemingly callous about it now—Julia had not known how far off, therefore cruel, it was possible for parents to be. Except for the tutors and "poor Lily" Magnus had grown up in near silence, abandoned in the glassy marble tomb of a house in Hampshire. His childhood was heartbreaking for Julia, whose own father, unlike Sir Greville Lofting, had been intrusive, verbal, and commanding. Magnus' childhood, that early isolation, she thought, went a long way toward explaining Magnus' compulsions; as a young man, he had apparently been ruthless about his professional life, and even now he invested it with enough psychic energy to power a steam engine. Magnus' childhood not only helped to explain Magnus to Julia, and thereby make him more accessible, but it also helped to humanize him. At first, that Magnus had once *had* parents seemed impossible, slightly shocking; that he had "poor Lily" and a much younger adopted brother, Mark, seemed a revelation.

She was further surprised by the depth of his attachment to "poor Lily." But again, their childhood made it accessible. Magnus and Lily had grown up a society of two, intensely devoted to one another, each other's only company. They had invented a language ("Durm") in which at playful moments they could still converse. They were "Magnim" and "Lilim." They had constructed elaborate games using every portion of the house and grounds, games in which Magnus apparently from the age of five or six had taken the commanding role—king, general, prime minister, Coriolanus, Odysseus, Priam. This had endured up to the time Magnus entered Cambridge. Lily had never married, and Julia learned that Magnus spent at least one afternoon or evening a week with his sister. In fact, she thought that the inevitable usage of "poor Lily" had been adopted less from any intrinsic absurdity of Lily's than from a wish to counter any jealousy Julia might be expected to feel. Despite her oddities, her spiritualism, her general appearance of genteel dissipation, Lily did not deserve the epithet. She proved, when Julia finally met her, grayhaired, undoubtedly lovely, and so finely made that separate facial muscles were visible beneath her skin. Lily made Julia feel awkward and hot, probably smudged in some conspicuous place. And it was only two years later, after the birth of Kate, that Lily became friendly.

Mark, the son of a young friend of Sir Greville's, a consular official in Africa who had killed himself, was another matter. The Loftings had adopted the child, then two years old, out of an uncharacteristic generosity, having promised his mother, dying in a tropical hospital, that they would care for him. Their notion of care was to send the child and nurse to England, with only a telegram and a breezy following letter to warn fifteen-year-old Magnus and sixteen-year-old Lily that a new brother was to be dumped in among them. They hated him. Their world had been a sacred alliance of two for too long to admit a third. Magnus invariably referred to Mark as a "waster" and a "troublemaker"; Lily too remained suspicious of Mark. Sometimes he was "bad, very bad," which Julia supposed was a reference to his having impregnated a girl in the Hampshire village when he was fifteen. It might also have referred to the first action of his adult life, having his name altered by deed poll from Lofting back to Berkeley—a mute comment on the Lofting methods of childrearing. Mark was a disappointment: he had never learned their secret language, never having been given much chance to learn it; he had obtained a third-class degree at Cambridge; he was now lecturing at a polytechnic in sociology, a field Magnus claimed did not exist. Mark had flirted with fringe political groups all his life, he had marched and passed out leaflets, and he was now supposed to be a Maoist—Magnus had once scornfully seen him carrying a copy of *Red Star Over China*.

—Well, I don't see what's wrong with reading any book. And neither do you.

—I didn't say he was reading it. He was carrying it. For effect. In his circle, it's the equivalent of a Rolling Stones record.

—Now, honestly, I'm not defending Mark, but you are being malicious and unfair. You condemn him whether he's reading the book or not.

—Does it matter what I say about some Notting Hill Maoist?

Mark generally dressed in blue jeans and a chambray

work shirt; he lived in the same rooms in Notting Hill
Gate he had taken after leaving Cambridge, sleeping
there, in a fabulous mess, on a mattress on the floor.
Julia had heard most of this from Lily, with Magnus
grunting disapproving asides, over a period of three or
four months. She herself did not meet Mark until the
day he appeared at Magnus' house on Gayton Road,
three weeks before Julia's wedding, saying that he
wanted to meet the victim. She heard his light, wry voice
—a very un-Lofting voice—from the front steps, and
then heard Magnus say, "The what? I take it you mean
my fiancée."

"Your victim, Magnus."

She heard Magnus sigh. "Well, you might as well
come in then, since you're here."

"You are typically generous, Magnus."

Julia had thought of Mark as a potential ally since
she had heard Lily and Magnus first disparage him; he
was at least flawed and might be expected to be sympathetic to her. Her heart beating a little quickly, she
thrust the *Guardian* behind her chair and stood to meet
him.

Magnus came scowling into the room, leading a tall
young man with long, shining black hair. Julia saw
Magnus' grimace at the sight of the wrinkled newspaper,
wadded up behind the chair; then she saw that Mark
Berkeley was the kind of man women might turn around
to stare at in the street. He was beautiful—sexually
beautiful. The long dark hair framed a face a few shades
lighter than olive, with high Mongol cheekbones and a
full, curving mouth. Beneath black eyebrows, in the
dark amused face, his eyes were unbelievably blue.
When he held out his hand, she noticed that his finger-
nails were filthy.

"You're almost as pretty as Lily said you were," he
said. "I wish I'd seen you first. Be nice to have another
beautiful woman in the family, won't it, Magnus? Now
that Lily is getting a bit past it."

Holding his rather grubby hand, Julia felt, as an
undercurrent to Mark's remarks, that he was looking

straight through her; he might be an ally, but not of the sort she had anticipated. Mark too was formidable. Yet he seemed far from unsympathetic. As Julia felt herself warming to her fiancé's younger brother, a number of impressions went rapidly through her mind. Mark seemed more like Magnus' son than his brother: he had an air of irresponsibility which seemed nearly cultivated. It was impossible to imagine Mark holding a job—any job but lecturing. And she considered, still holding his hand, that perhaps she was being conned by an expert. It was certainly all too easy to find oneself instantly liking someone so attractive. She disengaged her hand. She was not sure that she approved of men as beautiful as this.

"Really, Magnus," Mark said, "doesn't she look like a vision Lily might see in one of her crystal balls? What an extraordinary person she must be to want to marry you."

"Oh," she said, trying to save the situation, "sometimes I think half the women in London want to marry Magnus."

But Magnus had turned impatiently away from her. The rest of the afternoon had staggered painfully along, Mark taunting Magnus, Magnus becoming increasingly blustery. Julia had not known at all how to read Mark.

A year later, when Julia realized, sickened, that Magnus had not ceased to see his other women for as much as a month, she had angrily, furiously proposed to him that she could begin taking up with his brother. "Why should you have all the fun?" she had demanded, raging.

Magnus had gripped her hard enough to raise bruises on her arm: she saw, trembling with both fear and anger, that he was barely restraining himself from clubbing her. Then the pressure lessened, his jaw unclamped, and he moved a step backward. "I'd happily kill you if you ever slept with Mark," he said. His tone was so cold that she believed him at once: despite all that talk about "unbalanced" Mark, she had never before seen that he hated his brother. At least, that was what she thought she had seen.

It was not long after this explosion that they began to discuss having a child.

Kate was born the following summer. For the next nine years, the Loftings lived conventionally in Hampstead, traveling abroad—Magnus bought a farmhouse a mile from the Dordogne River, and they spent three summers doing it up—seeing Lily at intervals, seeing Mark two or three times a year when he dropped in unannounced. Clearly, he was kept informed of events in the Lofting house by Lily: he sent a beautiful dollhouse on Kate's first birthday, he frequently telephoned when Magnus was out of town, and conducted cool, flirtatious conversations with Julia. Magnus undoubtedly carried on his affairs, but they had lost much of their power to wound Julia. They seemed entirely peripheral, taking little away from Julia and Kate. Still unpredictable, still sometimes frightening, Magnus loved Kate absolutely. Julia spent the nine years of Kate's life in a homebound trance, superficially content. Once, at a party, she had heard herself say, "Can't live for another person? Of course you can live for another person, I live for my . . ." She was on the verge of saying "daughter," but saw Magnus staring at her, and substituted "family."

Now she thought: I'm going to start being myself, freely myself, and discover what that means. And if I go crazy that's okay too.

Julia stood at her bedroom window, the shades parted, looking out at the play area, filled with desultory children, and the green of the park beyond. She pushed up the window and leaned out, thinking *a woman on the verge of a new life leaned from her window. . . .* The room was unbearably stuffy. The air drifting across Holland Park seemed cooler, more invigorating despite the warmth of the day. Unpacking her clothing, untying the books, Julia had felt damp, sticky, and oddly ruthless— the clothing could go anywhere, since the bedroom, like the entire house, was solely hers. When she put the box of dolls for the moment in one of the bedroom closets, she sat on the edge of the bed for a moment, feeling heat rise from her in layers like steam. Julia felt the presence of the house about her, for a moment almost oppressive in its size. Yet she had wanted it, and she had it. The McClintocks' furniture was old-fashioned and a bit worn, but comfortable, tending toward plush and cushions. In time, she would get rid of it and buy new furniture, but for the moment she was as pleased with the old furniture as with the house, since it had the same settled, familial look of prosperous comfort.

It was odd, the way this house had claimed her. At first, she had thought of moving to a service flat, probably somewhere in Knightsbridge; the temporariness of such a home depressed her, however, even in imagination, and she had gone to a real-estate agent's office, thinking vaguely of buying a lease on a flat. But having seen the house on Ilchester Place—"quite unsuitable, of course," the man had said—she had known that she had to have it. It was nearly the first time in her life that Julia had used her money in a high-handed, reckless fashion. With Kate dead, did it matter how much she spent? The image of Kate's last minutes threatened to rise up again, and to put it off Julia moved quickly away from the window. She had been half-consciously looking for the girl she had seen that morning, the blond girl. How lovely it would be if buying the house brought her into contact, friendship, with another child, a girl like Kate, with whom she could have an easy, relaxed companionship.

But that was impossible: she could not make a stranger's daughter her own. She really was getting less realistic, less responsible to the world of ordinary truths. Was it possible that instead of beginning a new life, she had merely further confused and muddled the old one?

She could not afford to think that way. If she had been garrulous, disorganized, sloppy, everything that Magnus had accused her of being, perhaps these qualities were wrong only to Magnus: she had a right to her own foibles. And even now, free from him for only two

days, Julia could simply feel how oppressive Magnus
—Magnus' values—had been. She said to herself, I
think it means my marriage is over, and surprised herself with the thought. Leaving Magnus had everything
to do with Kate's death, of course, that horrific scene on
the kitchen floor, Kate's blood everywhere, boiling out
of her panicked body—but leaving him, Julia now
thought, might also come from a deep knowledge that
marriage to Magnus was no longer possible. Really,
Kate had kept them together. Kate had been their focus.

Interesting, she thought, and then realized that she
had spoken the word aloud. "I'm going to be the kind
of woman who talks to herself," she said. "Well, why
shouldn't I?" She turned to the McClintocks' mirror
and began to arrange her long hair, which now glowed
a little in the light pouring in the bedroom window.

When she had put everything away, scrubbed the already spotless kitchen and vacuumed the living room
carpet, Julia took a shower and afterward left the
house. She had been making up her mind that she would
see Lily after all—Lily now lived in Plane Tree House,
just across Holland Park. Surely she could persuade
Lily not to betray her to Magnus. "Poor Lily" had become, during the past nine years, a good friend: one of
the attractions of Ilchester Place was that it was so close
to Plane Tree House. In fact, Julia had moved near to
both of the other members of the Lofting family. Mark's
flat in Notting Hill was so close that she could walk to
it.

Julia made sure she had her key in her pocket, and
then turned up into the park. Almost immediately, she
saw the blond girl again. The child was sitting on the
ground at some distance from a group of other children,
boys and girls, who were carefully watching her. Julia
stopped walking, almost fearing that she would inter-
rupt whatever performance was going on if the child
should notice her. The blond girl was working intently
at something with her hands, wholly concentrated on it.
Her face was sweetly serious. Julia could not see what

it was that required such concentration, but the other
children were as grave as the little girl, indeed scarcely
breathing. This was what gave the scene the aspect of a
performance. Thinking of Kate, who could keep a dozen
other children still while she loosed some fantastic
story from her imagination, Julia, smiling, stepped off
the path on the side opposite to the play area, so that
she was perhaps twenty yards from the girl and her
audience, and sat on the grass. The girl was seated, her
legs straight out before her, in the sandy overspill from
one of the sandboxes: a sort of pit like a golfer's sand
trap. She was speaking softly now to her audience,
ranged on the scrubby grass before her in groups of
three and four. The other children playing in the sand
took no notice of them. They were certainly unnaturally quiet, completely taken up by the girl's theatrics.

Julia forgot that she was going to see Lily: she forgot
all about Lily. It was five thirty and still very hot; Julia
felt the sun's great weight on her forehead and arms.
Like most London women, she was as white as if she
lived under permanent clouds, and for a second considered that for the first time in years, she might get
some color. Watching the child continue her intricate
movements and brief, admonitory-looking bursts of
speech, Julia felt peaceful, slowed by the sun, her tension for the moment gone. She *had* been right to buy
the house; she had turned a corner, and could begin to
live differently. For a second she thought the blond girl
had darted a quick glance at her, but it was far more
likely that she had merely looked sideways, aimlessly.
There could be no doubt that she was the same blond
girl Julia had seen before, floating along up the street:
she did not really look like Kate, except for the accident
of that silky, innocent, nearly white shade of hair, but
she somehow suggested Kate. Oddly, watching her was
not painful for Julia: Instead, there was a rootless ex-
hilaration in it. Julia felt disconnected from everything,
watching the girl, a pure, happy, sun-struck disengage-
ment. The girl's face, at Julia's distance, looked aristo-
cratically fine featured: her profile was heartbreakingly

clear. She seemed to be not so much storytelling as lecturing—holding the others by force of personality.

Her hands were moving; something was held in her right hand. That was where the other children were looking. The girl laughed excitedly, and Julia saw some object flash in her left hand. She applied it to the thing in her right hand, apparently a square of green. The green square flipped in the air; it was like a rag. A little girl in the audience bent her head, and Julia saw her shoulders shake, as if she were overcome with giggles. The blond girl spoke a few sharp words, and the other girl raised her head. Now the group of children had a huddled look; they were creeping forward, fascinated . . . but fascination, Julia saw, was not quite the correct word. It was as though, almost, they felt trepidation about getting nearer the girl: she was undoubtedly their leader.

Now the girl spoke quickly to the others, pointing an index finger. It was extraordinarily like a classroom. She gestured with the limp green thing. One of the other girls flinched. Then the blond girl continued working with her hands, the other children slowly gathering about her. Julia strained her neck to see what they were doing, but could see only the crown of the girl's head. One of the smaller children began to cry.

In another second the performance had ended. The other children drifted away, some of them running, excited, shouting. Others moved slowly, going toward the first sandbox, where they aimlessly milled about, scattering sand. These continued to glance at the blond girl, who remained sitting where she had been, her back to them. She was smoothing the sand with the palm of her hand, seemingly filling in a hollow she had made. It was clear from her posture that she knew she was being looked at, and that she expected it; she was at once self-conscious and unconcerned. When she had patted and smoothed the sand, she stood up in one motion and briskly wiped her hands. She seemed regal, lifting her head, and Julia's heart contracted for her. The girl walked out of the little sand trap toward the path, moving directly toward Julia. Her face still bore an expression of watchful self-awareness. What complicated roles and rituals children have, Julia thought. She knew the girl would not look at her, and she did not. Once on the path, the girl turned deeper into the park, and after walking a few determined steps, broke into a run. In a moment she was traveling at top speed, racing up the path; in another moment, she had vanished before a knot of teenage girls whose long straight hair flipped like the tails of horses.

Julia stood—less gracefully than the blond girl had done—and went across the path into the play area. She still felt a little disoriented, as if she had just awakened after deep sleep. The sun felt unusually strong on her face. She wanted to see where the blond girl had been playing.

A small black girl, two or three, with a curly ruff of hair and huge mournful eyes appeared directly in front of Julia. She clasped her hands before the bib of her overalls and tilted back her head, staring up at Julia with her mouth open.

"What's your name?" she asked.

"Julia."

The girl's mouth opened a fraction wider.

"Doolya?"

Julia raised her hand for a moment to the child's springy ruff of hair. "What's your name?"

"Mona."

"Do you know the girl who was just playing in here? The girl with blond hair who was sitting and talking?"

Mona nodded.

"Do you know her name?"

Mona nodded again. "Doolya."

"Julia?"

"Mona. Take me with you."

"Mona, what was that girl doing? Was she telling a story?"

"She does. Things." The girl blinked. "Take me with you. Pick me up."

Julia bent down. "She does what? What does she do?"

Mona expressionlessly backed away a few steps, continuing to stare at Julia. "Poo," she said. She giggled, revealing small perfect teeth. "Poo." She turned away too quickly, fell on her bottom, and then struggled up on her feet and staggered off.

Julia looked after Mona for a moment, wobbling in the direction of the next sandbox, and went to where she thought the blond girl had been sitting. Julia knelt down above the spot. For a second she hesitated, wondering if she were trespassing on a secret or a code, and then she drew her hand along the sand as the girl had done. Her hand met no resistance. She repeated the action. Then she delicately scooped a little of the sand to one side, using the side of her hand. With her fingertips, she pushed another small amount of sand out of the hollow she had made. Very slowly, she continued to drag her fingertips through the little hollow. When the depression was three or four inches deep, her fingers touched something hard and metallic, and she dug cautiously around it, still using only one hand. Gradually she uncovered a small knife. Gummy sand was sticking to its blade. Julia looked at the knife in puzzlement and then scraped more sand from the hollow. Her fingers caught an edge of something hard, and almost without any pressure, she levered up from the sand the corpse of a small turtle of the size that had been sold to children for a quarter in Julia's own childhood. It took her a moment to see that it had been mutilated.

Vomit rushed up from the floor of Julia's stomach, and dropping the mutilated turtle and the small knife back into the hollow, she swallowed the bitter stuff back down again. With her foot she scattered sand over the turtle and the knife. Julia left the sand trap quickly, fearing she might faint, and moved toward a shaded bench on the main path through the center of the park. I'll just sit here and catch my breath, she thought, before I see Lily. She unthinkingly rubbed her hands on her dress, and after a few minutes noticed that she had left a small smear of blood along one seam. Sweat had broken out over her face; Julia blotted it on her sleeve, which instantly showed a series of dark crescents and ragged blotches. She made her mind empty: she concentrated on the sun, on the prickling she felt along her forearms and on her forehead. She was unable to look at the children.

After some minutes had passed, Julia raised her head and closed her eyes against the strong sunlight. She needed sunglasses. Somewhere, she had sunglasses. They were back at Gayton Road. She could visualize them, their bows crossed, lying on a formica counter in the kitchen. She'd buy another pair. Yes, she thought, I jumped into reacting, I did not think. There was no proof the girl had killed the turtle or cut it up that way. Julia may even have been probing the wrong spot in the sand. Little girls so pretty did not do things like that: it was an unfair psychological rule that handsome children were healthier and more stable than ugly ones. In fact—Julia allowed the idea to seep cautiously into articulation—she had been upset because the sight of the turtle reminded her of what had happened to Kate.

She could speak of none of this to Lily. Making that resolution, Julia stood up from the bench and cut across the long stretch of grass, going toward Plane Tree House. She really did feel peculiar.

2

The two women sat on Lily's terrace in the sun, now milder than it had been an hour before. "Poor Lily's" hair, prematurely gray like Magnus', had been cropped since Julia had last seen her sister-in-law, and it lay flat and short as a boy's, emphasizing the fragile lines of her

face and making her look more than ever at an oblique
relationship to the rest of the world. Yet Lily had remained unruffled by Julia's news and Julia's high-
pitched, taut mood. For half an hour, Julia had
considered that Lily might be pleased that she would
have Magnus to herself again, but she knew that this
was grossly uncharitable: Lily simply did not respond
as other people did. In the end, her news given, Julia
had allowed herself to relax, cosseted by Lily's hospitality—she was now drinking her third gin and bitter
lemon, served in a tall glass chiming with ice—and
Lily's unpredictability.

"You *are* extraordinary, though," Lily was saying.
"Extraordinary and precipitous. You're a regular hero-
ine. I can't imagine myself ever doing anything so reckless and brave."

"God knows I'm not brave," Julia said, laughing.

"Oh, but you are. You have a brave soul."

"Then I'm a coward with a brave soul."

"You mustn't think it is cowardly to fear Magnus.
Magnus is not like anyone else. He has always been a
terribly apart sort of person. He has *command*. Sometimes I think that Magnus is not from this world at all,
or that he is thousands of years old, preserved by some
black magic. I've had a reservoir of fear of Magnus
since he was three years old. Even then, Magnus had
an ancient, powerful soul. Of course, I think you were
wrong to leave him, and I hope with all my strength
that you will return to him." Lily was drinking tea, and
she followed these words by taking a birdlike sip at it,
making it clear that she had at least one more thing to
say. Julia, listening to this description of her husband,
wondered how many times Lily had pondered in just
this way on Magnus' "ancient, powerful soul." It was
typical of her romanticizing of her brother. "But as my
advice is universally ignored, I don't suppose that you
will immediately follow it."

"You heard from him, Lily? What was he like?"

"Desperate, simply desperate. Of course, I couldn't
give him a crumb of solace. And his solace, you know,

would be mine—I'd be desolate for him if I thought you were never going back to him."

"I can't."

"He loves you. Since the only other person, apart from Kate, that Magnus has ever loved is myself, I am able to be quite certain."

"Lily," Julia insisted, "please don't. I can't take that now."

After a moment while both women looked away from one another toward the park, Julia asked, "Was he angry?"

"I wouldn't call it anger," Lily said. "He was distressed."

"Lily," Julia said, "you have to promise me that you won't tell him where I am. Never mind what you think is in my best interest or Magnus', please don't tell him. Promise me. Please."

"I'll promise you anything you like. But I'd be happier about it if you made me a promise too. I'd like you to tell me that you will consider going back to your husband."

"Lily, I've bought a house," said Julia, almost laughing. "I've bought *furniture*. It's just . . . just impossible for me to face Magnus. I can't make a promise like that to you. I can't even think about Magnus."

"On the contrary, it is my impression that you think of him all the time." She looked interrogatively at Julia.

When Julia said nothing Lily went on. "It was no one's fault about Kate, darling. You both very bravely did what you had to do. Magnus and you were both commended at the inquest, you know."

"I can't help that."

"But it's a pity that you were unable to hear it." Conscious that she was too crudely leading Julia into an area she would be unable to enter for perhaps months, Lily resisted the impulse to be Magnus' advocate in the matter of Kate's death. The facts of her niece's death were at least as clear in Lily's mind as in Julia's, and Lily knew, and could fully understand, that Julia had broken down afterward. In fact, Lily realized, she must have begun looking at houses only a day or two after she had come out of the hospital where she had been kept under sedation. Julia had left the hospital only to attend Kate's funeral; even that had been a mistake. That pale, confused, drugged creature stalked through the rain by photographers—it was unlikely Julia had any memory of that morning. Apparently she had begun to make arrangements for bolting on her first day back at Gayton Road: Lily supposed that she had been unable even to look at Magnus straight. Of course, Kate's death had been horrible. She had choked on a piece of meat, and Magnus and Julia, after dialing 999 and waiting minutes for an ambulance while their daughter fought uselessly for breath, had frantically decided to attempt an emergency tracheotomy. Kate had bled to death by the time the ambulance arrived. By Magnus' report, Julia had been very calm, very controlled throughout: only the next day did she get funny. Even now she looked flushed and breathless; and was drinking far too much gin.

"Well, tell me about this house of yours," Lily said. "What number in Ilchester Place is it?"

"Twenty-five."

"How odd that you should move to that street. Perhaps it is not odd at all, given that London is the sort of place in which all sorts of recurrences and coincidences occur."

"Lily, what are you trying to say?"

"My brother used to visit a house in Ilchester Place, a long time ago. It was while he was at Cambridge. I believe he had a friend there."

This comment fed a familiar stream of bitterness in Julia, who said, "Magnus and his friends. How boring all of that is. Maybe it comes from his having such an old, powerful soul."

"Yes, it does," said Lily, who seemed to be a little hurt.

"Lily, I'm sorry," Julia quickly said. "Can't we two be friends, without any relationship to Magnus? I want to begin a new life, I have to live on my own, I can't stand to think of Magnus and I'm afraid to see him, so that's done, but I want your friendship very much."

"Why, my dear," said Lily, "of course you have it. I want what is best for you. We *are* friends."

Julia felt close to tears. "I'm going to have a new life," she said, almost defiantly. "I want your help."

"Of course," Lily said, reaching out and taking Julia's hand. It was cold from her icy glass, and some grains of sand still clung to it. She allowed Julia to weep for a few moments in silence.

"You need something to do, you know," she said after Julia's noiseless crying had ended. "Only bores suggest their interests to other people, but how would you like to attend our next gathering? Mrs. Fludd is our new interpreter. She was a real find, the most *sensitive* sensitive I've met since poor dear Mr. Carmen died. Not personally, of course. She is a real old cockney, tough as a boot. But she has the gift to an astounding degree. I am very enthusiastic about her—but if you scoff at these old-fashioned performances, my feelings won't be bruised. It would be something for you to do, however."

Ordinarily Julia would have made some excuse, but she was touched by Lily's kindness, and this made her feel guilty for her earlier deliberate rudeness. "Just tell me where and when," she said. "It might be fun." Then a troubling thought occurred to her. "They won't . . . she won't . . . do anything about getting in touch with . . . I mean. . . ."

"There's no question of it," Lily said firmly. "Really, people have the most obsolete idea about what we do. I suppose you expect ectoplasm leaking from shadowy cabinets."

"Okay," Julia said, smiling. "Just call me whenever your gang has its next meeting."

"Fine," Lily said, clearly pleased. "Now I think I want to give you a present. In return, I hope you will allow me to snoop enviously through your house as soon as possible. Now excuse me."

Lily left the terrace, and Julia closed her eyes for a moment. We make a wonderful pair, Lily and I, Julia thought, we're both out of our tiny minds. She thought of going round to see Mark, and then she ceased to think of anything at all.

Lily awakened her by stroking her shoulder. She was carrying a large yellow book under her arm, and had a pair of scissors in her other hand. "My dear, you've been asleep for half an hour," she said.

"I've just been thinking about Mark," Julia said. "I'd like to see Mark." She felt once more full of energy.

"That might not be very clever, dear," Lily immediately said. "You'd be far wiser to leave Mark alone."

Lily, having lost one brother to Julia, did not wish to lose the other; she had come closer to her adoptive brother over the past ten years, as Magnus had not; "poor Lily's" defensive psychology seemed quite clear to her sister-in-law.

"Mark is so interesting," Julia said, "and I hardly feel that I know him. Magnus scarcely let him in the house. He used to telephone me sometimes and we'd have these long, sweet conversations. He's probably the only man I've flirted with since I married Magnus."

"He would be," said Lily. "Let me give you these presents. I'm sorry I haven't more to welcome you into your new house, but it's on such short notice. First, here's a lovely big book full of pictures, and it's all about your new neighborhood." She held the big volume before Julia's eyes: *The Royal Borough of Kensington,* by Eda Rolph. "Full of astonishing tales. Haven't read the book in years. The other present is some of these flowers." She waved her hand at the small, vibrant garden growing in boxes at the end of her terrace.

"Oh, I can't let you cut these beautiful flowers," said Julia, who disliked all cut flowers. "That would be a terrible crime. You can't cut them for me."

"But I can," said Lily, bending down and beginning to snip off nearly a dozen flowers. "Some tulips, some of these beautiful begonias, some of my favorites here, these monstrous pinks, and a few more of everything else. Now. Take these home and put them in water," she said, giving Julia the double handful of bright flowers, "and they'll stay fresh for as long as you like."

Julia looked apprehensively at the flower boxes, but was relieved to see that the loss of her dozen scarcely affected their appearance at all: the flowers grew there in such abundance that only a few small gaps were now visible. The massed scent of the flowers in her hands made her light-headed. They were overwhelmingly sensual. One of the fleshy tulips brushed her face.

"I don't mean to look as though I'm sending you away," Lily said. "These flowers can always be put in water here until you leave. Why don't you have dinner with me tonight? I've got . . . let's see, some nice little chops. Or was this one of my vegetarian nights? There is enough food, anyhow. Afterwards we could watch a delicious new series on the television. One of those wonderful costume dramas. I've never read much Trollope, you know, but it means so much more all acted out. And the language is so beautiful, none of the vulgarity the younger playwrights go in for now. Will you watch it with me? It's fascinating, and I could tell you what's happened in the earlier five hundred episodes."

"I'm out of the television habit," Julia said, smiling. "Your brother wouldn't allow one in the house. I do think I'll go home. Thank you for everything, Lily."

"Have you a telephone?"

"I'm not supposed to, but I do," said Julia. "It's still in the name of William McClintock. But I could practically shout across the park to you."

Lily nodded, apparently satisfied.

Julia slipped the book under her arm and, still holding the flowers with both hands, turned to leave the terrace.

"Now remember your promise!" she called over her shoulder to Lily.

Later, Julia regretted that she had not accepted Lily's offer of nut cutlets and *The Pallisers*. She had fallen asleep on the McClintocks' enormous gray velvet couch just after lying down on it to rest her feet; she had been

trying to read a novel she had bought and begun in the
Knightsbridge hotel the night previous, a Penguin edition of *Herzog,* but had fallen asleep after two pages.
When she awakened, the smell of Lily's flowers pervading the large room, her mouth felt unpleasantly thick.
She was very hungry, despite a dull pain just behind the
frontal bone of her forehead. She marked her place in
the book with a wrinkled tissue from the pocket of her
dress and went through the long room to the kitchen.

The light bounced, harshly white, from the gleaming
surfaces of the oven and refrigerator. Julia looked in the
cupboard for a glass, but realized despairingly that the
McClintocks had taken all of the kitchen and dining
things with them, as well as all the linen. The kitchen
held no food, no drink. And now it was hours past closing time for shops. Julia turned on the cold water from
the taps over the sink and applied some of it to her face;
then she cupped her hands and tried to drink from them,
but she could not hold enough water in her palms. Eventually she reduced the flow of water from the tap and
bent her head so that she could drink directly from it.
The water tasted metallic and brackish: she let it run
for a minute, and tried it again. Now it was slightly
better, but it still tasted as though it were full of metal
particles. She supposed she would have to buy bottled
water; but maybe she would get used to the taste.

Julia dried her hands and mouth on the long reddish
drapes over the outsize hall window. While doing this,
she remembered the bloodstain from the morning and
looked down at the side seam of her dress. The light-
blue seersucker showed a stiff brownish crescent an inch
long. The stain seemed larger than it had that afternoon.
What an odd scene that was, reflected Julia; surely she
had found those things in the sand by some bizarre accident, she had probably been nowhere near the place
where the girl had been playing. No child would do a
thing like that—well, a boy might. She could imagine
Magnus cutting up live turtles as a boy.

Did hot or cold water remove bloodstains? She had
been told a hundred times, but could never remember.

It was the one you didn't think it was, so she decided to
try cold water. Julia went back through the hall to the
big ground-floor bathroom, the one the McClintocks
had lined with rose-tinted mirrors. (The McClintocks,
in most ways utterly conventional and even a shade
stuffy in their tastes, had revealed a secret decadence in
their bathrooms. The tubs and sinks were marble, the
upstairs tub shaped like a huge sunken shell; the taps
were swans' necks, gold. Most surprising were the walls,
lined with tinted mirrors. Julia's bathroom upstairs had
black mirrors, against which the gold faucets dully
gleamed.) Julia took off her dress and draped it over the
edge of the sink, so the stained portion would soak, and
then filled the sink with water. Cold was right, she
thought.

She turned away from the sink and caught sight of
herself in the wall mirrors. Funny to see yourself front
and back, half nude. Julia wore only underpants and
tights. *My shell*, she thought. She was beginning to get
a little fat: she would have to be careful about pants.
But, she told herself, you don't look so bad, considering:
if no Playmate, no matron either. The rose tint made her
skin look darker and healthier than it was; Julia decided to get more sun this summer. It was a vision of
Magnus-free peace—to be able to sprawl in the sun in
the park outside her home.

Leaving the bathroom, she sprinted up the stairs to
the bedroom she had chosen that morning. Though it
was still not dark, she turned on the lights in the hall
and bedroom. This gave the house a cavernous, echoing
aspect which made Julia realize how little she knew her
new dwelling. She crossed to the windows of the bedroom, pulled the drapes together, and began to dress.
In a few minutes, buttoning on a floppy blue blouse she
had always liked, Julia realized that it had become very
warm in her bedroom; she was perspiring as she had
outside. The rest of the house had not seemed so warm.
She drew apart the drapes and opened the window by
pulling it up from the bottom. The air which streamed
in seemed magically cooler than the air within the room.

It could have been because the house had been empty for a month; or could it have been something else?

Julia went to the storage heater set against the wall and touched it with the flat of her hand. She snatched it back in pain. The heater had been turned up to the full. The real-estate agent must have turned it on, Julia thought, so that he would not be showing customers a chilly house. Perhaps some of the downstairs heaters were on as well. She switched off the bedroom heater at the wall and went into the black-mirrored bathroom to comb her hair. The small heater in this room, she discovered, was also on. She flicked it off at the wall, and straightened up to look at herself. In these bathrooms it was impossible *not* to look at oneself. Julia wondered what sybaritic tricks the McClintocks had got up to before these sinister black mirrors. Yet her hair shone in them: and she supposed that she looked good enough for a restaurant. There was a decent-looking French restaurant, she remembered, just off Kensington High Street on Abingdon Road. And hadn't she seen a Chinese restaurant too? Now, she was embarrassed that she had cried, however briefly, before Lily; Lily had, though, demonstrated an almost otherworldly kindness. It seemed to Julia that she had very little to weep about —the sensation of debating between restaurants was one she had not had since her wedding, and it was charged with a nostalgic, delicious liberty. Still drowsy, hungry as she had not been in years, Julia felt for the moment young and capable of anything.

She decided, once on Kensington High Street, to try the French restaurant, remembering that it had been awarded a Michelin rosette some months before. On this first night, she could afford to be lavish with herself. She had, in the past, argued bitterly with Magnus about restaurants; spending twenty pounds on a meal for two at Keats was obscene; but surely tonight she had something to celebrate. Julia drifted down the busy street, looking in the shop windows, conscious of the multitude of cars surging past on her right, noting where she might buy things she needed for the house. She saw a bank: she would transfer her own account here and leave Magnus what she had put into their joint account. Up ahead was a W. H. Smith for buying books. She noticed a surprising number of package stores. At length she reached Abingdon Road and crossed the High Street to walk up toward the restaurant. The night air moved languorously about her, slipping past her skin. As she opened the door of the restaurant, a beautiful black-haired girl wearing large tinted glasses coming down Abingdon Road smiled at her, and Julia smiled back, feeling as though the girl had given her the liberty of the neighborhood. She too was a capable young woman, living alone in Kensington.

After dining luxuriously and slowly, relishing every mouthful of her snails, then half a seafood pancake, and finally a *suprême de volaille,* Julia paid for her meal with a check and walked back along the crowded street. Traffic seemed perpetual here, gnashing and snarling past as if it too were on its way to a meal. Only when she reached the quiet corner of Ilchester Place did she remember she had left the house key in the pocket of the dress now soaking in the sink.

"Christ," she moaned. She went up the steps and tried the front door. It was locked. Julia looked up at the windows and saw that she had left lights burning in the bathroom and bedroom. At the rear of the house, she had left the bedroom window open, but it was far out of reach. Perhaps a window in the kitchen or dining room might be unlatched. Julia walked around the side of the house, pushing randomly at the windows she could reach. After she had walked down the entire length of the right side of her house, she looked down in frustration and saw that she had trampled many of the little flowers the McClintocks had grown in a border around the house—small, brilliant flowers with thought-less, optimistic faces. They lay crushed and broken in a weaving line down the side of the house, just visible in the darkness. Julia felt as though the massive dark bulk of the house were rebuking her—it was a strong but momentary impression: she did not deserve this house and the house knew it now. "Oh, please," she breathed, and pushed at another window. It resisted her.

Julia rounded the corner at the back of the house and found herself in her moonlit back garden. The grass looked spectral, some color between green and black. Indeed, the entire garden looked unearthly in the dark light, the flower banks at the far end massive and colorless, like stationary clouds. Behind them reared the brick wall at the end of her property. Julia had a momentary tremor of fear that someone besides herself was concealed in the garden, but pushed this from her mind by the decisive action of vigorously trying each of the windows in turn. At the far end she discovered that the small window in the bathroom was opened out at the bottom, unlocked and with its ratchet set so that the window protruded two or three inches beyond the frame.

She reached in and released the ratchet, freeing the window so that it swung freely, opening a space about a foot high and fifteen or sixteen inches long, set in the wall at the height of her head. When she threw up the window and poked her head beneath it, she could see, in the rose mirror opposite, the light space of the window filled with the black orb of her head. Ordinarily, she would not think it possible that she could lift and squeeze her body through this small space, but now she had no other choice. The air in the bathroom felt silkily warm to her facial skin; she had to crawl in this way. The only alternative was to break a window, and she shrank before doing violence to the house.

On the verge of pulling her trunk up to force her shoulders through the window, Julia again sensed that another person was somewhere in the back garden: her stomach frozen with fear, she whirled about. No one was visible. The grass, tinted that expressionless color, lay unbroken to the mass of the flowers. Nothing moved. Julia narrowed her eyes and tried to see into the McClintocks' flowers. She braced her legs and felt some of the zinnias of the border crush beneath her feet. "I

know you're there," she said. "Come on out. Now." She
felt both foolish and courageous, uttering these words
in as commanding a voice as she could summon. Still
there was no movement from the featureless dark bank
of the flowers. After another long scrutiny, she felt safe
enough to turn her back to the garden.

Again she felt the heavy warmth emanating from her
house. She braced her elbows, bowed her head, and
scrabbled up the wall with her feet while pushing her
shoulders through the window frame. The window, let
loose, dug her painfully in the back of the neck. Hitch-
ing up on one arm, she banged the aluminum border of
the window with her other hand; this gave her enough
leverage to push herself through the window nearly to
her waist.

She wriggled, dropping her upper body so that her
weight might drag her bottom through. Instead, she
stuck in the window like a swollen fruit. She jerked forward twice, abrading the skin at her hips: from sudden
though tolerable pain, she knew she had begun to bleed.
Julia pushed with all her strength at the wall, bending
with as much torque as she could muster, and felt her
hips slide through another half inch. With one further
push and bend, she came through, banging her heels
on the protruding window, and fell to the bathroom
carpet on her right shoulder. She had lost both shoes.

She lay for several minutes on the bathroom floor,
breathing heavily. Her fingers found the cool marble of
the tub. Her hips ached; her stomach fluttered. For
some minutes Julia was unable to move, fearing she
might be sick. The skin of her face and hands felt very
hot. Eventually she sat upright and rested her back
against the bathtub. Through the material of the blue
blouse, the marble felt very cool. Modern urban people,
peaceful and sedentary, are crippled by shock when they
receive otherwise ordinary physical distress; Julia had
read this theory in a magazine recently, and she now
ruefully reflected that it seemed true in her case. She
could nearly feel the blood beating in her facial skin.

Supporting herself with one hand on the rim of the tub, she unsteadily stood up. The wall mirrors reflected a tangle-headed, stooping female figure in pale, ripped trousers. Everything glowed darkly, pinkly, as if through a haze. What she could see of her face looked black. Julia moved slowly to the sink. She tugged at the scersucker dress and let it drop wetly to the carpet; then she pulled the plug, not moving until the standing water had been sucked away, and ran fresh water, which she splashed on her face. The water smelled like greasy coins. When she peeled off her trousers, she saw that she had scraped skin from both hips; the trousers, bloodied, were ruined. By morning, she would have the beginnings of spectacular bruises on both hips. Julia bent down to the sodden dress, extracted her key from the pocket, and turned on trembling legs to the door. Then she had a second thought, and patted the heater by the door. It nearly burned her fingers, and she flipped up the wall switch to turn it off. Before leaving the bathroom, she remembered to place the blue dress back in a sinkful of fresh water.

The entire house seemed sluggishly hot; Julia thought it might take her an entire morning to find all of the heaters. Yet the warmth spread seductively throughout the living room, and she sat on the gray couch to relax for a second before attempting the stairs. Her hips ached. One of the downstairs heaters was set into the wall beside the big windows; yet another smaller heater was in the kitchen. Julia leaned back in the couch, stretching her legs out before her. She closed her eyes. Her hips smarted, but at least had stopped bleeding from the abrasions. Then she blinked, imagining that she had heard a series of sharp clicking noises from the dining room. Perhaps they had come from the kitchen: refrigerators made all sorts of noises. She heard one sudden, definite clicking noise, and her eyes opened involuntarily. It had come from the dining room—the noise had sounded like someone tapping at the window. Julia looked across the width of the living room into

the dining room, directly off it. Its large French windows
were set in line with the living room windows, so that a
passerby could look through the house into the garden.
The dining room drapes hung a foot apart. Through the
gap, Julia could see nothing but black. She felt an extreme disquiet; she wore only the blue blouse and underpants, and sat in view of the window. Perhaps someone had been hiding in the garden after all.

Her heart accelerated. Julia bounded up from the
couch and ran through the hall to the bathroom and
latched the window through which she had crawled.
Then she crept back through the warm house to the
dining room and peered out, concealing her body behind
the drapes. A second later, she thought she had distinguished a standing figure—it was a darker shape
posed before the mass of the flower beds. It moved
slightly. She had no impression of height or sex; she
needed none. Julia knew that it must be Magnus. She
fell to the floor as if by instinct. Julia lay there for some
minutes in a panic before she recognized that she must
have been wrong. Magnus did not know where she
lived.

If it were Magnus, and he wanted to hurt her, he
would have assaulted her in the garden. He could
scarcely have missed her scramble through the bathroom
window. And it was possible that no one was in the
garden. The motion might have been a bush, moved by
some breeze.

Julia opened her eyes and peered out to the garden,
her face at ground level. The garden held nothing un-
toward. Her heart had begun to beat normally once
again, and Julia sat up, blotting her face with the heavy
drape. The grass still had that spectral, shining blackness, and she could see the brick wall quite clearly.
Nothing between the house and the wall was moving.
Julia stood up and, holding one hand to her chest, went
back into the living room, moving slowly in the darkness. *Heaters,* she thought, and glided across the room
to the big storage heater set into the wall. It too had

been turned on, and she flipped up the switch set into the wall.

Julia woke with a start several hours later: she had been dreaming, and the dream eluded her from the second of her waking. She could hear noises from below; at the same moment she was aware of the noises, she became conscious of the heat in her bedroom. The window remained open, but the bedroom had not cooled since Julia had left for the restaurant. Her entire body was perspiring; this connected in some way to her dream, which had been frightful. She went taut with attention, listening, but heard nothing more. But there had been noises. She had not imagined them—rustling, soft, hushed noises, as of some person moving about in the dark. Her first thought was *Kate's up,* but this was only a half-conscious formulation on the surface of her mind when she thrust it away, aware that Kate had been in her dream, somehow threatened. Spurred by the image of Kate in peril, Julia sat up in bed, listening. She could hear no further noises. She rose from her bed and moved to the doorway. Standing halfway out into the hall, she loudly said, "I'm going to telephone the police. Did you hear me, Magnus? I'm telephoning the police."

Not knowing if she were to be attacked in the next instant, she hung in her doorway, listening with her entire soul. Sweat ran in a distinct line down her back to her buttocks. The hall seemed a shade cooler than her bedroom, less concentrated and dense. Julia remained poised in the doorway a long moment, hearing nothing, her mind empty of all but physical sensations. She began to count silently to one hundred, forcing herself to pause between numbers; when she reached one hundred, she went on to two hundred. Still she heard nothing. She must have been mistaken; yet she was too frightened to go downstairs to check. In the end, she went back inside the bedroom and locked the door. Then she thrust up the window and let the cooler night air pour over her. In her garden, in the visible areas of the park, all was

still. Eventually she returned to her bed and lay down
on the damp mattress.

The next morning, while Julia was writing a provi-
sional shopping list on the back of her checkbook, the
only paper she could find in her bag apart from a few
wrinkled tissues, the telephone shrilled in the living
room. Her first thought was that Markham and Reeves
were ringing with some question about the house; but
realizing that Markham and Reeves were likely to ignore her until she annoyed them with yet another request, Julia thought that Lily must be telephoning her.
She put down her checkbook and went from the kitchen
into the living room. Light streamed slantwise through
the big south windows and the front of the house. The
terrors of the previous night had seemed unreal and
slightly hysterical to her, waking uncovered in the sunny
house and moving through it during the morning, deciding what she needed to buy—food, dishes, glasses, pots
and pans, sheets, towels, blankets, eating utensils. For
the time being, bottled water. Books and whiskey.

"Hello?" she said, looking at the windows across the
street. A man down the block washed his car, sluicing
water across its top. Who were these people, who were
her neighbors?

In the next instant all the optimism was battered out
of her by the sound of Magnus' voice. "Julia, I expect
you know who this is. I want you to leave that building
and come back to Gayton Road. That's where we *live*.
I've been on to the estate agents, and I made it clear to
them that no contract you could sign would be considered binding, so we might just emerge from this ludicrous deal of yours with only a small loss. At the
moment, Julia, I consider you incompetent to handle
your own affairs, and certainly incompetent to make
decisions about our future. In the meantime I want you
here where you belong. You must leave that house. It
is unthinkable—"

She hung up.

When the telephone rang again, she plucked the receiver from the hook and held it away from her ear. Magnus' voice went harshly on, but she could distinguish only isolated words. *Irresponsible . . . featherbrained . . . Kate . . . marriage . . .*

"I don't consider myself married to you any longer," she said into the receiver. "You frighten me. You're a bully. I can't think of you without seeing Kate. So I can't look at you, live with you, be married to you. Please leave me alone, please. Stay away, Magnus."

"Like hell I will," she heard him say. "You're disturbed—when you face up to certain things—"

She shouted, "If I catch you hanging around my house, in the garden or anywhere else, I call the police." Then she snapped the receiver down.

She stood over the telephone, waiting for him to ring again, threatening, bullying, lying to her. When a minute passed without his making a third call, she thought: he ripped the phone out of the wall.

Yet, a few seconds later, he did ring again.

"Julia, Magnus. Don't ring off. I was so angry I couldn't telephone back immediately. Julia, I want you here. I want you with me. I fear for you. You're in danger down there, alone."

Julia felt herself stiffen. "Why am I in danger, Magnus?"

"Because you're alone. Because you need help."

"On the contrary, Magnus," she said. "I feel safe for the first time in two months. Lily promised me she wouldn't call you, and now that she has, the only danger I can imagine is from you. Maybe I'll move again. I know you were here last night. You were watching me. When we have something to talk about, I'll invite you to my house. Until then, stay away. Or you will be in embarrassing trouble."

She could visualize his response to this: his hands tightening into fists, his face reddening, his mouth compressing.

"Damn you," he said. To Julia, it was as though the weight of their ten years together was behind his curse. She made no reply; a second later, Magnus hung up.

Now she felt as though in battle with Magnus—perhaps the chiefest effect of eleven years of marriage was that threats and curses were no longer suppressed by politeness. They knew each other too well for politeness.

Twenty minutes later when for the first time she heard the sound of her doorbell, Julia started violently, spilling the contents of her bag. It was just long enough since her telephone call for Magnus to have driven down from Hampstead, intent on forcing her back to the house—or back to the hospital. There was no question that Magnus was capable of clapping her back in a hospital bed, muddled by drugs: in the meantime he could find some legal maneuver that would make her his prisoner. This was a new thought, and Julia, stuffing things back into her bag, resolved that she would fight him physically, violently, rather than submit to being dragged away.

She crept behind a large brown chair and peered around the drapes to the front steps. She could see only a squat, foreshortened shadow. Then the person took a backward step and came into view. It was Mark Berkeley. Julia jumped up from behind the chair and hurried to the door. She threw it open just as Mark, still walking backward and looking up at the house, had reached the steps to the pavement.

"Mark, you darling," she said. "What a wonderful surprise. I thought you were Magnus. Please come in."

Mark stood in the sunlight grinning at her. He really was incredibly handsome. His denim shirt and trousers were so faded they might have been the same ones he had been wearing when she first met him.

"Do you mind my knowing your secret?" he said. "Lily rang me yesterday evening. She's full of admiration for you, and I must say I am too. What a beautiful house. It's perfect."

"Lily has a terribly big mouth, but in your case, I don't mind." Julia held the door as Mark came into the hall beside her. For a moment she had a strong impression that he was about to embrace her, and she moved fractionally away from him. Mark put one warm hand on her back.

"She called Magnus too? So he knows where you are?" Julia nodded.

"He rang me up two nights ago, in an utter rage. He accused me of hiding you from him."

"Damn him." Julia was shocked, and then considered that such a suspicion was characteristic of Magnus. "Oh, I'm so sorry, Mark. I don't want you to be bothered by him. Well, come on in and sit down. Can I get you anything? Actually, I can't. I don't have a thing in the house and I was just about to go shopping. Oh, I'm so happy to see you, you're just like fresh air."

"Why do you keep this house at nursery temperature? It's warmer in here than outside." Mark flopped onto the couch. "Julia, you know you needn't be apologetic about Magnus with me—I've known him even longer than you have. In fact, I was never quite sure why you stayed with him all those years. I suppose I can say that now."

"You can say anything you like," said Julia, though she did not actually wish it, and disliked his remark. Almost against her will, she added, "We did have Kate," and then thought that her marriage really was over if she could make such a statement. Seeing handsome, banished Mark at rest in her home, his scuffed boots crossed on her carpet, Julia felt alarmingly free of Magnus. She said, "I can't bear to think of him right now, Mark. I'm still frightened of him. But I'm getting stronger. You do think I did the right thing?"

"Julia released from bondage," Mark said, laughing. "Of course you did the right thing. I'm just worried that he won't let you be. Do you think he won't bother you?"

"I don't know," Julia admitted. "I think he might have been sneaking around the house last night. It was just an impression, something I saw out in the garden, a figure. In fact, he as much as admitted it this morning on the telephone. He scared me out of my wits." Mark was regarding her very seriously, which gave Julia's narrative some impetus: she would have hated Mark's easy dismissal of her fears.

"But that's terrible," he said. "That's just what I was afraid of. You have to keep him away. To be frank, I wouldn't trust anything he says. It would be just like Magnus to try to frighten you into returning to him."

"Oh, let's not talk about Magnus," Julia pleaded. "I want to show you my house. Do you really like it? I bought it in such a rush that I'm not sure myself. I've never done anything like this by myself before."

"It's perfect for you," he said. "But where did you get all this astounding furniture?"

"It belonged to the people who used to live here," she said. "I like it. I don't want to have to think about furniture."

"Then you're all right," he said, smiling.

Julia led him through the house, taking him into each room in turn until they came finally to her bedroom.

"But it's roasting in here," Mark said. "Even with the windows open. You must have the heaters on. Where are they?"

"No, I switched them off yesterday," Julia said, going across the green carpet to the big gray block of the heater. She looked at the wall outlet and saw that the switch was in the down position. "That's funny, I thought. . . ." She paused. "Maybe I switched it on. No, I couldn't have, because it was so hot when I moved in. I must have been mistaken in some way." She bent down and flipped up the switch. "Up is off, isn't it? On these switches."

"Usually," Mark said. He went across the room and lightly touched the top of the heater. "Well, that's on, anyhow. It's turned up all the way. Maybe you have a poltergeist."

"Oh, I hope so," Julia said. "That's nice. You just smile when I say something drippy and girlish like that. Magnus would look disgusted."

"Magnus has Standards."

"And a powerful soul."

"Hah! Do you forgive her for letting me know your secret?"

"For telling you, but not for telling Magnus. He gave me a wretched night."

"Let me go shopping with you, and I'll help you put Magnus right out of your mind."

"You're a dear. I'll need lots of help carrying heavy things."

"Consider my back yours." These words, coming from Mark, had an almost explicit sexual overtone; Julia took his arm as answer. No one as irresponsible as Mark could ever be threatening.

"If you help me, maybe I'll return the favor by helping you clear up that legendary mess of yours in Notting Hill."

"Agreed," Mark said.

3

Even later, Julia could look back on that afternoon of shopping with nostalgic, regretful pleasure. It had been as though she really were free of all ties, unattached, spendthrift and carefree—the girl she might have become ten years ago if she had not been mesmerized by Magnus Lofting. She and Mark had taken the Rover first to Oxford Street, where Julia bought towels and sheets and some kitchen things she needed, and then to Harrod's. Mark had insisted on buying her an odd little green bracelet, not expensive by Harrod's standards. Finally they had gone to Fortnum and Mason's, where Julia spent a ridiculously happy, ridiculously costly hour buying exotic groceries. Julia several times caught other shoppers looking at her queerly and realized she was making a lot of noise but for once did not feel embarrassed or rebuked; Mark, for his part, seemed delighted

by her effusiveness. His enjoyment of her high spirits
fed them: Julia felt nearly intoxicated with pleasure,
uncomplicated and cloudless. She and Mark had tea at
Fortnum's; then they abandoned the laden Rover in a
parking garage and went to a pub; in the evening he
took her to a small restaurant in Notting Hill. Magnus
had never entered a pub in all his adult life—Magnus
would have fled The Ark (providing that he could have
been coaxed into any restaurant in Notting Hill) at
first sight of the menu which was chalked on boards
hung on the walls. After dinner, now in a second pub,
Mark rather shyly invited Julia to his flat: "Room, actually. You've never been there."

"Some other time, dear Mark. I have all those things
to put away. And I've had too much liquor to trust myself in your room."

That night her dreams were lurid. She was walking
slowly, ploddingly, through Holland Park—a Holland
Park full of statues and bronze monuments. She was
alone; Magnus had vanished somewhere, and Julia knew
that he was seeing another woman. Kate gamboled up
ahead, her head bobbing, her white dress winking in the
gray-green light. Julia tried to walk faster, in order to
protect Kate, but each step took enormous effort, as
though she was walking through a bog. Then, looking
ahead, she saw that Kate had a companion, the blond
girl she had seen on her first day in the park. The two
girls danced ahead of her, unheeding. Their identical
heads, each white gold, flew through the dense air. Far
ahead of Julia, on a long hill, they sat down. Julia tried
to run, but her legs were as if paralyzed. The second
girl was speaking rapidly to Kate, uttering some vile
business—Kate sat enthralled. When Julia came nearer,
the girls turned their faces toward her, their identical
eyes glowing. "Go away, Mother," Kate said.

Then she was carrying Kate's body through a city.
The blond girl, as before, danced ahead of her, leading.
Julia followed after, crossing busy streets in bright sunshine, until they had left the crowded downtown part of
the city and were in a sinister, dilapidated area: grimy,

sunless courts and filthy brick buildings with boarded windows. A hunchbacked man scuttled past, grinning at her. The blond girl entered one of the buildings through an open arch. Julia, frightened, forced herself to follow. She found herself somehow on a rooftop, stared at by shabbily dressed, lounging men. Her arms were in great pain and Kate had got very heavy. The blond girl had vanished through another arch. Julia understood that she would have to stand on the rooftop, holding her daughter's corpse and gazed at by the shabby men—she would have to stand there for hours. The entire scene had a despairing, criminal atmosphere of moral failure; Julia wanted to leave, but she could not.

She awakened in the hot room. The despairing flavor of the dream still clung to her. Julia missed Kate terribly: at the moment, as she stared up into blackness, her life seemed empty of anything but loss and uncertainty. With a tiny shock of disapproval, she realized that she wanted Mark's company, not sexually, but for the fact of his sleeping near, his chest rising and falling. She turned over on her other side and buried her head deep into her pillow, which still smelled of the shop; the single blanket she had put on the bed had been kicked off during her sleep. She closed her eyes, trying to overcome the mood of the dream. Then she heard the noise which had awakened her the night before. It was a soft, rustling, rushing noise, coming from the hall or the stairway. Julia tightened, then relaxed. It must have been a breeze on the drapes in the hall.

A crash from downstairs made her sit bolt upright in bed—she immediately thought that Magnus had broken in and was now storming about, breaking things. At first she felt her familiar fear of him, but as she listened, her fear hardened into anger: she would not have Magnus in this house. She lifted her wrist near to her face and squinted at her watch. It was past two in the morning. If Magnus were out at this hour, he was probably drunk. In the past years, he had begun to drink more heavily and often came home to Gayton Road smolderingly intoxicated, incensed by something that had happened in the night. She slid from bed, pulled a nightdress over her head, and then wrapped herself in her bath- robe. When she opened the door to the hall she listened intently, cautiously, but heard nothing.

Julia left her bedroom and crept into the hall, moving as quietly as possible. When she reached the head of the stairs, she heard the rustling noise again, and her heart nearly stopped. She flailed out with her right hand and banged the switch for the stairway light. No one was there. She could see the edge of the drapes over the downstairs hall window; they hung straight and still. The rustling noise had suggested rapid movement, a two-legged presence; yet it was a feminine noise, and it was impossible to imagine Magnus producing it. Julia went quietly and slowly down the stairs and paused in the hall. She heard nothing from any of the rooms. Still using the light emanating from the staircase, she pushed open the door to the living room. Moonlight lay over the couch and carpet, silvery and weightless. The yellow cover of Lily's book shone from the floor. "Magnus," she enunciated, taking a step into the room. *"Magnus."* There was no answer. Julia became aware that her eyes hurt; her flanks, too, throbbed where she had abraded them the previous night. "Say something, Magnus," she said. It would be very unlike Magnus to crouch silently in a dark room. Much more in his style would be to seize her, shouting.

Julia glanced rapidly around the room, but saw noth- ing amiss; the living room looked drugged, impersonal, not hers; the McClintocks' furniture lay like heavy beasts sleeping around a water hole. She walked through the moonlight to the dining room. These drapes too were open, and she could see out into the garden, eerie in the silvery light. There too nothing moved. Julia turned around to look into the corners of the room.

And then she saw what had made the noise. Lily's flowers lay in a puddle on the carpet, the vase she had put them in shattered into four or five large irregular pieces. Julia stifled a scream rising in her throat, and put one hand to her mouth: someone had smashed the

vase against the mahogany table and then thrown the
flowers to the carpet. She ran to the windows and tugged
at the handle; it moved smoothly down, and the window
swung out into the garden, admitting a wave of cool
night air. It was unlocked. Last night, outside, she had
pushed at the handle, and it had not budged. Now she
turned the key, locking the window again. Magnus must
have entered somehow—had found his way in here—
and after smashing the vase, had fled through the garden. The scene, in her imagination, had the same stench
of moral failure, the same hopelessness, as the moment
on the rooftop in her dream—it was overwhelmingly
despairing.

Julia bent to the soaking carpet and picked up the
sections of the McClintocks' vase. These she took into
the kitchen and set on the counter. Later she would try
to glue them together. When she returned to the dining
room she gathered the foolish broken flowers, took them
into the kitchen and pitched them into the small bin beneath the sink. She thought of Magnus reeling homo,
furious, talking to himself, staggering bearlike up Kensington High Street. She supposed that he would visit
one of his women.

After she had blotted up some of the water with a
dish towel, Julia went back upstairs to her bedroom.
She felt flushed and restless and lay down in her bed to
await morning. It would be impossible to sleep, she
thought, but her eyes, heavy, began to close almost immediately. Just before she dozed, she imagined she
heard far off laughter—an unfriendly, mocking noise.
Heat settled on her in layers; in one of the broken
dreams she had between intervals of wakefulness, she
dreamed that she and Kate were birds, gliding birds,
riding currents of warm air. Up there, they were free:
no one would notice them. She desired anonymity, apart-
ness, isolation. Perhaps, she thought, she really did
want to go mad.

"Well, I told you I wanted to see your house," said
Lily. They were speaking on the telephone, shortly be-

fore noon. "And it would be a heaven-sent answer to
our problem. Normally we meet at Mr. Piggot's rooms
in Shepherd's Bush, but he's been doing some painting
and the flat simply reeks of it—extremely unsuitable, as
you can imagine. Mrs. Fludd won't come to Plane Tree
House because she insists on working in a ground-floor
room, and I don't imagine we should occupy the lobby,
do you? Miss Pinner and Miss Tooth live together in a
bed-sitter in West Hampstead, but that too is on the
second floor. Mr. Arkwright says his wife won't hear of
having our session at his house. So, my dear, you see
our position. Might we meet at your house? I know it's
an intrusion, especially as it's your first experience, but
I'm at my wit's end trying to invent a ground-floor room
which simply does not exist."

"No, it's my pleasure, really," said Julia, who was in
fact dubious about having Mrs. Fludd and the rest of
Lily's circle in her house. Then she thought that if Magnus were hanging about outside, watching the house, it
would serve him right to see a crowd of people drive up.
She saw the house from his point of view, all its lights
blazing, cars parked outside on both sides of the street:
it would be an emblem of her independence from him.
She said, "I'd be happy to help out. What time do you
usually meet?"

"You *angel*," breathed Lily. "Nine o'clock. The
others will be so gratified."

"Should I have any refreshments? Anything to eat?"

"Coffee or tea. Some biscuits. We're not a very particular set."

For the rest of the morning Julia sat out in the sun
in her garden, alternately reading *Herzog* and dozing;
after lunch she went again into the garden, taking with
her an iced glass of gin and bitter lemon. The drink, the
hot sun, reminded her of summer afternoons in America, at home or at Smith, afternoons of Nat Cole on the
radio, boys appearing to sprawl on the grass. In this
mood of nostalgic, sun-drugged leisure, Julia passed the
afternoon, reading steadily through *Herzog*.

At four, struck by an idea, she went into the house through the dining room and telephoned Mark.

"It's probably totally crazy," she said, feeling a little dishonest. "Lily practically insisted that I join her gang of devil-worshipers or whatever they are, and now that they're meeting here I feel sort of swamped by them. Could you come over to hold my hand?"

"Lily won't like that," said Mark.

"Bugger Lily. I haven't even mentioned to her that she broke her promise to me by telephoning Magnus. I know she couldn't help it. Besides, I don't know that she wouldn't like it if you were here. Aren't you two friends these days? I thought you and Lily were getting on?"

"She's got some peculiar ideas about me," Mark laughed. "I think Lily fancies herself my warden."

"As mine too," she said. "Please come. We're all meeting at nine, but you could come over earlier."

"Done. Do you want me to bring anything?"

"Bring yourself," Julia said.

Lily and a squat, red-faced woman in a flowered dress covered by a shapeless, ancient gray tweed overcoat straining at one large button arrived at eight fifty. As a pair they were unavoidably comic: Lily like some aging, silky moth accompanied by this little bulldog of a woman who needed only a carthorse's straw hat to complete her ensemble. And Julia could not keep from smiling at the two of them when she had opened her door. Of all the women who looked like Lily, she thought, only Lily would appear in public with this person. They looked like a vaudeville team—Lily would be the "aristocrat" who is doused with water and slapped with cream pies.

"Mrs. Fludd and I had a lovely walk through the last of the sun," Lily said. "Julia Lofting, Mrs. Fludd."

"How do you do?" Julia said. "Please come in. Did you walk through the park?"

"Holland Park is locked at sunset," said Lily. "It's tight as a drum. Mrs. Fludd wanted to see the neighborhood."

"It ain't half hot," said Mrs. Fludd. "It's tropical, I call it. Still, it's nearer than Shepherd's Bush. Not exactly cool in here either, is it?"

Julia apologized, explaining about the heaters.

"You want to go to a nice air-conditioned bingo," said Mrs. Fludd.

She bumped to a halt following Lily into the living room. Mark rose from the couch, grinning. "Nice to see you again, Lily," he said. "And you must be the wonderful Mrs. Fludd I've heard so much about."

Lily glanced at him, and then at Julia; her disapproval clear, she turned to attend to Mrs. Fludd, who appeared to have become even redder and more squat in shock.

"There's two new ones," she complained. "You said one. You never said two new ones. I come all this way for nothing. Too much interference with two new ones."

"This is my brother, Mark Berkeley," Lily quickly said. "He's a friend of Mrs. Lofting's. Mrs. Fludd, please don't say it's impossible. All the others will be arriving soon. And I wanted Mrs. Lofting to witness our transcendances."

"No transcendances with two new ones," Mrs. Fludd said firmly. "No transformations, no interpenetrations, and no consummations neither. This one"—she pointed at Julia with a stubby finger—"is skeptic. All the vibrations will be muddled. Aren't you skeptic, dear?"

Julia looked at Lily, not sure what to say. Lily was no help. She was still upset by Mark's presence. "I suppose I am," she finally said.

"Of course you are. Your aura's dark—dark as pitch. Confusion and despair in the seventh plane. That's the plane of domesticity. Right, dear?"

"Well. . . ."

"Right, then. And there's another cloudy aura," nodding to Mark. "Dirty as an old pond. But that one's open to things. He's receptive. Maybe too open. Pretty men are like that. He needs special care, he does."

"Does that mean you won't do it?" said Julia. She was charmed by Mrs. Fludd.

"Did I say I wouldn't? I said, no transcendances, no transformations, no interpenetrations and no consummations. You couldn't follow them proper anyhow, being skeptic. But *he* could—he's open. He wants to be filled, like a bottle."

Mark laughed delightedly and said, "Mrs. Fludd, you're a genius. You're worth twice your fee."

"Don't take money," said Mrs. Fludd, unbuttoning the single button and permitting the front of the tweed overcoat to spring apart. "Money soils the gift. I take tea, though. PG Tips is my drink." She moved unhesitatingly toward the couch. "Mr. Piggot makes a wonderful cup of tea." She sat, exposing thick white calves and a pair of tight, black policeman's boots, and looked expectantly at Julia.

"Oh, I'm sorry," Julia said, "but I don't have any tea. I bought coffee, thinking. . . ." She looked again at Lily, who merely shrugged, still distressed by Mark's presence. She had moved far across the room from him, and after her gesture to Julia, pretended to examine the garden through the long dining-room windows.

"Can't drink that muck," said Mrs. Fludd. "Sometimes I take a little Ribena. Smashing for the upper regions, Ribena is."

"I don't have any Ribena either," Julia said, nearly wailing.

"Humph."

"Sherry?"

Mrs. Fludd cocked her head and considered. "Well, as there's to be no special tricks tonight, I could accept a tiny amount of sherry, yes. Next time, you want PG Tips, love. We all drink tea here. Miss Pinner and Miss Tooth dote on Mr. Piggot's tea. Here's my coat, love."

When Julia was going toward the kitchen for the sherry the doorbell rang, and she asked Lily to open it for her. When she returned to the living room, a tall spindly man in his sixties with a severe long face and a little Hitler mustache was regarding Mark with an expression of grave disquiet. "Two will never do, Miss Lofting," he was saying. The man had thrust his hands into the pockets of his long tan canvas coat—a coat like a park attendant's or a movie IRA man's—and showed no inclination to remove it or his large-brimmed hat of the same color. Mark, perfectly at ease, merely smiled back at the man.

"Now, Mr. Piggot," Lily coaxed, "Mrs. Fludd is willing to go ahead, and so. . . . And here is Mrs. Lofting, our hostess. Mr. Piggot, Julia."

Mr. Piggot glanced sharply at Julia, softened a bit, and removed his hat. His hair grew in a graying mousy fringe above his ears, leaving a high, mottled bald scalp which looked as fragile as an eggshell. "Well," he said. "Looks like she makes a good cup of tea."

"Have a nice glass of sherry, Mr. Piggot," Julia said, trying desperately to win over the old scarecrow.

"Sherry, is it? We generally imbibe tea at these gatherings. PG Tips, I use. Mrs. Fludd fancies it, don't you, Mrs. Fludd? But I won't say no to a nice sherry, not from your hands. British, is it?"

"Uh, Spanish," Julia said. "Manzanilla."

Mr. Piggot's face contracted. "Well, it'll wet the whistle. I feel a bit dry after cycling over here from Shepherd's Bush. We generally have these sessions at my place, you know. Expect your—aunt?—has told you that. But Mrs. Fludd won't go into a place that's been painted too recently. Distorts the reverberations."

"Something horrible," Mrs. Fludd cheerfully agreed, accepting her sherry. "Throws me whole system off."

"There's Mr. Arkwright," said Mr. Piggot when the bell rang again. "Punctual as the Irish Guards is Mr. Arkwright."

Julia said, "Will you let him in, Lily?" She took a third glass of sherry to Mark, who said something sardonic about filling up his bottle and moved over to sit beside Mrs. Fludd. Mr. Piggot still gazed at him with affronted blue eyes, spaced rather too closely together.

"Hullo, all." A compact little gentleman in a frayed gray gabardine suit bounced into the room a few paces ahead of Lily. He too had a mustache and a bald head, but his mustache was larger than Mr. Piggot's, and his cranium seemed almost aggressively solid. Julia noticed a medal pinned to his jacket before she saw that one of his sleeves was pinned up. "Am I the last?" He looked around briskly, paused at Mark, and then made for Julia. "See the West Hampstead ladies aren't here yet. You must be Julia Lofting. Pleased to meet you. The name's Arkwright. Nigel Arkwright. And you have sherry, how thoughtful. Lovely house you have here, eh? My cousin Penny Grimes-Bragg took a house in this neighborhood many years ago, over in Allen Street. Not far from here, is it?"

"No, not at all," Julia said, wondering if Mr. Arkwright got out of the house much. But she had decided that he was an "ally" against the unpredictable Mrs. Fludd and the as yet unknown West Hampstead ladies.

"No more than a brisk walk," he was saying. "Driving my old bus down here, I was just thinking of the old days when Penny and I—"

"Do join me, Mr. Arkwright," Lily broke in. Her innate sociability had apparently overcome her resentment of her brother's presence, for she smiled at Julia once Mr. Arkwright turned his back.

"With pleasure, Miss L.," he chirped. "Ah, Mrs. Fludd, two new ones tonight. That'll limit the old bag of tricks, won't it?"

"Drink your sherry, Nigel," said Mrs. Fludd amicably. She had moved some inches away from Mark, who was now slumped far down on the couch so that his bottom seemed in danger of slipping to the floor. He looked profoundly bored, but Julia sensed some area of tension—unreleased, concealed—in him. Mrs. Fludd too appeared to have been accumulating psychic power, for she glanced toward the door a second before the bell rang again.

Julia went into the hall and opened the door. Two women, both thin and elderly and dressed in long, threadbare black coats, stood on the doorstep. Behind them Julia glimpsed an ancient black bicycle propped against the curb, and an even older-looking, rusty Morris Minor behind it which must have been Mr.

Arkwright's "bus." The West Hampstead ladies had presumably taken a combination of buses. If Magnus were lurking outside, watching the various arrivals, the effect would not be what she had intended. In fact, she saw, the effect would be the reverse of her intention: Magnus would suppose her to have slipped over the edge into total incompetence. Still, she found a smile for the two women.

"I'm Julia Lofting. You must be Miss Pinner and Miss Tooth."

"Such a long way."

"But not as far as Shepherd's Bush."

Miss Pinner and Miss Tooth entered Julia's house, remarking upon its niceness. When they reached the living room, they darted in tandem across to Mrs. Fludd, spoke a few words to her, and then turned around to smile at the others of their group. When Miss Pinner finally saw Mark, her smile disappeared. Miss Tooth, however, cast him a glance full of vague benevolence.

"Who is this young man?" asked Miss Pinner.

"Now, Norah," said Miss Tooth.

"Who is he?"

"Mrs. Lofting's brother, Mark. Very dark in the aura, he is. *Your* aura's very strong tonight, Miss Pinner. Bright orange, the color of powerful movements in the fourth house. Perhaps we shall have luck tonight." Saying this, Mrs. Fludd looked about the room, her attention visibly distracted from Miss Pinner; she had grown, since Julia had last looked at her, slightly apprehensive.

"There will be no question of the higher states with two new ones," said Miss Pinner.

Lily said from Mr. Arkwright's side, "Mrs. Fludd has very graciously agreed to limit herself to the elementals."

As Julia looked at the two old women their faces, which had seemed so similar at the doorway, separated. Miss Pinner bore a certain resemblance to Mr. Piggot, at that moment engaged in describing to Lily and Mr.

Arkwright how he caught fish in Hyde Park by fixing bread to his fishhooks: both of them had long narrow faces and small bright-blue eyes like chips of sky. Miss Tooth looked rather dusty and faded, with her small, deeply-lined face the image of a retired governess. Miss Pinner could have been an exheadmistress noted for her disciplinary acumen. Julia took all the coats to the hall closet and returned with sherry for the two women. Miss Tooth glanced at Miss Pinner before accepting hers and, receiving a nod, took the glass in her small, trembling hand.

Mark gave Julia a despairing look and rose from the couch to join Lily, listening to Mr. Piggot describe his illicit fishing experiences. For these old people the spiritualist gatherings were social occasions; Mr. Arkwright kept punctuating Mr. Piggot's adventures with loud bursts of soldierly laughter. His rush of talk hadn't denoted any special sympathy for Julia, but demonstrated instead pleasure at his release from loneliness. Julia's house was filled with people whose company she could not enjoy; even Mark was sullen. Miss Pinner and Miss Tooth were now examining Julia's furniture. They were in an ecstasy of approval, everything being "so nice." Julia wished she could leave and lock the door behind her; but she took a sip of her sherry and sat beside Mrs. Fludd on the couch.

"I shouldn't stay here," said Mrs. Fludd.

"No? Mrs. Fludd, I'd be so grateful if you could. Lily has been looking forward so much. . . ."

"You needn't be false to me, Mrs. Lofting, you'd be happy if the lot of us went home. But you don't take my meaning. I shouldn't stay here if I were you. Shouldn't stay in this house."

Julia looked at the woman's red puggish face in surprise; she was further surprised to notice that Mrs. Fludd's eyes were shrewd and perceptive, not at all vague. It was as though she had seen that Mrs. Fludd was actually a man, wearing that absurd clothing; the shock was as great as that. She had been seeing Mrs. Fludd as a "character," someone not to be taken seriously, and this quick glance of recognition made her blush for her assumptions. If the others of Lily's gang were lonely eccentrics, Mrs. Fludd's cool, startling gaze revealed a person composed of flintier materials than the gibberish about transcendances and interpenetrations had suggested.

"Something's funny in this house," she said.

"You think I should leave?" said Julia, transfixed.

"Do you see anything? Hear any noises? Has anything unexplained occurred?" Even her diction had altered.

"I don't know," Julia confessed. "Sometimes I think I hear things—"

"Yes." Mrs. Fludd nodded sharply.

Remembering something Mark had said, Julia asked, "What are poltergeists, exactly? I feel sort of foolish, asking you, but is it possible that there might be one here?"

"Never any harm in a poltergeist," replied Mrs. Fludd. "They move things, sometimes break a mirror or a vase—mischievous creatures. You'd be in danger only if you were very receptive, like your pretty friend across the room. Or if you were dominated by some strong destructive emotion. Hate. Envy. Then, if the spirit wished revenge, it might influence you. That's rare, but it does happen, if the spirit is particularly malefic. Or if some coincidence links you to it. In Wapping, a thief dead for fifty years set fire to a house containing a burglar's family. Killed them all."

"But how do you know?" asked Julia.

"I felt it. I knew."

Such monolithic assurance always influenced Julia. In any case, it permitted no argument. "You feel something here?" she asked.

Mrs. Fludd nodded. "Something. Can't pin it down yet. But I don't like this house, Mrs. Lofting. Who lived here before you?"

"A couple named McClintock. He made carpets. I bought this furniture from them."

"Any deaths in their family? Any tragedies?"

"I don't know. They were childless people."

"But you've seen something. Things in this house."

"Well, I'm afraid it might be my husband," Julia said, and laughed.

Mrs. Fludd immediately closed up, separating herself from Julia; then, relenting, she took Julia's hand. "Ring me if you ever want advice," she said. From her bag she extracted a white card which read *Rosa Fludd, Interpreter and Parapsychologist.* Printed at the bottom was a telephone number.

Mr. Piggot approached the couch, followed by the perky Mr. Arkwright. "It *is* time?" said Mr. Piggot. "I'm eager to investigate some theories I had at the shop since our last meeting."

"Of course, love," said Mrs. Fludd, firmly back in her former role. She clapped her hands together twice and conversation in the room ceased. Miss Pinner and Miss Tooth turned their white faces raptly to the couch.

"Time," breathed Miss Tooth.

At opposite ends of the room, Lily and Mark also turned to face Mrs. Fludd; Lily with an expression combining eagerness with satisfaction, Mark wearily. Julia had time to wonder what was wrong with Mark before Lily asked her to turn off the lights.

She jumped up and went quickly to the light switch. Glowing gray light entered the room from the big windows; in this soft diffused semidarkness, Julia could see the fixed, rapt expressions on the faces of the "group." She and Mark were outsiders here, and she moved to his side.

"Have you a candle or small lamp, Mrs. Lofting?"

Julia went into the dining room and turned on a little ceramic lamp in the shape of a toby jug.

"Move it further away, please," commanded Mrs. Fludd. "I must ask you all to join hands at the beginning. Look at the light behind me. Cleanse your minds."

The little lamp cast only a feeble light into the living room. Julia, joining the group, found herself being gripped by Mark on her right; he was holding her hand tight enough to hurt her. On her left Mr. Piggot's hand was surprisingly soft and damp. His wafery skull shone palely in the twilight.

The group members, once they had joined hands, moved to sit on the floor, awkwardly, pulling Julia and Mark down with them. Only little Miss Tooth accomplished the move from standing to sitting with grace, seemingly floating to a cross-legged position; Miss Pinner moved with a machinelike efficiency. Julia, covertly watching her, thought she could smell oil and gears.

Once on the floor, the group members looked past Mrs. Fludd's head to the soft light emanating from the toby jug lamp. Mark, brooding, had set his face into a mask of weary tolerance. Both apprehensive and skeptical, Julia too looked at the lamp. After a bit her eyes began to burn. When she glanced at the others, she saw that the group members had closed their eyes; their faces hung in the air like death masks. Mrs. Fludd sat in a perfectly ordinary position on the couch before them, her hands folded in her lap. In the pane of the tall back window, her head and the lamp glowed against the darker glass. Whitish clouds scudded above the flame-like, dissolving orb of the lamp.

"Close your eyes," said Mrs. Fludd, her voice very slow and quiet. Mr. Piggot, to Julia's left, sighed and slumped backward, tugging her hand. "You may open them later if you wish."

She closed her eyes. About her she heard breathing. Mark gripped her right hand even harder, and she shook her hand in his, signaling him to loosen; he pinned her hand yet more tightly.

"One of us is having trouble," said Mrs. Fludd. "Who is it?"

Mark said, "I'm getting out of this." He broke contact with Julia and stood up.

"Close the group," said Mrs. Fludd. "Mr. Berkeley, you will sit quietly outside the group and observe."

Julia hitched sideways and grasped Lily's cool hand. It lay passively in hers. Lily had not opened her eyes when Mark had spoken, though all of the others had. Mark now sat behind them, still facing Mrs. Fludd.

"I need your help, Mrs. Lofting," said Mrs. Fludd softly. "Make your mind empty, completely empty and white. Let nothing enter it." Her voice was slowing and becoming deeper in timbre. Julia opened one eye and saw, looking up toward the couch, Mrs. Fludd's heavy jowls outlined by the soft light behind her. Her hair was a white gauze. She seemed to have become heavier and older. Julia closed her eyes again and thought of a white saucer.

Miss Tooth, at the left end of the seated line, began to breathe stertorously. Lily's hand still lay utterly passively in Julia's. After a bit, Julia felt an ache in her thighs. Her eyes closed, she began to see flashes of scenes, people's faces or landscapes appearing momentarily before her and then melting into other scenes. Moses Herzog, his face that of an elderly English professor at Smith, metamorphosed into Blake's flea. The hideous features of the flea in turn were transformed into Magnus' face. By an effort of will, Julia dismissed this last vision—she thought of clouds covering that big, powerful face, obscuring it. When the clouds blew off, they revealed one of the lounging, shabby men who had been in her dream. Now the man was her father, and he examined her with an expression of exhausted pity. She could see herself standing on the black tarpaper of the rooftop, Kate dead in her arms. Both of her thighs ached; the right was on the verge of cramp. Julia lurched to one side and twisted her legs out before her. Mr. Piggot twitched at her hand in rebuke.

Opening her eyes, Julia again saw Mrs. Fludd, who now sat slumped in the chair as if she had fallen asleep. Her mouth was open, black and toothless in the fleshy mass of her face surrounded by the penumbra of her hair. The woman's squat body was as if compressed— "slumped" was the wrong word, for she appeared to be under gathering tension.

"Close eyes," she said in a gravelly voice. Julia, startled, immediately pressed her eyes shut. She heard Mrs.

Fludd's heavy boots scuffing on the carpet. She was again on the rooftop, now alone with the men. Her father, who had died one summer while she and Magnus were in Perigord, turned his face from her. Internally, she began to speak to him, as she frequently did when moved by guilt. *You were a decent man, but too forceful. I can see that now. I married Magnus because he had your power, he could dominate like you, and then I saw what a weapon your power was. But Daddy, I loved you. I would have gone to your funeral if I had known, I want you to forgive me for being away, I loved you always, please forgive me, grant me that. . . .* As the words became rote, the vision dissolved. She was alone on the roof, oppressed by the comprehensive atmosphere of moral loss. All was grimy, all was inferior and flawed. She bent her head. The scene turned to opaque blackness through which she fell: Julia was dizzied, and seemed actually to be slowly falling. The room seemed to have turned about; surely she was now facing the front window instead of Mrs. Fludd? She resisted the temptation to open her eyes. Again, she imagined the white saucer—cool, without blemish, entirely surface—and filled her mind with it.

For a time the only noises in the room were Miss Tooth's strained breathing and the hushing noise of Mrs. Fludd's boots scuffing the carpet. Julia grew calmer and wondered what Mark, behind them, was doing and thinking in the darkness. He had begun to be uneasy after he had crossed the room to sit beside Mrs. Fludd. She must have said something to him—as she had to Julia. And now how did they look to him, seated on the carpet like fools before the massive image of Mrs. Fludd? She could scarcely restrain the impulse to turn her head to look for him. Mr. Piggot's boneless hand, stirring momentarily in hers, returned her to her context.

"*Agh. Agh.*" The soft choking noise came, Julia thought, from Miss Tooth. Then she heard a wail which was unmistakably Miss Tooth's and realized that the insistent choking noise was made in Mr. Arkwright's throat. Lily too was making a noise; the most mothlike, ladylike of noises, an exhalation of breath carrying the slightest coloration of voice. This was astonishingly sexual. Julia's hands were tugged forward and back, and soon she too began to rock. Her legs had once more begun to ache, but she could not think of interrupting the resistless rocking motion to swivel them back under her. Daringly, she slitted her eyes and saw, as in a haze, the dark heads on either side bobbing forward and back. Each was making some low noise, rhythmical and insistent. Miss Pinner was growling like a cat. Before them sat Mrs. Fludd, her feet now still, her face distorted. Mr. Piggot's hand had grown very sweaty. Julia closed her eyes and resumed rocking back and forth. Not wishing to remember the image of Mrs. Fludd's face, she made her mind utterly void of thought. She thought of the thought of nothing. Soon she was a rocking particle of nothing.

Then she saw Kate—Kate with her back turned to her.

A deep croaking voice stopped them all. *"Aah, stop."* Jolted back to herself, shaken by the vision of Kate, Julia withdrew her hand from Mr. Piggot's while still clinging to Lily's. She opened her eyes. Mrs. Fludd was pressed back against the cushions of the couch, her face nearly purple. She had none of the repose Julia associated with the notion of mediumistic trance: her eyes bulged, her mouth worked. *"Stop. Stop."*

"Something's wrong," whispered Mr. Piggot.

Together they watched Mrs. Fludd struggling, not knowing what should be done. Lily tugged at Julia's hand, indicating that she was not to rise. Gradually Mrs. Fludd's face cleared of purple and her eyes closed; she lay back drained and apparently powerless, her face heavy and dead. As Julia watched, the old woman's face became chalky. "It's over," she uttered, her voice low as it had been earlier in the evening. Yet it seemed to shake. Her hands, too, trembled as she placed them on her chest, forcing herself to breathe regularly.

"Over?" inquired Miss Pinner. "Why, we were just—"

"This must stop," said Mrs. Fludd in her trembling voice. "I'm sorry. I can't do more. I can't finish." The woman, Julia saw, was terrified. "Get my coat," she ordered. She was trying to struggle up from the sofa. "No more tonight. My coat. Please." She fell back exhausted, and Julia saw with horror that the old woman had begun to blink back tears.

The group members stood about in the darkness, uncertain and disturbed. Only Miss Pinner seemed indignant. While she hissed something to Miss Tooth, Lily approached Mrs. Fludd. "Get my coat," said Mrs. Fludd. Now she was openly weeping.

"Somebody get some water, please," Lily said, and Miss Pinner looked up from her intense talk with her companion. Julia stood by, frozen, incapable of movement.

"What happened?" she asked. "Mrs. Fludd, what happened to you?"

"Get out of this house," Mrs. Fludd whispered. She lolled back on the cushions, her mouth dryly opening and closing. Tears continued to roll down her meaty cheeks. "Some water." She began to whimper.

Miss Pinner exasperatedly went from the room. Julia noticed that she was going not to the kitchen, but in the direction of the hall bathroom.

"She's frightened," Lily whispered to Julia. "What was that she said to you?"

Julia shook her head. Mrs. Fludd was again trying to speak. She bent near. Foul breath assaulted her. "Danger. I'm in danger. You too." The woman was trembling violently. A sharp, acetic odor floated up to Julia, and she recognized it only when Mrs. Fludd gasped and made a violent, thrashing attempt to get up from the couch. Now she was both humiliated and terrified, and Julia, the sour odor swirling about her like ammonia, could not hold her to the couch. She looked into the dark recesses of the living room, over the heads of Miss Tooth, Mr. Piggot and Mr. Arkwright, but

Mark was nowhere in the room. He had left the house unseen.

Miss Pinner's shriek stopped her speculation and froze her as she stood, her arms on Mrs. Fludd's shoulders. Miss Tooth rushed from the room. Mrs. Fludd too had heard the scream, and sank back into the couch, closing her eyes. Julia ran after Miss Tooth. When she reached the bathroom, she saw Miss Pinner supine just inside the door; Miss Tooth was cradling her friend's head. Julia stepped over Miss Pinner's body and entered the bathroom. The mirrors reflected her startled, wide-eyed round face, making her look unnaturally healthy and beautiful. Then, momentarily, flickeringly, she saw someone behind her move out of her field of vision: she whirled around, but no one else was in the room. And if anyone had been there, Miss Tooth would have seen him. Julia turned back to the mirror; and there the figure was again just slipping from sight. Yet Julia, like everyone, had seen this happen before: it was a common experience brought on by nerves. It was no more unusual than hearing one's name called in the street. Surely, this or something similar had startled Miss Pinner. Julia approached the sink for a glass of water and saw that her blue seersucker dress, forgotten, still soaked; the water in the basin had turned the color of rust, but the dress still bore its stain.

4

When Julia finally returned home that night, shortly after eleven, she went early to her bed. She felt as though she would be apprehensive all the rest of her life—and half of the disquiet lay in the inability to be definite about what was its source. She and Lily had

taken the quaking Mrs. Fludd to her flat in a taxi; driven
through the grim, hopeless streets which were so much
like the streets of her dream, they had come to Mrs.
Fludd's block of flats, in a cul-de-sac off the Mile End
Road. The street-lamps had all been broken, and whitish shards of glass shone up from the dirty pavements;
the road too was littered with broken glass, the pebbled
green spray of shattered windshields. A lighted plaque
on Mrs. Fludd's building announced that the gray,
prisonlike structure, one of a series of similar buildings
forming a compound, bore the name Baston; before
Baston, roving gangs of boys in rolled-up Levi's passed
back and forth, shouting in raucous voices. Several of
them stopped to gape at the taxi. When they saw Mrs.
Fludd they began to hoot. "Bloody ol' witch! Bloody
ol' witch!" Mrs. Fludd had not spoken a word during
the long ride from Kensington, though Julia had twice
asked her what had happened to her, what had she seen.
The old woman's mouth had tightened with such pressure her upper lip went white. The gang of boys terror-
ized her even further, and she initially refused to leave
the cab. Lily, on the street side, got out and at first disconcerted the boys. When they began again to hoot, it
was at Lily. She ignored them and, together, she and
Julia coaxed Mrs. Fludd from the taxi. "Wait for us,"
Lily said to the driver, and the two women helped Mrs.
Fludd into the open court. Several of the boys trailed
along behind, calling out obscenities. "Here," said Mrs.
Fludd, flipping up a hand at an entrance: she lived on
the building's ground floor, as Julia had expected.

Julia supported her through the small, antiseptic flat
to the tiny bedroom where a dusty budgerigar slept in its
cage. The bedroom, no larger than a big closet, contained a single bed and a dwarfish chest of drawers. On
the white walls hung crosses, star charts, a dozen odd
paintings which Julia scarcely noticed. Lily had gone
into the kitchen to see if anything could be found for
Mrs. Fludd, and Julia helped the old woman down onto
the cramped bed and bent to unlace her boots.

Bending and struggling with the tight knots, Julia

felt a pudgy hand settle on the nape of her neck. "Get out of here," Mrs. Fludd croaked.

"I just thought I could help," Julia said, looking up into the old woman's flaring face—she wondered if Mrs. Fludd's heart was all right.

"No. I mean, get out of this country," muttered Mrs. Fludd. Her breath was like a buzzard's. "Go back to America. Where. You belong. There's danger here. Don't stay."

"Danger here in England?"

Mrs. Fludd nodded as if to a backward child, and rolled onto her bed.

"Does it have to do with what we were talking about? What did you see?"

"A child and a man," Mrs. Fludd said. "Be careful. Things could happen to you." She closed her eyes and began to breathe heavily through her mouth. Julia, looking up at the wall, found herself looking at a Keane print.

"Is the man my husband?" she asked.

"The house is yours," Mrs. Fludd said. "You must leave."

Then she turned her heavy face again directly to Julia and gripped both of her hands. "Listen. I do. Fake things. Frauds. For the others. Mr Piggot and Miss Pinner. Expect it. Not all. All that about transcendance —it's fraud. But I do see. Things. Auras. I *do*. But I hypnotize them, like. Now I'm scared. They were a man and a girl. They put you in danger. Me. In danger. They're evil. Just evil."

"Is the man my husband?"

"Get out," Mrs. Fludd groaned. "Please."

"Please, Mrs. Fludd, who is the girl? You must tell me."

The old woman rolled on her side, groaning. A wave of corrupt air rose from her body. "Go."

On the ride home Lily demanded to know what had happened. "She was frightened out of her wits. What did she say to you?"

"I'm not sure I understand it," Julia defensively said.

Soon after this the cabdriver confessed that he was lost,
and they switched back and forth on dark, oppressive
streets before finding their way again. Julia got out of
the taxi at Plane Tree House and paid the fare over
Lily's protests: it took most of the money in her purse.
Then she walked home, skirting the park, where voices
and laughter came to her from the dark regions beyond
the locked gates.

Once in her house, she went into every room, looking
for she knew not what and finding nothing: most of the
lights had been left burning, and the house had a blank,
emptied, waiting air, as if no one lived in it. Half-filled
sherry glasses adhered to the tables. One had tipped
over, and poured an irregular dark stain onto the carpet.
Probably because of what Mrs. Fludd had said to her,
the house seemed malevolent: "malefic"—that extraordinary word the old woman had used.

In the unused bedrooms, where the furniture had
been covered with dust sheets and vacancy lived like a
guest, Julia felt insubstantial, drifting without purpose,
looking for what she knew she would not find. Dusty
and untouched, these rooms seemed chilled by their
emptiness. When she checked, she saw that the heaters
here had been left in the "off" position. Yet the house
was a giant structure, a huge form, which hedged her
out and kept her at bay: it would resist her impositions,
it would not yield to her. Her sense of the house's
obduracy was immense. She felt, more than ever, that
she was living inside a comprehensive error, the mistake
that her life had become: bigger forces lay without, waiting. A child and a man.

This hopelessness drove her finally to her hot, claus-
trophobic bedroom. She undressed quickly and threw
her clothing over a chair; before she got into bed, she
looked at the heater's wall switch. The switch was down.
Julia remembered having flicked it up yesterday morning when Mark was in the room; certainly she had not
turned it on since. She touched the metal surface of the
heater, and found that it was as hot as if it had never
been turned off. That meant that it had been on last

night, since these heaters did not function during the day; yet hadn't she looked, last night? She cursed her memory. But last night Magnus had been *in the house*. Could he be so childish as to go about turning on the heaters?—but if he could stoop to smashing things up, terrorizing her as bluntly as the boys had Mrs. Fludd, it was impossible to say what he might not do. Angry, Magnus was capable of anything. She turned the heater off once again; then, on an afterthought, took a roll of tape from her closet and taped the switch to the fixture.

Though she shrank from the very idea, Magnus had to be faced: as did her feeling about him. What *were* those feelings? Julia felt at once as though she were on the crumbling lip of a precipice; her control, her hold on things sound and normal, was fragile; she knew that much of her seeming calm and placidity was a performance. Horror lay beneath the surface—horror was what inhabited the abyss below the precipice. The image of Magnus murdering Kate, that sight of him plunging the knife into Kate's throat while she thrashed on the floor, could rise in her at any time, as it had before she had been taken to the hospital and drugged into insensibility. Even then she had been tortured by waking dreams. Over and over, her wrists strapped to the side of the bed, she had imagined grasping Magnus' arm and turning the knife to her own throat. That image too had haunted her. Dying for Kate—she would gladly die for Kate. Instead, she had passively watched the clumsiest of murders. Magnus was inextricably tied to this horror, the horror of inanition, of drift which meant loss, of lying, of emptiness without end or meaning: that was death indeed, and it seemed to crawl forth from the walls of this house.

A child and a man. Kate and Magnus. Mrs. Fludd had seen them. And what had she said, before the trance? It had been something about hate or envy—they were what made a spirit "malefic." Kate was present; Kate lay behind Magnus' mad forays into Ilchester Place. She was unforgiving. Logic took her relentlessly to this illogical conclusion. Julia began to rock from side to side on her bed, moaning. She was breaking down. It was an image, again, of the precipice where she had so carefully walked, of clods and pebbles shredding away, breaking up on the long fall down. It was Kate. Mrs. Fludd had seen Kate. In some vivid, dream-like way, Magnus was dominated by Kate; he was an unthinkable danger to her mind.

Unable to sleep, unable to control her thoughts, Julia snapped on the reading lamp at the head of the bed. She forced herself to extend her arms alongside her body. Flatten the fingers so the palms touch the sheet, extend the thumbs. Relax. She breathed deeply, twice. She would talk to Mrs. Fludd. If she had to leave the house to escape the danger Magnus posed, she was capable of leaving. For now, sleep was impossible: but she would not leave this bedroom. This room was hers. If she were to be driven from the room, she would leave the house.

Julia turned her head to see the books on the little stand beside the bed. She had finished the Bellow novel, and now had *The Millstone, The White House Transcripts, The Golden Notebook* and *The Unicorn* on the table; she needed something less stimulating than any of these. Kate and Magnus: Mrs. Fludd's hints and warnings outlined a dread possibility. Kate's spirit still living, hating her and using Magnus' anger, feeding that anger, Kate's spirit seething through this house. . . . All of this was real, happening to her.

Julia had to call Miss Pinner as well as Mrs. Fludd; before the departure of the West Hampstead ladies, Miss Pinner had been too shaky and distraught to describe what she had seen in the bathroom.

Then she saw another book which she had recently placed on the bedside table, hidden behind the little stack of paperbacks. It was *The Royal Borough of Kensington,* Lily's present to her. A sober, judicious list of facts, a few anecdotes, color plates—it was just what she needed, a book about as tangy as a suet pudding, a sleeping pill of a book. She lifted the heavy

volume into her lap and began to flip the pages, reading
paragraphs at random.

Prominent inhabitants of Kensington in the eigh-
teenth century . . . Kensington as a village . . . political
history of the royal borough . . . the planning of Kensington Gardens . . . merchant princes included . . . a
notorious Mr. Price, hanged for the theft of a whip-
pet. . . . Flipping a page after reading about the fate of
Mr. Price, Julia saw a heading which read "Crime,
Ghosts and Hauntings." At first she turned over several
pages, not trusting herself to read such a chapter, but
her curiosity was too great, and she went back to the
heading and began to read.

At first she found nothing more exciting than had
been the lists of prominent Kensington aldermen and
merchants; the author had tracked down a number of
conventional haunted-house anecdotes and set them
down in colorless straightforward style. The ghost of a
headless nun in a "manorial" building on Lexham Gardens; two sisters who had killed themselves in adjoining
houses on Pembroke Place and had been seen crossing
the gardens, hand in hand, by moonlight; the Edwardes
Square "paterfamilias" of 1912 who had been possessed
by the spirit of his mad great-grandfather and taken to
dressing in the extravagant style of a century before and
had finally murdered his children; Julia read all of these
stories with a dulled interest.

Then a sentence and a street name burst from the
text.

One of the most vexed and troubling of all
Kensington murders [Julia read] was that of the
case of Heather and Olivia Rudge, of 25 Ilchester
Place. One of the last women to be sentenced to
death in England, Heather Rudge, an American,
had purchased the house on Ilchester Place from
the architect, who had built it for himself in 1927
but in two years wished to move, due to family
troubles; at the time, Mrs. Rudge, who was separated from her husband, had a reputation as a

brilliant, rather reckless hostess, and was considered by many inhabitants of her social world as "fast." [Eda Rolph implied a fondness for handsome younger men and wealthy businessmen from the City.] One contemporary, the author of several mild books of verse and a once-popular series of theological novels, described her as possessing "a small, vivid, distinctly alarming face in which beauty and avidity fatally conjoined. *Vanitas* indeed: yet we found in her a helter-skelter charm." The birth of a daughter, Olivia, twelve years after the purchase of the Ilchester Place house, occurred in wartime, and so did little to affect her already damaged career as a hostess—the morals of a rich, aging playgirl whose greatest notoriety had passed six or seven years before interested only a few.

The parties continued, at intervals and with considerably less splendor than previously, and then ceased altogether; little was heard of the Rudges until 1950. In that year, the nine-year-old Olivia Rudge was mentioned in connection with the death by suffocation in Holland Park of a four-year-old child, Geoffrey Braden of Abbotsbury Close. Olivia Rudge and what the popular press briefly referred to as the "Holland Park Child Terror Mob"—a group of ten or twelve children apparently led by Olivia—had been seen tormenting young Braden on the day before his death. The following morning, Olivia and several others, according to a park attendant, had again pursued young Braden and abused him. The attendant had chased away the gang of older children and advised young Braden to go home; when he had returned to that area of the park, he had found the boy's body lying in a shadowed place beside a wall. Public and police interest shifted from the gang of children when it was learned that young Braden had been sexually injured before his death; and subsequently a vagrant was hanged for his murder.

Two months following the execution of the vagrant, Heather Rudge telephoned the Kensington police station to confess to the murder of her daughter. Police arriving at the house found Olivia stabbed to death in her bed; the coroner later reported more than fifty stab wounds to the body. Mrs. Rudge was immediately taken into custody and hence was protected from the crowd of journalists who wished to harry her—the murder of Olivia Rudge had quickly become a front-page speciality of the scandal press which had soon unearthed the past of Olivia's mother. ("Society Sex Queen Murders Daughter.") In time, Heather was convicted of murder and sentenced to death. Later her sentence was commuted to life in prison.

Certain questions remain. Why did Heather Rudge kill her daughter? Why was her sentence commuted? Was there a connection with the murder, a year previous, of Geoffrey Braden? Certainly the press had implied such a connection. Newspapers had seized on the case, claiming that Heather Rudge had been driven mad by her daughter; the more sensational papers asserted that Olivia had taunted her mother with her knowledge of the Braden murder, and that Heather had decided that her daughter could not be permitted to live. In time, Heather, now represented as a victim herself, was found to be insane by a special examining board. She is at present an old woman living in the permanent seclusion of a private mental hospital in Surrey. The questions remain unanswered. Heather Rudge will take the secrets of her daughter's involvement in the Braden case to her grave. Forgotten by the public, her mind shadowed and confused, Heather Rudge is a living ghost.

Julia's first thought, after reading this, was an irrelevance: so that's where those mirrors came from—Heather Rudge, with her wild parties staffed with young men, not the proper McClintocks. Then in the next half second, she knew that she would find out, that she was

compelled to find out, everything there was to know
about Heather and Olivia Rudge. She read the two pages
over again quickly, then flipped back and read them
once more, slowly and carefully. Eda Rolph nowhere
stated directly that Olivia Rudge had murdered or had
helped to murder the Braden boy: what grounds were
there for the implication? Julia immediately began to
think of how she could discover information about the
Rudge case. Newspapers: surely the British Museum, if
not a branch library, had newspaper files on microfilm.
Could Heather Rudge be living still? She turned to the
first pages of the book to look at the publishing information. *The Royal Borough of Kensington* had been
published by the Lompoc Press in 1969, five years ago.
She might easily be still alive. ". . . a private mental
hospital in Surrey." How could she find the name of
the hospital? Heather Rudge had lived in this house,
she had slept in this bedroom; in sleep, her body had
occupied the very space Julia's body now did. Julia
seemed to be spinning through time; time seemed plastic, distorted, unsafe: the past seemed to rise up all
about her, like a foul gas.

Then she sat upright, her heart speeding. Perhaps
Heather Rudge had stabbed Olivia in this very bedroom. Olivia dying as Kate had died, bleeding as though
blood willed to depart the living body, her blood foam-
ing out over this spot around a hidden corner in
time. . . . Julia nearly bolted from her bed.

But it could not be true. This must have been
Heather's bedroom, she thought; her daughter would
have had one of the smaller bedrooms down the hall.
And that was where the murder would have been done.

Why am I so interested in this, in these people? Julia
thought. Because it will be an explanation.

Julia felt wide-awake, as stimulated as if she'd just
had three cups of strong coffee. She wanted to telephone
Mark, to see Lily—she wanted to telephone Eda Rolph,
to ask her the name of the hospital where Heather
Rudge had been kept for the past twenty-four years. But

she is here too, Julia thought, she is part of the character of this house, and she lives here still, moving up and down the stairs, her skirt rustling, turning down a bed, running to the door to greet a lover or a friend, locked in the bubble of her time. Every moment lives parallel with every other moment. What *had* Miss Pinner seen, to make her faint?

As if in answer, a clicking noise came to her from downstairs. It was the same noise she had heard before when, crouching beside the drapes, she had seen Magnus standing motionless in her garden. It was the noise of something outside wishing to come in. Julia realized that, paradoxically, she was now less afraid of Magnus than she had been before reading about Heather and Olivia Rudge—Magnus was flesh, Magnus was blood. All about her moved intimations of the past of the house, those echoes of her own past. She lay in bed listening to the soft rapping at the downstairs windows. Some minutes later she picked up *The White House Transcripts;* she read doggedly for two hours, getting through very nearly half of the book, before she finally fell asleep, her light still burning. The rapping, patient and insistent, continued to sound through the house.

Sweating, she dreamed of Kate.

Julia came drowsily awake two hours later feeling that she had just been touched: no, caressed. Her light still burned. She reached up to switch it off. The bedroom was even hotter than it had been when she had first come in; her entire body seemed filmed with sweat. The bedroom curtains hung straight and unmoving; in this room, air refused to circulate, but piled atop itself, densely. The sky shone through the window, lighter than the dark of the bedroom. Julia could still feel, along her bruised left side, the afterimage of a hand, stroking lightly. The caress was gentle, seductively soothing. Of course there was no one else in the room; she had conjured up the caress herself, summoned it up out of her needs.

Julia settled down into the sheets again, deliberately

relaxing. The rapping from below had ceased: Magnus had gone home, unable to bring her wandering and calling through the house, having failed at least this once. She closed her eyes and crossed her hands on her midriff. Perhaps Heather Rudge had nursed Olivia in this room, talking to her daughter in baby talk . . . perhaps Mrs. Fludd had seen Heather doing violence to her daughter. Surely such an event still lingers in its physical setting, still reverberating there. . . . Julia's mind began to drift. She heard a snatch of music playing: it was big band music, tinny, as if on a radio, and then it dissolved, along with everything else. She fell immediately into dreams which were indistinguishable from semiwakefulness. Once again she was being caressed. She was being touched by lingering, stroking hands beside her own hands. Small hands moved lightly down her body. They paused, and began again, stroking. Julia saw Kate beside her: they clasped one another. Kate was with her. The caresses were like music—soft, moving, layered. Julia felt infinitely quietened, infinitely soothed; the small, moving hands were like tongues, lapping at her. She gave herself to this comfort. Broken dreams, fed by these long caresses, filtered through her mind. She and Mark sat side by side on the gray couch, speaking words she could not hear. Mark's hand surrounded hers. She was swimming in warm water, a pool of water as warm as a bath. She wore no bathing suit, and the water slipped about her like oil. Her skin was opening. She was beneath strong sun. The flickering touches ran insinuatingly over her opening body. Mark and Kate: then, shockingly, only Kate. *"No,"* she said, groaning, and her voice brought her up through sleep. "No." She could still feel the last touch of the hand, stroking between her thighs: she felt sickened and frightened, roused. Now she was absolutely awake.

She had been dreaming of Kate. What horrible thing had she dreamed? She listened for the sound of Heather Rudge slipping down the stairs. Now, the thought of Kate was fearful: Kate, she realized, must hate her. She was caught in a terrific dislocation, her body mov-

ing toward its resolution, her consciousness stunned
by what was logically inexplicable. Slowly, feeling as
though soiled for life, Julia slipped her hand to the part
of her body which needed its touch, and with hard cir-
cular movements of two fingers brought herself over the
edge. She felt like the unappeased ghost of the living
Heather Rudge. Her body smelled of loss and failure,
of airless exertions.

The next morning, with trembling hands, she dialed
the number Rosa Fludd had left with her. For the first
time in her life, she had taken a drink in the morning—
a smoky, unwatered slug of malt whiskey, choked down
while she was still in her robe. She had immediately
wanted another. The quick explosion of warmth, in-
timating relaxation and pointing to an eventual extin-
guishing of consciousness, was uncannily like being back
in the hospital, seconds after her morning injection.
Now, she thought, I know why people drink in the
morning. It's better than breakfast. She had quickly
screwed the top back on the bottle and gone to the telephone. Beside it was the white card Mrs. Fludd had
given her.

She heard the telephone going *brrr brrr* in Mrs.
Fludd's white antiseptic flat. It trilled six, then seven
times without answer. Was she still there, watched over
by her budgerigar and the huge sentimental eyes of the
girl in the Keane print? It was imperative that Julia
speak to her: what would the old woman have said to
her—admitted to her—if Julia had known about
Heather and Olivia Rudge last night? On the tenth ring
the telephone was answered.

"Yes," said a young woman.

"I'd like to speak to Mrs. Fludd, Rosa Fludd. My
name is Julia Lofting."

"Wait a minute." Julia heard muffled voices; the
young woman had covered the receiver while turning to
speak to someone else in the room.

"My aunt says she can't talk to you."

"Is anything wrong?" Julia asked.

"Anything wrong? You should know. You were one of them brought her home." The girl's accent was so strong that Julia had difficulty distinguishing the words. "You're one of them put her in a state."

"A stite? Oh."

"A *state*. You and them others. You bunch of airy-fairies near drove 'her out of 'her mind, didn't you? That's not proper, is it? Poor woman don't even take money to jolly you lot along, and. . . ."

Another voice was raised in the background and the hand again clamped over the receiver.

"Tell her I have more information," Julia said. "This is terribly important."

". . . she says she has more information. You sure? You want to?"

In a moment Mrs. Fludd had taken the telephone. "I'm here," she said. Her voice sounded tightly contained.

"Mrs. Fludd, this is Julia Lofting. Are you all right? I've been worried about you."

"You can't waste your worry," said Mrs. Fludd. "What did you want to tell me?"

"Well, I read, just by accident, a story about my house in a book on Kensington, and I had to tell you what it said. Mrs. Fludd? This house used to be owned by a woman named Heather Rudge, an American, who had a daughter named Olivia. Mrs. Fludd, she stabbed her daughter to death. My own daughter was stabbed to death—my husband wanted to save her life, she was choking to death, and he killed 'her. The other little girl was killed right in this house more than twenty years ago. Is that what you saw? Is that what Miss Pinner saw in the bathroom?"

"Don't know about Miss Pinner," said Mrs. Fludd.

"Mrs. Fludd, could—could my own daughter be haunting me? Could she try to harm me? Is that what you meant the other night? Did she try to harm *you*? Is my daughter behind this?" Hysteria and tears mounted in her, and she stopped talking to force calm into her voice. "Can't you help me, Mrs. Fludd?"

"Go back to your own country."

"Can't you tell me what you saw?"

"I didn't see anything."

"But you said—a child and a man. Kate and Magnus."

"I saw *nothing*. Miss Pinner is an old fool, and she saw nothing either. Get out of that house, get out of this country. That's all I can tell you."

"Mrs. Fludd, please don't hang up. I've been doing so much thinking—I have so many things to ask you. How . . . how do people in the past work through people in the present? How do dead people control living people? Is that possible?"

"I told you that," said Mrs. Fludd. "You're wasting my time. Good-bye."

"You said hate or envy," Julia quickly said.

"You remember, then. Sometimes they might want to take something of yours, and to give you something. It helps the malefic spirit. But strong spirits don't need help, Mrs. Lofting. They does what they want to do. I can't talk, Mrs. Lofting. Please leave me alone."

She hung up and Julia kept the telephone pressed to her ear until she heard the dial tone.

She pressed the button, wanting to dial again, but in that instant her instrument shrilly rang. Julia released the button.

"Yes," she said softly.

"I'm going to get you back," came Magnus' deep voice. "You can't get away from me. Do you hear me? Do you hear me, Julia?"

Julia clapped the receiver down. Some figure behind and beside her seemed to move quickly away, just out of the line of her vision, and she whirled around, her breath caught in her throat. No one else was in the room. "Kate," she whispered, "Kate, don't."

When Julia went into the kitchen for a glass of water, she recoiled as soon as she turned on the tap. What gushed from the faucet was a foul brown stream, stinking like ordure. Julia clapped one hand to her mouth,

then twisted the knob and shut off the flow. Now it
smelled like metal, like coins. After a moment, testingly,
she turned it on again: the greasy stuff foamed from the
taps. Frantic, Julia again twisted the knob to make the
flow cease. Malvern water from the Safeway, a dozen
bottles, ranked beneath the sink, and she took one,
pried off the cap, and poured a glassful. It tasted incredibly sweet: drinking it, Julia realized how close she
had come to being sick. Even now from the sink rose
the stench of that rushing brown fluid, making her
stomach contract.

Then she remembered something, brought back by
her physical discomfort. The night she had climbed
through the bathroom window, she had lost her shoes;
they had fallen outside when she had finally pushed herself through the little frame. And out there they had
lain, to be found by Magnus: something taken, something given, Mrs. Fludd had said. Nearly everything she
owned had been given her by Magnus. She wore his
ring; he had bought earrings, pendants, beads, clothing
for her. Julia would nearly have to walk naked to divest
herself of everything given her by Magnus.

But how long had those shoes lain outside? Three
nights and two days. They might still be below the bathroom window. Julia ran out of the kitchen into the hall
and down the hall to the bathroom. Reflected in the
rose mirrors, she threw the rod off its ratchet and lifted
the window out. On tiptoe, she leaned forward, holding
the window with her left hand, and put her head out.
She looked down at broken white and yellow flowers,
some snapped off at their stalks, others trodden into the
soft dirt. She could not see her shoes. Julia leaned
farther out of the window—she leaned forward as far
as she could go. Still she could not see the shoes. They
were gone: someone had taken them. It seemed like a
proof. A girl and a man. They wished to do her harm.

For some moments Julia thrashed back and forth in
the bathroom, out of control. She knew she was making
some low, dreadful noise; the noise could not be
stopped, and it echoed within the mirrored room, bounc-

ing back and forth like her body. *I have to stop this,* she told herself, and forced herself to sit on the floor. The noise came out in hiccoughs and then concentrated itself in her throat, where she could stop it. When she became aware that she had been drooling, she wiped her mouth.

She looked dumbly around the bathroom. She was sitting, glassy-eyed, her mouth open, near the tub: her face in the rose mirrors looked slack, exotic. Magnus had taken the shoes.

Julia unsteadily rose, gripping the sink with both hands. Within it, the seersucker dress still lay in an orangey-brown pool. She could still see the bloodstain; it seemed to have got larger. Now it appeared to be several inches long. Julia tore the dress out of the sink, pulled the plug, and squeezed the soaked material while the discolored, odorous water was sucked away.

She was not really thinking. She knew that she had to destroy the blue dress, and the knowledge instantly became action, bypassing thought. She had to burn the dress.

Julia carried the dress through to the kitchen where she picked up matches and then continued on to the fireplace in the living room. She dropped the dress onto the grate and applied a lighted match to a dry corner of fabric. The dress did not light. Julia lit a second match and held it to the same point; this time, the thin material flared up, crumpling and darkening beneath the spreading corner of flame. An acrid odor spread into the living room, followed by smoke. About half the dress burned before the flames guttered out on sodden material. The room stank of charred fabric—it was the smell of burning fur. Julia scarcely noticed this stench. She tried holding matches beneath the wet remaining half of the dress, but the fabric merely blackened, still wet.

Then she saw the morning's *Guardian* on a table near the couch and moved across the room to get it. She shook four pages loose, and stuffed them beneath the dress in the grate. When she picked up the sodden lump

of dress, ashes and soot clinging to it, she saw the large,
rust-colored bloodstain leaking out from the seam. She
thrust papers over the dress and tossed matches into
them. Greasy yellowish smoke boiled out from beneath
the papers. Julia threw match after match onto the
smouldering newspaper, but the damp fabric would not
burn. Her hands were black with ash.

Abandoning the effort to burn the dress, Julia went
into the kitchen for one of the big black plastic garbage
bags, which she flipped open and carried back to the
fireplace. Using the small ornamental shovel, she
scooped the mess of ashes and charred spongy fabric
into the mouth of the bag. She then twisted it shut and
carried it outside into the path beside the house.

Sunlight and warmth surprised her. The past half
hour—hour?—seemed to have been visited upon her.
She had been dominated by an urgent, thoughtless revulsion she had been unable to resist. Julia felt her
pulse slow; she became aware of sensation again, the
light defining a million blades of grass, the sun's warmth
penetrating her hair. Julia began to breathe more regularly, suddenly conscious that she had been panting.
That *thing* in the black bag: she had had to destroy it
as though it were alive. Now, grasping the neck of the
bag, she felt all of her revulsion once more and thrust
it into the bin and clapped the lid over it. Big smudges
of ash dirtied her quilted robe. Other smears of ash
covered her legs. Julia felt as though she had just run
a race.

Magnus: she had lost all reasoning consciousness
when he had appeared, as if by evil magic, on the telephone. Now she could not even remember his words,
but she remembered their import. They had been threatening. He had her shoes. She flew back into the warm
confines of her house.

Twenty minutes later, another visitation: this young
woman standing before her, a neighbor, living in Number 23, the house next door. Smaller than Julia, her
hair nearly as short as Lily's, a creamy, shy, smiling

face only just beginning to show wrinkles. Her name, Hazel Mullineaux. From the woman's first words ("I don't know if I should bother you now"), Julia suffered from an acute awareness of her smudged robe and blackened hands. Her face too—from Mrs. Mullineaux's glances at her cheeks and forehead, Julia knew she was a patchwork of filth. She hid her hands behind her back.

"You seem so busy that I don't know if I should take up your time like this." A smile.

Julia, bent on appearing normal, did not think to invite this hesitant young woman inside. "Oh, I have all the time in the world," she said, and then cursed herself for overstatement.

"It's just that we thought we should ask. We thought you should know," she amended, and then gave a further amendment. "And of course we wanted to meet our new neighbor."

"Thank you."

"I didn't really catch your name, I'm sorry."

She had not given it. "I'm Julia Lofting."

Hazel Mullineaux peered past Julia to see the interior. "You are a Canadian? I'm trying to catch the accent. . . ."

"I'm American," Julia said. "But I've lived here a long time."

"That explains why it isn't so broad."

"Oh," Julia said, "I never think about it at all, it's changing all the time, I guess. My husband used to say that I sounded like an Iowa farmhand, and I've never been in Iowa in my life, but then neither was he." She babbled, smelling the reek the burning dress had made: for ten minutes, she had fanned a newspaper in the living room, but the smell hung on, as though she had burned a cat.

Mrs. Mullineaux seemed disconcerted by this chatter about Iowa. "Well, as I said, we thought you should know about it. Last night my husband saw a man standing outside your house."

Julia froze. "What time was that?"

"At ten, when he came home from his office. Like all

publishers, he works too late. Then at ten thirty he happened to look out the window, and he saw you going into your house and the man was still there. Perry said he didn't look like a criminal, but he had moved further down the block and was beside the tree in front of number seventeen, the Armbrusters' house. Perry was curious, so he kept watching the man, and after you'd gone in, he began to come up the block toward your house again. Then he just stood across the street and watched the house. Perry said he stood there for at least an hour. Of course, there's no law against looking at a person's house, but it did seem odd. He asked me if I thought he should have telephoned the police. I said I would speak to you about it. In case he returns. I hope you don't think we have been prying into your—circumstances."

"No, oh, no," Julia said. Now she could smell the burned-cat odor all too definitely, and she saw that Hazel Mullineaux also had caught it: the creamy little woman looked at her oddly, and moved a step backward. "I've been doing some cleaning," Julia said. "I know I'm a mess."

"Yes. I mean, no, of course not. But *as* this man seemed to hang about so long, I did want to tell you. I hope you don't think we did wrong not to ring the police."

"It was my husband," said Julia. "I think he's watching me. I know he is."

"Watching . . . ?" Hazel Mullineaux's face expressed a perfect incomprehension.

"He doesn't live here," Julia supplied, feeling herself slip into a bog of explanations and not knowing how to avoid it. "You see, I bought this house for myself. I can't see him—he's been bothering me, making telephone calls. I think he broke in here one night. . . ."

Mrs. Mullineaux now radiated shock and disapproval.

"Oh, please, I want us to be friends," Julia said. "Neighbors should be friends, don't you think? I haven't even invited you in. Would you like a cup of coffee?

You were so kind to tell me what you saw. I don't know
if the police should be called or not. I don't know if
there's any danger. . . . Everything's gotten so confused
in the past couple of days, it's because of Kate, our
daughter, I mean late daughter. . . . Really, I'm terrified
of him, but I don't think I should call the police, it's not
a story they'd understand. But thank your husband for
me, for worrying about me, that was a friendly act. . . ."
She looked at Hazel Mullineaux's rather dazed expression. "Won't you come in for a cup of coffee? I'll have
to air out the living room to get rid of that terrible
smell, but we could sit in the kitchen, or even in the
back garden."

"I can't right now, thanks," said the other woman.
She was already moving down the steps. "Some other
time."

"Oh, I have to ask you," Julia said before the other
woman could get away. "Did you know the people who
used to live here?"

"Of course we knew the McClintocks," said Mrs.
Mullineaux. "They were older, and a bit remote, but
quite nice, really."

"No, not the McClintocks," Julia broke in. "I mean
the ones before them. Mrs. Rudge. Heather Rudge. She
had a daughter."

"Before the McClintocks? We moved here in 1967,
and the McClintocks had been here for twenty years,
we thought."

"Yes, of course. Of course. You couldn't possibly
have known her."

Mrs. Mullineaux turned away, went down the steps,
and before walking down the pavement to her house,
looked back at Julia. Her face twitched into a grimace
approximating a smile.

That woman thinks I'm crazy, Julia thought. And
then she thought of Magnus, patrolling the street. He
had rapped at the dining room window for hours last
night—Magnus was trying to push her over the precipice. She wanted Mark's easy presence, Mark's care-
less masculinity: he was a talisman against Magnus.

Even Lily could not be trusted to save her from Magnus. She heard Hazel Mullineaux slam her front door. Against that, too, Mark would stand as protection.

"I think you need help, darling. You're under so much pressure, and I can't blame you for being apprehensive, even suspicious."

"Apprehensive, Lily? Of course I'm apprehensive. That performance the other night put me right at ease. . . ."

"That's *just* what I mean. I rang poor dear Mrs. Fludd this noon, and the telephone just kept ringing. She never goes out, never, except for her sessions. Something terrible has happened, I'm sure. I can't help it, I'm worried for the old dear."

"Well, I'm worried for myself. Magnus was seen loitering outside the house last night. I'm sure he broke in here two nights ago. He's trying to drive me back to him. He's out of his mind, and I think I might be too. Do you want to know what I think? I think Kate is punishing me. It's what Mrs. Fludd said—a man and a girl. Kate is in Magnus' mind. Sometimes she's in this house too, and she hates me. She believes Magnus' lies."

"Oh, darling. . . ."

"You want him for yourself, don't you? You want Mark for yourself too. You'd like Magnus to think I'm going crazy. I suppose you'll call him right now and tell him what I said, but you won't get him because he's probably hanging around here, watching the house."

"Julia, you can't think that of me. . . ."

"You called him. You broke your word."

"Because I wanted you to be back with him."

"But you do want him for yourself, don't you? And Mark."

"Julia, this does us no good. That is terribly unfair. Please listen, Julia. Kate has no reason to hate you, nothing you did was meant to injure her. You were brave."

"Magnus killed Kate. Magnus hates me for leaving him, and now Kate hates me. Mrs. Fludd saw them."

"Julia, why don't you come over here so we can talk about that day? Please come over. That's at the bottom of everything. . . ."

"What do you mean by that? What are you trying to get me to say?"

"Nothing, Julia, nothing. I just thought that talking about it would do you good—if not to Magnus then at least to me—but if you're not ready yet, that's fine. I still think you should come over and stay with me for a few days so. . . ."

Julia had a sudden, clear vision of a man in a white jacket jabbing a hypodermic into her arm.

"Good-bye, Lily. Sorry."

She hung up, trembling so severely the receiver rattled out of the cradle and fell to the floor. She had to get out of the house.

Julia ran upstairs to her bedroom and threw off the filthy robe, in her bathroom, she hurriedly showered, avoiding looking at herself as much as she could avoid it, afraid that a glance into the mirrors would show a slight figure just flickering from her sight. The telephone began to ring as she was toweling herself, and Julia let the bell shrill, counting the number of rings. After twenty, it stopped. She continued dressing, deliberately not thinking of what Lily had said to her. She thought, instead, with longing of more books—of buying books—of slipping into a narrative of other people's lives. *That* was release.

It led her, as she went rapidly along Kensington High Street twenty minutes later, her damp hair adhering to her neck, to sudden, vivid memories of her girlhood: of summers at their home in New Hampshire, where it had been as warm as this every day. Her great-grandfather had bought the estate after he had retired from the board of his railroad company, having made several hundred million dollars in the boom; the soil itself, the texture of the air had seemed different there, wholly, innocently absorbed into her family's life. For

an instant, Julia ached to be back in America. She stood
on Kensington High Street, between a package store
and W. H. Smith's, the sound of car horns dividing the
air, and was transfixed by the particular memory of a
New Hampshire valley. And beyond the valley, the end-
less innocent unrolling of the continent: but it was not
like that any more, she knew. It was her own past for
which she had ached. Yet there lay in her an undigested
yearning for the visionary and fruitful continent; her
childhood, it seemed to her, had been spent there. She
turned into W. H. Smith's and bought a fat paperback
of *Gravity's Rainbow*.

Toting the book, Julia passed through the crowds on
the High Street. It really was as hot as New Hampshire
in August. She debated walking up Kensington Church
Street to Notting Hill Gate, to see if Mark were home.
She remembered his address, and thought she knew
where the flat was; it was on one of the long curved
streets, Pembridge something, intercepting Notting Hill
Gate, one of the streets lined with large houses now
broken up into bed-sitting-rooms and two-room flats.
Mark's was a "garden flat": it was in the basement. She
imagined a flight of steep steps down from the pavement
into a dank lightless room—the vision was enough to
turn her back to Holland Park, where she could lie in
the sun. She did not feel ready, yet, to visit Mark's flat.
To go there unbidden would entail a chain of con-
sequences of which she was a little apprehensive.

As she walked along past the row of shops, Julia
scanned the crowds for a glimpse of Magnus. He could
easily be facing a window, unseen, tailing after her;
certainly she had to assume that Magnus had taken to
such tactics. Or, even more unsettling, perhaps he was
now forcing his way into her house. But she could not
rush back to inspect the house, she would never catch
him there, she was sure of that. Still, Julia could not
rid herself of the image of Magnus hovering behind her.
In front of the long piazza of the Commonwealth Institute, she whirled around quickly, and caught a priest
in the stomach with her elbow. While they each apolo-

gized, they recognized one another as Americans; the priest, a neat dark man with a witty face, looked at her oddly as they swapped pleasantries. She could only surmise that he was responding to something in her own manner or regard. What was wrong with her, that even a pleasant stranger found her peculiar? Julia brought one hand up to wipe her forehead and saw the hand tremble. Her forehead dripped sweat. "It's nothing," she said to the priest. "Just anxiety. I'm a normal person. I don't usually punch men in the stomach."

She turned up into Holland Park. The paths were crowded, and every five feet of ground supported a new body. A pack of children ran squealing on the long sward, breaking apart into pinwheeling clusters and then, clamoring, reforming. Boys in jeans, girls in long filmy dresses, girls in jeans, Germans strapped into cameras and expensive clothes. She skirted a party of twenty Japanese, singing to one another. A young couple directly before her exchanged a long kiss while the boy rubbed and kneaded the girl's buttocks, uncaring of the crowds. Julia felt a hot, direct physical pang until she saw the American priest, walking quickly up ahead without looking back. She deliberately thrust down the memory of her last night's dream and its aftermath. Without purpose, she began to drift after the American priest. The book felt very heavy in her hand.

The priest turned off the main path to enter the smaller walk which, Julia recalled, passed the area where peacocks and other birds strutted beneath dark trees. Julia followed, watching the black suit as if it held a meaning. The priest paused to look at the peacocks for a second and then continued walking toward the woods which circled the top half of the park. He strode along briskly, and soon was disappearing around a corner into the sparse woods. Three women pushing baby carriages, accompanied by a single man carrying an open winebottle, crossed before Julia, and the priest was gone from sight. Then she saw Magnus.

He was sitting on a bench, not looking at her. He looked very tired. Julia froze; she took two cautious

steps backward, and then turned around, the vision of
Magnus in a light-gray suit, bending forward, his face
rumpled, burning into her: if he turned his head, he
would see her. At first she took light quick steps, gliding up the path; when she passed around the bend, she
moved more slowly until she dared to look over her
shoulder. He had not followed her. Julia looked across
the park—an exit lay ahead and to her right, just before Plane Tree House. She would circle the park to
get home. Julia trotted down the path, ignoring the
stares of men she met, setting her face.

There was no longer any question of staying in the
park to read her book: she had to get home and lock
the door. But just before she reached the final stage of
the path to the side gate, she saw the tiny black girl
who had been in the park that first day. The girl was
staring up at her just as she had that day.

"Hello, Mona," Julia said. "Do you remember me?"

"Poo," said Mona, smiling open-mouthed at Julia.
Her eyes shone.

"That's not a nice word."

"Poo. Shit." Mona giggled and turned away. "Fuck
you."

Julia stared at the tiny girl.

"Fuck you. Shit. Fuck."

"What. . . ." Julia turned and found herself looking
into the face of the little blond girl. She was touching a
bicycle which was leaning against the fence bordering
the park, and she was looking straight into Julia's face.
No other children were near; the closest people were a
man and a woman twenty yards away, asleep on the
grass with their faces to the sun. About Julia and the
blond girl a charged timeless vacuum seemed to exist.
The child wore curiously old-fashioned denim trousers,
with a high elastic waist and floppy legs. The resemblance to Kate made Julia's heart pulse with fear. They
stood looking at each other, not speaking; Julia had
nearly the sense that the girl had been waiting for her
in this secluded place.

Then the girl smiled, and her resemblance to Kate

vanished. One of her front teeth had been broken in half, chipped away in a rising arc which left her smile uncentered and asymmetrical.

"Who are you?" Julia said.

The girl's smile tightened in a curiously adult, challenging way. Her joined hands moved, or something in them moved. When Julia looked at her hands, she saw that the girl was not actually touching the bicycle, but holding her hands near the rear wheel. It took her a moment to see what the girl held captured between her cupped palms. Only when the small brown creature quivered did Julia see that it was a bird.

"Is that bird injured?" Julia asked.

The child made no response, but continued to stare at Julia, smiling her adult, unbalanced smile. The whole being of the child seemed hurtled together, compacted.

In one quick sure movement the girl thrust the bird into the wheel of the bicycle, jamming it securely between the spokes and the metal rods which held the mudguards to the wheel. The scene printed itself with utter clarity on Julia's mind: as in the second before some foreknown disaster, time seemed as fixed as the girl's smile. Julia stared at the bird, the instant before the girl jerked the bicycle forward— it was held between the two metal rods, not in the wheel as she had first supposed. Its body projected through the spokes.

"Don't . . . no . . ." she stammered.

The girl jerked the bicycle and the bird instantly became a pulp of bloody feathers. Its head fell softly to the ground.

Julia snapped her head up to look at the girl, who was now mounting her bicycle. She did not immediately ride away but straddled the bike, intently staring at Julia.

Julia opened her mouth to speak, but caught sight of the bird's head lying with open eyes beside the rear wheel, and felt her stomach irresistibly begin to draw itself upward. She turned away and vomited into the dust.

When she had finished, the girl was no longer beside

her. The bicycle was rolling away through the gate, the girl pedaling slowly and unconcernedly; soon she had slipped into crowds and traffic.

Julia took a step and found that her knees shook: she forced herself to run. Heedless of Magnus, she raced directly toward her home, her mouth open, her body jouncing, her breath straining at her ribs. She flew across the green, narrowly missing the curious who parted to let her pass, and into the path which curved around past the children's play area. By then her mouth had turned to cotton and her side felt pierced by swords.

She came racing around the corner of Ilchester Place and stumbled to a walk. Her breath dragging in her, face pumping with blood, she went up the three steps to her walk. The house seemed impassive, unwelcoming; she wanted no more than to fall into her bed and close out the whole world in sleep. The book in her hand seemed to have tripled in weight.

When Julia reached her front door she felt in her pocket and touched a used paper tissue, an earring with the pin broken, a loose mint, two small coins. The key, she remembered, lay at the bottom of her bag, on a counter in the kitchen. Her knees seemed to disappear altogether. Her body pitched into the springy grass. Before her eyes went shut, she saw the creamy startled face of Hazel Mullineaux staring at her through a side window of Number 23.

The old woman sat up in her narrow bed; a long, white page of moonlight lay folded at the juncture of wall and floor. Pulling her gently from sleep, a low voice had uttered her name repeatedly, lightly, as if teasing her. It came again, this time from a greater distance, somewhere else in the house. The woman did not want to follow the voice; she clung to the sheets, resisting. But she knew that she could not resist long. The voice was cool water, long blue slices of water she needed. The weak muscles in her arms began to tremble. And she knew who it was. Her tongue dryly scraped her teeth. Her name issued teasingly from the hallway. At last her body ceased to strain. Without her guidance, the woman's arms parted the upper sheet from her body and folded it back. Her legs swung over the edge of the bed.

She rose on unsteady legs which knew where to take her. The voice seemed the only thing in her mind. Her feet found her low shoes and slipped within them. She moved out of the hallway and saw the open door. Just outside, luminous in yellow light, stood her visitor, calling.

The woman moved down the hall. Knowledge lay ahead, knowledge and peace. Her hand moved to grasp the heavy tweed coat as she passed the coat hooks. Silly hand; silly coat; not needed. It was only to cover her nightdress. She pulled it across the bulge of her belly and fastened the single button.

Teasing, gentle, the visitor waited. Seductive—extraordinarily seductive. The woman padded toward the door, then passed through it into a wide familiar space.

The visitor moved quickly, walking backward, beckoning. White light on hair, on the beckoning backs of hands. All about the visitor was indistinct and hazy. Other voices filtered to her, but she did not turn her head.

The teasing voice was the last thing she heard.

Part Two

The Search: Heather

5

"I almost understood everything," Julia said. "I was lying in bed, reading that book you gave me, and when I came to the bit about Heather and Olivia Rudge, I knew that I was getting close to understanding what's been happening to me—because I *haven't* just been making it up, Lily. It was all mixed up with Kate and a little girl I saw before I fainted—I was so close, I had this amazing rush of energy and I almost called you, I had so many ideas. There's something about the house that Mrs. Fludd saw, and it's important because of what Magnus did to Kate. Somehow, the energy in this house is focused on me because of that. Mrs. Fludd *knew* she was in danger, and she said I was too. Doesn't that convince you I'm not just making it all up?"

There was a long pause on the line while Lily balanced the effects of several statements. Finally she said, "Darling, Mrs. Fludd was killed in an accident. It was a hit and run, very near her house. Apparently she just wandered out into the traffic on the Mile End Road, and the car was gone before anybody knew what had happened. It's always best to look for a reasonable, rational explanation before . . . before deciding on the other."

"I know. But some things don't have rational explanations."

"Darling, there is nothing supernatural about a hit and run. As tragic as it is."

"Evil isn't rational. Lily, I know that something hates me—something in this house. Mrs. Fludd felt it too—it's what she kept saying to me. I was so close to understanding everything that night I read about the Rudges. I almost broke through—I had all of these thoughts and ideas—I could feel the past all around me. The past is *in this house.* Don't you see that I'm connected to that story? Because of Kate? It's the key to everything."

"Well, as to the key to everything," Lily began, and then stopped. She had promised Magnus (they had worked it out together, with some strong advice from Julia's doctor) that she would not lead Julia into that territory; if Julia were ever to admit the truth about Kate's death, she would have to come to it herself. So she finished her sentence by saying, "I think it is in your state of mind." Immediately she regretted her choice of words.

"My state of mind? That's nice of you, Lily. Thanks."

"I didn't mean that the way it sounded. That's the truth, my dear."

"I can't believe that you of all people won't even discuss the possibility that something out of the ordinary is happening. Lily, if Mrs. Fludd saw something or felt something, as she did, isn't that just in your line? Isn't that just the sort of thing you *do* accept?"

"Only under the proper circumstances, Julia. You know I have a firm belief in the supernatural, but. . . ."

"And how about Heather and Olivia Rudge? Lily, there are no accidents. *There are no accidents.* These things have been happening to me for a reason. Maybe it takes a coincidence to set it off, maybe there's some kind of plan, I don't know, but I've been doing a lot of looking into the Rudge case for the past few days, and

I'm sure that's the direction I have to go. I found out the name of the clinic where Heather Rudge has been kept, the Breadlands Clinic, and I wrote to her, asking if I could see her."

"How did you find it?"

"It was in an old copy of the *Times*. My neighbor, Perry Mullineaux, got me a reader's ticket for the British Museum's periodical collection, and I've spent the past three days going through old newspapers. Remember telling me that I needed some interest? Well, I've sure got it. I tell you, sometimes I almost see the two of them, I can feel them all around me in this house—I hear the music they listened to, sometimes I think they've just left a room the moment before I entered it —did you know about the heaters? I kept turning them off without ever turning them on, someone else was doing that, I thought Magnus, but eventually the only room where it happened was my bedroom and I taped the switch to the wall and the heater still wouldn't go off. So I cut the wires, and the thing still stays hot. That's just a small thing I know, but then there was that bloodstain on my blue seersucker that wouldn't go away and kept getting bigger, there are the flashes of someone I keep seeing in the mirrors and the way the water has been getting so foul, it simply reeks, it's like shit, like diarrhea but full of *money,* sometimes it smells like greasy old American pennies, I haven't taken a real bath in a week. Then there are the noises and the whole general feel of the house—it wants me here, but it doesn't like me. Lily, why did I buy this house? *This* house? Don't you think I have a right to find out? That's why Mrs. Fludd was killed, it's horrible, it's awful, that intelligent old woman was killed to keep me from knowing too soon. I'm going to see Heather Rudge, and I'm going to find everyone I can who knew Olivia—I keep seeing signs of evil in children, not just malevolence but real evil, Lily. Kate's behind all this, she's evil now she's dead and I have to work at it, I have to see what I can do, it's so unfair. . . ."

"Julia," Lily said when Julia's voice had broken

down into a series of excited hiccoughs, "I want you to move over here with me. I don't think you should be on your own."

"I can't leave. Everything I'm interested in is here."

"Julia, have you been drinking?"

"Not much. Why? It doesn't matter. Magnus drinks."

"I want you to come to stay with me, Julia."

"That's funny, everybody wants me to live with them. I'm very popular with the entire Lofting family. I can't tell you how wanted that makes me feel."

"Are you sleeping?"

"I don't need sleep anymore. I'm too excited to sleep. Well, I suppose I get a couple of hours a night. I've been having the most amazing dreams—I keep dreaming about that girl I saw in Holland Park. She's a sort of metaphor for Kate, I guess. She seems totally without any redeeming virtues."

"Julia, guilt shouldn't. . . ."

"I have no guilt. I leave that to your brother."

Julia hung up.

Worried, Lily took her watering can into her efficient little kitchen and filled it at the tap. She carried the can out onto the terrace and began to sprinkle water over the flowers, which had lately showed the effects of the past month of hot dry days—particularly intense weather for a London summer. Eventually the weather would break, she supposed. Lily's clearest memory of such a long spell of hot weather was a summer more than twenty years before; she remembered it because that had been the year Magnus bought the house on Gayton Road. He had not been so fat then, and he had told her that he liked to go on Hampstead Heath and take off his shirt. One day she had met him in Gayton Road and walked over the Heath with him; in a green sloping vale Magnus had removed his shirt and fallen asleep in the sun. He had looked enormous, hieratic to her, his big pink trunk and massive, handsome head against the brilliant green of the grass. Lily had watched him for an hour, admiring how even in sleep Magnus seemed more powerful, more authoritative than other men. Of course, he was cruel, though not to her. "Magnim," she had said, stroking one of his bristling eyebrows—it was his name in their private language. She had been happy that he had women, but equally happy that he seemed incapable of marriage. Lily, in those days, had thought that most women would know better than to desire marriage with Magnus.

Julia had been a shock: at that time, an innocent, radiant girl with beautiful hair and a modest manner absurdly at variance with her general air of healthiness, she had been eminently the type of the girl Magnus seduced (physically, she was rather an American Sonia Mitchell-Mitchie, then Hoxton), but far from the kind of woman he might reasonably have married. Lily had for some reason always thought that were Magnus to marry he would take a woman older than himself. "It's her Burne-Jones eyes," Mark had suggested—poor envious Mark would have wanted any woman Magnus claimed as his own, even if she had looked like Mrs. Pankhurst. Later she had discovered the extent of Julia's wealth, and Magnus' marriage had become far more comprehensible.

But not for years did it become less painful. Really, Kate had helped with that reconciliation, had perhaps effected it, since Magnus, while altering little in other ways, had revealed a surprising capacity for fatherhood. He had loved Kate so deeply that Lily could not herself do otherwise; and eventually she and Julia had become friends. That Julia from the beginning had wished for that friendship encouraged it; but perhaps the change had begun when Lily arrived one morning to find a nursing Julia reading not a baby manual but *Middlemarch*. Julia might have been absurdly young, almost too wealthy, but at least she had good taste in fiction. Eventually, Lily had given her some of her volumes on the occult—books recommended by Mr. Carmen and Miss Pinner—and had been pleased that Julia had read them carefully. (Though she had thought more of Mr. Carmen's Roheim and Mircea Eliade than Miss Pinner's books on astral projection.) Later, she had more reason

to be grateful for Julia, though Julia was unaware of it,
for she had purchased the flat in Plane Tree House
largely with money allotted to her by Magnus from his
joint account. And she knew without asking that it was
Julia's money which paid for most of Magnus' expensive presents to her.

The main thing, Lily thought, was to get Julia back
with Magnus—never mind how much money was lost
on the house and its contents. Both of them needed
healing. Lily knew perfectly well that she was at times
jealous of Magnus simply because he was a man, and
jealous of Julia because she had come between herself
and her brother as even Mark had never done, but it
was in everyone's interest that they begin to knit themselves together again. Magnus, this past week, had been
worse than Lily had ever seen him. Sometimes he did
seem almost to hate Julia—though, proud as he was,
he needed no supernatural assistance in that—while he
desperately wanted her cured, wanted her back.

And Julia needed Magnus far more than he needed
her. She had begun to look shockingly weak and ill.
Her marvelous hair had gone dull and limp, and her
face soft and pouchy. Sometimes she seemed hardly to
be listening to what you said to her. Julia was running
on sheer nervous energy. It was no surprise that she saw
evil children everywhere or that she had built up a sick
fantasy about Kate.

And now this obsession with the Rudge case, which
was perfectly explicable in the light of what Julia was
determinedly repressing. Lily imagined Julia in a reading room, flipping crazily through old newspapers, making mad notes—she must look like Ophelia floating
downstream on a sea of newsprint.

I have a duty to Julia and to myself, Lily thought.
When she had finished watering the plants she put the
can down on her terrace and went inside to telephone
Magnus.

Most importantly, she had to keep Julia from Mark.
There was something missing in Mark, a moral space
filled by his resentment of Magnus. Lily knew that

Mark would miss no opportunity to humiliate Magnus. Julia, now weakened and perhaps hysterical, would be more open to Mark's entreaties than she had ever been. That must be blocked.

She first dialed Gayton Road. When there was no answer, she tried his chambers, where a secretary had not seen him all day and had been told not to expect him. She knew what that meant. Lily went down a list of his drinking clubs, and finally reached him at the Marie Lloyd, a certain sign of trouble. Once at the Marie Lloyd, the least prepossessing of all the little clubs he patronized all over the city, he began looking for a fight—he had once knocked down a truck driver outside the club who had sneered at him. She had to carefully judge the state of his intoxication, and calibrate her statements to it. Magnus' spy, she also saw herself as Magnus' protector. From his first words, she knew that it would be dangerous to irritate him, and so Lily omitted from her account of her conversation with Julia most of the material about the Rudges.

"Yes, she's much better," she said. "I think she fainted from exhaustion, and she's been getting some rest. She has a project she wants to begin working on, and that will help her fill her time. It seems harmless enough. Magnus, you must not go to that house anymore. That is absolutely the wrong tactic."

"Were you there when she fainted? Did you see her?" This meant, Lily knew, that Magnus wished to ignore her advice.

"A neighbor saw her faint," Lily said. Now was not the time to inform Magnus that Mark had come along moments later. "Someone got word to me, and we helped her get inside. She'd locked herself out, but the French windows at the back were unlatched and we helped her in that way."

"Those damned windows are always open," Magnus grumbled. "I'm going to go down and see her. Take her home."

"I wouldn't," Lily hastily said. "In her frame of mind that would only hurt things."

"Bugger that."

"I think you should go home. I think you should let things go their own way for a few days, my love, until she has settled down a bit more. She's a terribly confused girl."

"She looks like hell," Magnus said. "I saw her. But who isn't confused?"

"Magnus, before long she will have to face what really happened to Kate. I know it is dreadfully unfair to you that she blames you for what happened, and my dear, I feel your pain, but I do think now that the best thing for you would be to go straight home and perhaps telephone her later and try to speak calmly to her. I'm certain that is the best tactic, in the long run."

"I have the feeling you're hiding something from me, Lily."

"No. I am not."

"What's this project?" Magnus belched loudly. "Christ, I have to pee. What's this project she's working on?"

"I gather it has something to do with that house she's taken."

"Christ," Magnus said and brutally rang off.

Julia, hanging up the telephone, still kept her mood of excited elation. This had little to do with liquor, despite Lily's implication, for she had only sipped at a watered whiskey during the afternoon after her return from the periodical collection in Colindale. Yet the feeling was akin to that of one stage of drunkenness—an optimistic, impulsive sense that wheels had begun to move, that a resolution was near. She had no doubt that this would have a connection with the Rudges: the Rudges were to help her exorcise Kate, help her finally lay Kate to rest. How this was to happen she did not know, but she felt a certainty that it would happen. In any case, she no longer had any choice—she was driven to discover the truth about Olivia Rudge.

The old copies of the *Times* and the *Evening Standard* she had read had convinced her of at least one thing. Olivia Rudge had been psychotic. One member of her group, the gang of children in Holland Park, had been anonymously quoted as saying that Olivia was "bent"; even a detached reporter had called her "disturbing." If Julia could determine the truth about the murder of young Geoffrey Braden, perhaps that would appease Kate. Wasn't proof of that the extraordinary change in her mood since she had read those pages in *The Royal Borough of Kensington?* She still had trouble focusing her mind on remembering what she was supposed to do from one moment to the next, but she felt as though she were riding a great wave, borne along on it resistlessly. She burned her dinners, left half-filled cups of coffee all over the house, but since she had thought to ask Perry Mullineaux to help her get a reader's card, she had one great sustaining purpose— even Magnus had receded in importance. Let him skulk about the neighborhood; he was merely in the present; he had no connection with what mattered.

Turning, still pleased with herself for her parting shot at Lily, vaguely toward the dining room and the doors to the garden, Julia reminded herself of an idea she'd had at the end of her day's stint at the library. Before she talked to Heather Rudge—she had no doubt that she would hear from her—she would look through old copies of *The Tatler.* Surely, in the hostessy period of her life, she had been photographed for that magazine; there might even be pictures of her parties.

Then she remembered something Mark had said when he had appeared, as if by sympathetic magic, at her side when she had fainted. She had come conscious to find herself cradled by Hazel Mullineaux, Mark holding her hand. Even then, groggy and confused, she had been aware that Mrs. Mullineaux was not blind to Mark's appearance, and she had tried to fight her way upright into parity. Mark had taken her hand more firmly and said to Hazel Mullineaux, "I don't know who you are, but as you're being so kind, do you think you could go across the park to fetch Julia's sister-in-law, Lily Lofting?" He gave her Lily's address and said he'd "stay

on" to watch over Julia—a little bemused, but glad to
be of use, Hazel had left them.

"That was neat, don't you think?" asked Mark.

"Do women always do what you tell them?"

"Nearly always. They're usually thoughtful enough
not to terrify me, too. I thought you were about to live
up to your mortuary eyes. Like that Burne-Jones girl
at the Tate you've always reminded me of."

"Mortuary eyes? Burne-Jones? What are you going
on about? I feel better already." Julia straightened up,
her grogginess nearly gone.

"The girl in *King Cophetua and the Beggar Maid*.
Same eyes. I noticed it years ago, when I first met you.
What brought on this fit?"

Then she had told him about the blond girl in the
park, rushing to finish the story before Lily's arrival.
The incident was so private that, at least then, it could
be shared only with Mark.

Julia threw some things in her bag and rushed out of
the house just as a taxi appeared at the far corner of
Ilchester Place. When it came near she hailed it and
told the driver, "The Tate Gallery, please." Better than
driving: she felt too excited to trust herself to the Rover.

When the taxi pulled up before the Tate she gave the
driver a pound note and went quickly up the gray stone
steps, passing the usual crowds of tourists, and went
through the entrance and turnstiles. She said to a guard,
"Could you tell me where to find the Pre-Raphaelites?
I'm looking for a specific painting. A Burne-Jones."

The man gave her detailed directions, and she went
down the stairs and eventually turned into the room the
man had indicated. She saw the painting immediately.
The girl sat, backed by a cushion, on a long shelf, shyly
holding some flowers; the King, seated on gold beneath
her, gazed up. She did look like the girl Burne-Jones
had painted. Mortuary eyes. Were hers so round? But
the King: the King, but for his short sharp beard, was
Mark. She gasped with pleasure. Julia stood before the
painting for ten minutes, and then, still looking at it,
moved to a bench where she could sit and keep looking

at it. The little room endured several waves of spectators, swelling in, circling, and then draining out again. Julia shifted her place on the bench whenever her view of the painting was blocked. Eventually, alone in the room once again, she silently began to cry.

She had Mark—at least she had Mark. Both of them were Magnus' victims. Mark's phrase encapsulated the futile history of her marriage; she did not know if she were crying for her nine wasted years or for relief that Mark, however slightly, had shown her a way out of them.

Mark, Mark.

When the next dribbling of strangers entered the room, Julia dabbed at her eyes and went up the stairs back through galleries to the entrance. She walked outside into warmth and light and the noises of automobiles, went down the stone steps, crossed the street to the embankment and began to walk along the river. After a time she ceased to walk and leaned on the railing to stare at the gray and sluggish water. Low tide had left some scraps of weed, a bicycle tire, a battered doll and a child's cloth cap stranded on the mud and gravel of the riverbed. Julia was certain that she would soon hear from Heather Rudge; she felt oddly disembodied, as though she were floating above the river muck. She found herself adopting the expression of the girl in the Burne-Jones painting.

That girl is going to pieces, Lily thought, and if she does, she'll ruin everything for all of us. Drying her hands, Lily tried to think if any explanation had been given for Mark's appearance by Julia's side. Had he been invited? Was he in the habit of calling on Julia? The first possibility was less dreadful than the second, but only marginally. In any case, she had to talk sense to Julia, she had to try to break her out of her wild and irrational mood. Julia had almost certainly come out of the hospital too soon. Magnus would be able to correct that. The girl had become fixated on the sordid Rudge case, of which Lily had a dim memory. It had been in the newspapers for several weeks a long time ago—now that she thought of it, all of that had happened the same summer Magnus had purchased his house. But it was merely one of those newspaper sensations, having no connection with herself. Surely it was a reflection of Julia's loss of control that she had focused on that ancient story.

No connection. Unless . . . no, that could not be. Despite Julia's frantic assertions, accidents and coincidences occurred all the time. You had only to think of Rosa Fludd to see that. Poor dear Rosa Fludd. Poor Rosa. The horrid niece had been very rude to Lily on the telephone.

Lily went through her living room to her bedroom, stopping on the way to regard the Stubbs drawing which had been Magnus' last birthday present to her. Perhaps she could still persuade Julia to sleep in the spare bedroom. She had to make some sort of assault on Julia— all of them had been too easy, too lenient with her brother's wife. The image in Lily's mind was of a butterfly battering itself against a window: to keep its colors safe, the butterfly had to be pressed between glass. Once Julia was safely in the extra bedroom at Plane Tree House, Magnus could be brought in to make her see good sense. Thinking of this, Lily thought of asking Magnus about the coincidence she'd had in mind a moment before, just to see if it could possibly be true— and if it were, might Julia discover it? Lily cursed herself mildly for her lack of knowledge of the details of Magnus' life. Where exactly had he gone when he had visited Ilchester Place? But surely it was stretching things to suppose . . . ? Lily shrugged the idea away and turned to her wardrobe closet. She had already decided to change her clothes.

The more soberly she were dressed, the more convincing she would be. Flipping through her clothes, Lily pulled a dark blue linen suit from the closet. She'd owned it eight years, and it still looked elegantly crisp. Then she opened her scarf drawer, sighed, and began to change.

Wearing the blue linen suit and an off-white blouse Julia had given her the year before, Lily returned to her scarf drawer. She tried on three before settling on a long rectangular Hermès scarf in a red and white pattern; then she regarded the effect in her long mirror. She looked slightly more practical than usual—like a retired lady lawyer, or the wife of a prosperous professional man. Now she had to rehearse what she would say to Julia. She glanced at her watch and saw that it had been half an hour since she had spoken to Julia on the telephone. Surely she would still be at home.

Use the Rosa Fludd story, Lily advised herself. Remind her that Mrs. Fludd told her to leave the house; now was the time to take hold of herself, very firmly, before things got utterly out of hand. She must not mention Kate unless Julia did so first. It was monstrously unfair to Magnus, but, as Lily reminded herself, Magnus had taken up the doctor's suggestion more quickly than she had herself—Lily would have put an end to Julia's fantasy.

Now Lily supposed that she'd have to use the plural. One fantasy had burgeoned into half a dozen. "Wants a little cold water thrown over her," Lily muttered, and checked the angle of her skirt in the mirror. She was ready.

Outside in the warm sun, she strode into the park. It was Friday afternoon, and Holland Park seemed always to be more crowded then than at any other time save the weekends. Lily's neat figure moved, her bag swinging in time with her heels, through crowds of young people. Layabouts, most of them. Students. Though what they found time to study she couldn't say. Of course there's one famous subject, she thought, seeing a couple kissing on the grass. Magnus should really have married someone his own age: a man like Magnus needed a respectable woman for a wife. And certainly not an American. Americans failed to understand so much, for all their automobiles and electric toothbrushes. Magnus should have been Queen's Counsel by now, but any chance of

that had disappeared when Julia became Mrs. Lofting.
She *was* a dear girl, of course, and no one could say
that all that money hadn't been helpful. But even that
had its shady side. The old rogue who'd made it was a
sort of pirate, from what Lily could gather. Julia's great-
grandfather had been one of those ruthless railroad
barons of the end of the last century—he had blood on
his hands up to the elbows, Magnus had said. The
grandfather was cut from the same cloth, apparently:
whole forests had been felled for him, rivers spoiled,
wars fought and companies stripped and men killed to
increase his holdings. There was a taint, an historical
stain, to Julia's money. Lily lifted her head and turned,
her heels making a neat staccato sound on the asphalt,
deeper into the park.

Descending a short flight of steps beside the little
gardens, Lily noticed a small blond girl leap up from
one of the benches where old people sunned themselves
and run in the direction she was now walking. After a
few yards, the girl began to walk. What a sweet old-
fashioned-looking child, Lily thought: she even looked
a little like Kate, at least from the back. After a moment
she recognized that it was the girl's trousers which gave
her the old-fashioned aspect: they were high-waisted
and elasticized around the top, like children's trousers of
twenty-five years before. The girl seemed almost to be
leading Lily to Julia's house. She began to skip ahead
of her, slowing to a walk whenever she got more than
fifteen or twenty yards away, and then, Lily approaching, skipped and ran once more—just as if, Lily
thought, she were on a leash.

When they reached the children's play area, within
sight of Julia's house, the girl vanished. Lily checked her
stride for a moment, puzzled. She looked over the children playing in the sandboxes and sporting beside the
trees, but saw no flash of that astonishing hair—that
hair like Kate's. To her left, on the long stretch of grass,
she saw only three small wailing children, none of them
the girl.

Lily glanced from side to side once more, then

shrugged and was about to resume walking when she felt a quick chill over her entire body. She had seen, she was now looking at, a stout elderly woman seated on a green bench, her profile to Lily. It was Rosa Fludd. She was far off to Lily's right, staring straight ahead of her, unmoving. She wore the hideous tweed coat she had worn the night of the last gathering. Lily slowly turned in the woman's direction; her stomach felt frozen, and the ends of her fingers were tingling. She realized that she was unable to speak.

By a violent effort of will, Lily turned her head away from Mrs. Fludd and looked back at the children. They played on, scrabbling in the sand. Their voices came clear and sweet to her. She snapped her head back to look at the park bench. It was now empty. Like the girl, Rosa Fludd had disappeared.

Lily's breath gradually returned to her body, as if it had been suspended for some minutes in the air before her. She self-consciously straightened her back and patted the back of her head. She looked once again at the bench. No one sat there. No sad gray fat lady. Of course. No one had ever been there. What an extraordinary thing, Lily thought. And to have an hallucination just at the time when she was preparing herself to drum sense into Julia! A less stable person than herself might immediately join Julia's fantasies and condemn himself forever to unreality. Lily permitted herself a smile at the thought of the response of Miss Pinner or Miss Tooth to the resurrection of Mrs. Fludd. Then she wondered just what Miss Pinner had seen in the bathroom on that awkward night; and then reminded herself on no account to bring up the subject with Julia. She found herself, she reflected, in the position of a priest taking a hard line on miracles with an overenthusiastic new convert.

By now Lily felt recovered; well, nearly recovered. The experience had been decidedly *dégoûtant*. She glanced once more at the bench—empty—and firmly marched on her way down the path.

On the corner of Ilchester Place Lily paused, trying

to marshal her arguments. She had nothing in mind as to
her exact words, but she knew she must have a lever—
Julia in effect had to be pried from that house. Perhaps
she could use Magnus. Some subtle threat was needed.
If she could drop the word "hospital" in the proper
way. . . . Lily stood for a moment, enjoying the unac-
customed flavors of power and connivance.

She glanced up at Julia's bedroom windows. Or were
those for the unused rooms? The house did have an
empty look: more romancing, Lily thought. That damnable hallucination had upset her. Yet she could look
obliquely through the side windows and see that at least
half the living room was empty. From directly across the
street she'd be able to look straight through the house:
and if the drapes were drawn, wouldn't that mean that
Julia was probably at home? Lily felt an inexplicable reluctance to begin her crusade immediately.

She took the ten paces across the street and looked
through the double set of windows to the garden which
glowed greenly, as if reduced in scale, through its frame.
She'd have to ring the bell. Why this odd reluctance?
Some memory pulsed below the level of consciousness
and then opened to her: Mrs. Weatherwax at a postwar
cocktail party (in the Albany, she remembered). A
giant hulk of a woman, the wife of a Minister, the queen
of her set, Mrs. Weatherwax had been in particularly
foul mood, and had occupied a settee, her face frozen
into disapproval—she had nearly dared anyone to approach her. Absurdly, the house had reminded her of
Mrs. Weatherwax, exuding hostility from a flowered
settee in the Albany. Those crushed flowers along the
side of the house: had it been some sort of visual pun?
Yet pun or not, the impression had been clear and
strong.

What nonsense, Lily thought, and took a step off the
pavement. Then she saw Magnus' face appear in the
light square of green at the back of the house, and she
froze in the attitude of taking her second step. She
quickly retreated backward. After a second, she moved
as far to one side as she would go while still watching

the windows at the rear of the house. Magnus was jerking on the handle, his mouth working. As Lily watched aghast, he took some sort of card from his wallet and slipped it into the frame where the two halves of the window joined. His arm pumped rapidly; the windows parted, and Magnus climbed into the house. Lily could watch no more.

6

Magnus stood in the sunny dining room, listening carefully. Somewhere in the empty house a switch moved, inspiring a hum from machinery hidden behind the walls. Magnus fumblingly replaced his Access card in his wallet. He lurched forward a step, then paused again and listened like an animal. Perhaps the buzzing noise came from inside his head. He'd had no more than seven or eight hours' sleep all week, fueling himself with whiskey, keeping his adrenalin flowing by imagining scenes with Julia—sleep was caught in his office between clients, on park benches; once he'd fallen asleep in the flowerbed in the garden, keeping watch on Julia's window. He could imagine beating Julia, making love to her, waking her up an hour before dawn and talking to her urgently, cogently. Like many gregarious men, Magnus hated to be alone, and at times this week, locked into his house, patrolling from room to room with a bottle in his hand, he had talked to Julia so earnestly that he seemed to see her before him, her own ghost. Twice he had heard her calling his name in distress or pain and sped drunkenly across town to park before the dark house on Ilchester Place. He didn't know what he expected to see—unless it was Julia pinned by Mark, fighting him off a final desperate

second before yielding. That scene came into his dreams
and sent him rocketing awake, his heart thudding. He
had begun to masturbate again, as he had not done
since adolescence. There was a woman five minutes
from this house, a former client who lived in Hammer-
smith, another woman nearly as close, the wife of a
man in prison, but Magnus knew that he went to them
largely because he frightened them; and they made
sense only as temporary alternatives to Julia. Without
her, they were useless to him. So he had come to lurk
outside this house at night, his anger and frustration un-
dimmed by whiskey, with no plan other than to speak
to Julia the words he could always find when alone. On
the telephone he could not control himself: she sounded
snippy and pert, dismissive. It infuriated him.

Now the memory of that anger, and the tone of
Julia's feigned coolness which inspired it, momentarily
helped Magnus to quiet his apprehensions. That, of all
the houses in London, Julia had chosen this one was
nearly enough to encourage belief in all of Lily's mysti-
cal claptrap. Twenty-five Ilchester Place contained too
many frustrating memories for him to feel comfortable
with Julia's living there. Even after all these years, it
was the past stirring again, wretchedly.

Now, Magnus thought, I should burn this place to its
miserable roots. This idea gave him a shade more courage, and he moved around in the dining room, picking
up things and putting them down. He would not be
spooked by the place. And now it was bright day, unlike
the other times when he had crouched outside, tapping
at the windows before trying to force his way in. Then
he had felt the house beating at him, almost—it was the
only way he could describe it.

Magnus pulled the little bottle of brandy from his
pocket and took a long swallow before entering the living room. Noticing that he had begun to perspire, he
loosened his tie and swabbed at his forehead with his
handkerchief. In the old days, the house had never been
so hot—if anything, it had been rather cold. Someone
had installed these damnably ugly storage heaters. This

warmth was unpleasant, oppressive. Magnus tore the tie from his neck and balled it up in his trouser pocket.

He called Julia's name. When no answer came, he staggered toward the couch and leaned on its cushiony back. He bellowed her name again, then swore when he heard only the soft, buzzing noises of the house. Looking toward the staircase, he saw double for a moment and forced himself to stand straight upright. He focused his eyes. Of course all the furniture was different. Years ago the room had been brighter, with satin wallpaper—could that be right? It had looked like satin. Her sheets had been satin too, and silk. Down here there had been small couches, bright paintings: the room had looked much larger. Everything gets smaller as we age, Magnus thought. This isn't a bit like the room where I came years ago—that room had been cheerful, frivolous, a bit silly. And we silly young men had thronged here. As an alternative to Cambridge, the house had attracted him by its carelessness, its perpetual atmosphere of carnival, the license he had thought of at the time as American. That was not to neglect the attractions of his hostess. He could visualize Heather Rudge slipping through the arch of the doorway with a cocktail shaker in her hand, a Sobranie cigarette wobbling in her charming mouth.

But all of that was what he wished to keep Julia from discovering. And what he must not think of. Magnus pushed himself away from the couch and went toward the kitchen.

There too everything had changed. Now all was white—white as a hospital. Magnus threw open several cupboards. Bottles of Malvern water, plates, glasses. A drawer of new silverware. To one side beneath the sink he found a clutch of whiskey bottles. The malt he'd taught her to like. He touched one of the bottles. They were somehow reassuring.

She must be dead by now, he thought. Then his mind blurred, and he thought he had meant Julia. The fear he had felt on the night he had broken the vase began to leak back into him. No, it was the other one who was

dead, not Julia. She must have died in that place where
she'd been put. That weak, foolish woman. He'd sent
her money for years. Presumably other men sent her
money too. She kept the same claim on all of them.
Magnus slammed the door to the liquor shelf, hoping to
chip away some of the white paint or damage the catch.

From the kitchen he stalked into the downstairs bathroom. He hovered just within the door, sensing that
someone was near. Cunningly, he glanced into the rose
mirrors. Something was just flickering out of sight. He
was drunk. There was nothing to be afraid of. His head
seemed to hum in sympathy with some deeper vibration.
Watching himself in the mirrors, he took another pull at
the brandy. And there it was again, just vanishing from
sight. "Damn you," Magnus uttered. His thick gray hair
lay across his forehead; his suit was spattered and wrinkled. He combed his hair with his fingers. "You're not
there," he said aloud. "Bugger yourself."

What was it that had frightened him that first night he
had come in from the garden? He had been slightly
more sober that night: he'd half wanted to pound sense
into Julia's fuzzy mind, half simply to sit in her house
and relish her atmosphere. He had lifted the vase of
flowers to smell them. The house was a particularly *taut*
web of noises, none of which he could identify. But he'd
thought he could hear Julia moving about upstairs, talking to herself. Then, at first quietly, almost modestly, a
feeling had grown in him that he was being watched, as
if by some little animal. A feeling of eyes on him. Irra-
tionally, this had grown: the mouse had become a tiger,
something baleful and immense and savage. He had
never felt such sudden terror. And it was as much
despair as fear—an utter and complete hopelessness.
Gripping the vase, he'd been afraid to turn around,
knowing that something loathsome crouched behind
him. Kate's death. That very second seemed to hang behind him, about to engulf him. His head had hurt in-
tolerably. Something rushed toward him, and he threw
down the vase, making an awful clatter, and raced outside into the little garden without looking around.

Now he repeated "Bugger yourself," and left the bath-room to stand at the foot of the stairs.

If Mark were up there he'd . . . he'd strangle him.

Magnus put a foot on the lowest stair.

Something was up there. His skin seemed hot.

He stepped back down to the carpet and felt an im-mediate release of pressure. Even the buzzing in his head diminished. The upstairs of the house was full of noises. A running, rushing noise: for reasons Magnus could not begin to define, this meant an appalling danger to him. He put his foot back on the stair and felt the atmosphere thicken about him. An iron band clamped about his forehead and tightened; his chest pulled for air.

He backed away further into the hall. Now the house almost palpably lay about him—to stay there would kill him. He felt it with utter certainty. He tried to pull his handkerchief from his pocket and found that his fingers were unable to close properly. His hand shook. The fingers could not coordinate. He was afraid to turn his back to the staircase. Eventually he made his way to the door.

When he stood outside on the front doorstep in the sun, Magnus wobbled a little and touched the bottle in his pocket, stroking it as a man pets a dog. Out of the side of his eye he saw a face peering through a window at him and he wheeled to face it. The woman's face, as pretty and mild as a saucer of cream, hung there by the drapes for a second and then jerked back. Magnus con-tracted his face at the spot where she had been. If he saw Julia, he'd beat the life out of her. Someone had to pay for this—humiliation. He'd batter anyone who got in his way.

The day after these events Julia drove her car south along the motorway, following the directions given her by the director of the clinic. She felt bright and il-luminated with sleeplessness, her consciousness high and clear. She was driving very fast, and became aware of her speed only when she accidentally glanced at the dashboard. It seemed to her that she had never driven

so well, with such confidence. Below the bright center
of her consciousness, her body piloted the little car like
an extension of her nerves.

In Guildford, the sight of a restaurant made Julia
suddenly aware that she was hungry. She had not eaten
since receiving the letter; two letters, actually, the short
scrawled note from Mrs. Rudge folded within a typed
sheet from the director. The first of these had read:

> Julia Lofting,
> Is that your real name and do you live in my old
> house? You remember my case. Visit me if you
> wish.
>
> HR

In her excitement she had been able only to skim the
covering letter, which claimed for its writer a great pleasure that Mrs. Rudge was to be visited after so many
years and that no official impediment would block such
a visit. There had once been a problem with the press,
who had treated "the patient" badly. It would be a
further pleasure to the director if he could meet Mrs.
Lofting after her talk with "the patient." This had the
whiff of a laden desk and busy secretary, behind them
the stronger odor of hospitals and ammonia, and Julia
had thrust it away after memorizing the directions to the
Breadlands Clinic. She had reread Heather Rudge's
scrawl a dozen times, looking for whatever she might
find in her cramped, spidery letters. It was, most notice-
ably, an American handwriting, without the copperplate
flourishes and separations of that generation's hand in
England.

Julia had spent that morning and afternoon foreseeing
her meeting with Mrs. Rudge—she was like a grey-
hound pulling at its leash, blind to everything but what
had just scrambled out of the bush. She had let the telephone ring unanswered, had finally left her home and
walked until dark, through dingy sections of Hammer-
smith and Chiswick; past eleven, she realized that she
was wandering near Gunnersbury Park, and took the

underground back to Kensington. Not even the increasing noises and furies in the house had frightened her: they were a sign that she was indeed getting closer to whatever was directing her life. She was at last able to act.

And the poltergeist, the spirit, was pleased. It was almost showing itself. Of course if it were Kate's spirit, it could not reveal itself until the very end—she was certain of that. But the heat in her bedroom had doubled in intensity and the noises at night—the rushing and rustling—were almost frantic. At times Julia heard voices, a woman's and a girl's, muttering from the hall. Snatches of music. Magnus had dwindled in her imagination. He was merely an outside force—baleful but not central to her. Magnus was a tool. Julia felt as though she were approaching the center of a blinding light too burning and intense to permit fear; she had to stand in the full clarity of that light, she had to understand all. Otherwise, Mrs. Fludd had died in vain. Perhaps even Kate's death would be for nothing. She felt the full weight of the past impelling her toward this hot center of light.

Just out of the center of Guildford Julia saw a Jolyon restaurant and her stomach again cramped savagely. She pulled up to the curb and went inside. Going down past the ranks of cafeteria food, she grabbed at whatever fell beneath her hand, at the cash desk finally paying for yogurt, chips, two sausages, an egg, toast and coffee. She carried her tray to one of the room's few clean tables and, scarcely bothering to look around her, began to bolt the food. After a few bites her hunger ceased as abruptly as it had begun, but she continued to eat until the sausages and egg had been consumed. The rest lay untouched on the table as she hurried out.

Half an hour later Julia saw the brass plate identifying the Breadlands Clinic and turned into the long narrow drive, which circled through a small wood before ending at a gray manor house. Julia's mouth was very dry: her heart seemed to be skipping beats, skittering. To calm herself she called up the photographs she had

seen of Heather Rudge. Finally she was able to open the
door of the Rover and walk across the crunching gravel
to the steps of the manor.

An elderly woman in white greeted her. "You are
Mrs. Lofting? Mrs. Rudge is *so* pleased that you wrote.
And you know that Dr. Phillips-Smith wishes to see you
afterward? Good. It's rather a long way away, so please
follow me—of course, the poor old dear's not so difficult, not any more, but we have to obey all the regula-
tions, don't we? Of course. And she does have her rough
spots. Keeps going on about her daughter, as I expect
you'll know. You look as though you could use a rest,
dear. Do you want to take a minute before you see
her?" Small, bright squirrel's eyes.

"No, please, no," Julia got out.

She received a professional smile which seemed to
conceal a good deal of metal. "Then please come this
way, Mrs. Lofting."

They went briskly down a featureless corridor, past
numbered doors. All eggshell-white. "We *were* able to
move her into E wing," the elderly woman said.

"Oh? How—how does she look?"

"Much better."

"Better. . . ."

As the nurse inserted a key into a locked metal door,
Julia turned her head and looked into a small white
room where a motionless form lay beneath a sheet. Beside the bed stood a steel table crowded with ampules
and hypodermics. Julia nearly stumbled. The food
bounced in her stomach like an angry cat.

"Just through here." At the end of the corridor, another heavy metal door. A large bald man in dirty white
hoisted himself from a stool. His stomach wobbled as
he came forward.

"Will you fetch Mrs. Rudge, Robert? I'll take Mrs.
Lofting to the visitor's room."

Robert nodded and moved slowly off. The nurse led
Julia through a small room bright with watercolors—a
few old men working about a scarred table gaped at
them. The men looked frightened, their faces oddly

smooth and unmarked. One wore dark glasses which froze his face into granite.

Why am I here? Julia thought. I can't stand this place.

The feeling grew as the nurse brought her through two more chambers, each with the unsettling contradiction of bright, haphazard walls and pale, stunned-looking inhabitants. Faces which fled from experience. . . . Julia felt trapped by their hunger.

"Here we are, dear." The nurse had turned another corner and was holding open a door to an anonymous little room where two chairs stood on either side of a green metal table. Gesturing at a tattered pile of magazines, the nurse said, "She will be right with you."

Julia took the far chair as the nurse pivoted from the room.

A second later footsteps came. The door opened on Robert, who then stood aside to allow a woman to pass by him. Julia at first thought he'd brought the wrong woman. The flabby creature in the faded housedress bore no resemblance to the photographs of Heather Rudge, who had been trim and oval-faced in her forties, clearly sensual. Julia glanced at Robert, but he had moved to the stool in the corner of the room and now sat with his hands locked across his belly. He stared at the floor.

The woman still stood just inside the door. She was the sister of the faded, hopeless women Julia had seen in the other rooms.

"What is your name?" the woman asked. Her words scattered Julia's first impressions.

"I'm sorry . . ." said Julia, rising from her chair. "I've wanted so badly to meet you. You are Heather Rudge?"

"Mrs. Lofting?"

They've tricked me, they've given me someone else, thought Julia.

"Mrs. Lofting?"

"Yes," Julia said. "I'm sorry, it's just such a moment,

meeting you—I bought your house, you know. I think about you. I think about you a lot."

The old woman shuffled across the floor and sat facing Julia. Her jowly face sprouted a few white whiskers.

"Why were you interested in my name?"

The woman looked slyly at Julia. "Nothing."

Julia leaned forward. "I don't know quite where to start. . . . Do you like having visitors? Do they treat you well here?"

"It's bad here. But better than prison. I was in prison, you know." Julia could hear in her voice the flat vowels of the Midwest. "You don't have to tell me about outside. They let us read—things."

"Oh, I should have brought you something, a book, something, or magazines, a stack of Penguins—I didn't think."

The blunt-faced woman stared impassively at her.

"I came to talk about you."

"I'm nothing. I'm safe here. Nothing happens to you here."

Julia could not speak. Finally she blurted, "My daughter is dead too. We have things we share, things in common, important things."

"You think mine is dead?" The old woman shot a quick sly glance across the table. "That's what they all think. But they didn't know her. Olivia isn't dead. And why should I care about your daughter, Mrs. Lofting?"

"Not dead? What. . . ."

"It isn't 'what.' It's what I said. Why are you interested in Olivia? Didn't you come here to talk to me, Mrs. Lofting?" Unexpectedly, the old woman chuckled. "You poor cunt. You don't know where you are."

The heavy food churned in Julia's stomach. "I have to begin at the beginning. . . ."

"First you have to know where it is."

"Something's been happening to me and I have to tell you about it. I've been reading about your case in the old newspapers, I've been reading them for days, I believe there is some connection between us. . . ."

"Look at me, Mrs. Lofting," said the other woman.

"I'm the one who is dead, not Olivia. Mrs. Lofting. Nice Mrs. Lofting visiting the crazy woman. Eat your own shit, Mrs. Lofting. Rub yourself with your shit. Then you'll know what I am."

Julia threw herself into it again. "I think I can help you too—part of you is caught in my house, I can hear you there sometimes. Does that make me crazy? Why did you talk about being safe?"

Now Mrs. Rudge's attention was wholly fixed on Julia. "I can't do anything for you, Mrs. High-and-Mighty Lofting. I scorn you." Her face grew distorted; she nearly spat her words. "Live in your house. I'll tell you about Olivia, Mrs. High-and-Mighty, Mrs. Nice. Do you want to know? Olivia was evil. She was an evil person. Evil isn't like ordinary people. It can't be got rid of. It gets revenge. Revenge is what it wants, and it gets it."

"What—what was her revenge?"

The silence was better than scorn.

"Do you mean that she made you do what you did?"

"She's laughing at me. She's laughing at you too. You hear her, don't you? You don't know anything." The flabby white face, contracted about a writhing mouth and narrowed eyes, loomed before Julia. "*I* did what I did, Mrs. Shit, because I saw what she was like. Do you have to ask me what her revenge was?"

"Mrs. Rudge," Julia pressed, "did she do what people thought she did?"

"What she was was worse than what she did. Ordinary people can't touch it. I'm happy to be in here, Mrs. Lofting. Do you want to know a secret?" Malevolence gleamed from her distorted face.

"I want to know," said Julia. She was leaning across the table, straining to hear the thick words.

"You'd be lucky to be me."

Robert snorted from the corner.

"You're stupid, Mrs. Shit. As stupid as us in here."

Julia bowed her head. Spittle shone on the table's battered surface. The room seemed horribly small. A

rank odor floated about her, and for a moment she felt
dizzy, assailed.

"Who else can I talk to?" she brought out. "Who
else knew you?"

"The Braden bitch," snarled Mrs. Rudge. "Talk to
that sauerkraut eater. Talk to my daughter's friends.
They'll have found out."

"What are their names?" Julia softly asked.

"Names. Minnie Leibrook. Francesca Temple. Paul
Winter. Johnny Aycroft. Do you want more? David
Swift. Freddy Reilly. Hah! Go ask them about your
problems, Mrs. Shit."

"Thank you," Julia said.

"You're just what I thought," said Mrs. Rudge. "You
belong in here. Stupid cunt. Now get out."

"You have eight minutes," said Robert from the
corner.

"No, I'd better. . . ." Julia began. She stood up.

"Stupid cunt bitch. Stupid murdering cunt bitch."

Julia bolted around the body of the old woman and
threw open the door. Robert looked up startled and
held out a pudgy hand. Julia ran down the corridor and
turned blindly at a corner. When she saw a large door
with a light over it, she rushed through; impelled by a
vision of Mrs. Rudge's sullen, working face and Robert
chasing heavily after her, Julia fled the hallways and
spun into a long hall filled with men and women.

Their faces were sagging and gray, or drawn and
gray. They had all swiveled to stare at her entrance.
Julia at first stopped, and then moved quietly among
them toward the far end of the hall. The men were bent;
their faces mooning and unconscious, they shuffled aside
to let her pass, some of them fumbling toward her with
unsteady hands. One cadaverous man grinned slackly
from beneath wild hair. Julia only half saw the Ping-
Pong table, the metal chairs pushed together to form
rows. The odors of clean linen and sour flesh and dis-
infectant swam about her, as if Heather Rudge had
leaped on her back. These faces—they looked as though
they would leak sawdust. A hand with enormous knuck-

les brushed at her wrist, snatching at her. Julia flinched, and the elephantine man at her left hissed at her. A squashed-looking woman with terrible bright hair joined his hissing. A man whose face was all drawn to one side, as if snagged by a hook, scuttled before Julia and grabbed for her elbows as she twisted to pass him. She felt as if drowning in grotesque, stinking flesh. . . . She pushed at the man in blind revulsion and ran to the end of the hall just as Robert appeared at the far corner.

She was in a long dim corridor. Behind her she could hear lurching bodies, heavy footfalls. She ran. At the corridor's end there was a flight of steps down to a narrower, darker hallway with a rough stone floor. Here she ran in darkness for half its length; then, holding her side and gasping for breath, Julia walked quickly to a large barred wooden door. She pushed aside the bolts and swung the door open, grunting with the effort. Three broad stone steps led upward to a grassy lawn. At the far end of the lawn, the wood began. The names Heather Rudge had spat at her came thrillingly into her mind. *Braden. Minnie Leibrook. Francesca Temple. Paul Winter. Johnny Aycroft. David Swift. Freddy Reilly.* She looked into the dark tangled wood and moved up over the steps toward the wood's darkness, repeating the names.

Magnus stood in shock beside the sandboxes, children all about him. He was staring up at the window of Julia's bedroom. It was impossible, what he had seen there for a moment. He touched the bottle in his jacket pocket. A little boy brushed against his legs and Magnus stepped backward, feeling sand grind beneath his heel. His pulse seemed to have stopped. Gradually, into the silent vacuum which had dropped over him like a bell jar, sounds began to come. He heard children's piping voices and the far-off booming wash of a jet. One of the children pressed against his left leg. He had walked through the park from Plane Tree House, irritated. Lily had been more than usually coy with him, as if she were keeping a secret. She'd assumed her you're-such-anaughty-boy manner, as she sometimes did when she had learned something upsetting about him, but she had refused to speak directly about his supposed transgression. Instead, she had babbled about Julia's "privacy," about her need for "an honest meeting" with Magnus, about "the needs of all concerned," all the while her eyes shining with bright, needling admonition. He had supposed that all this had to do with his drinking.

Then she had got onto his not being a Queen's Counsel again.

"For God's sake, Lily," he had said. "I've explained this to you a hundred times. If I wanted to be a QC I could be one. But all I would do would be to double my prices and drop my cases down to a fourth of what they are now. You don't understand what a Queen's Counsel is. For a man in my position it would be a ludicrous mistake."

"I want my distinguished brother to be a QC."

"You mean you want to be the sister of a QC without first understanding what it means. Absurd. And it has nothing to do with Julia. Can you get that into your head?"

"Magnim. . . ."

"And don't start to stroke me with Durm."

She had brightly pulled back. "You should have your clothes looked after. That suit looks as though you've slept in it."

"I probably did, damn it."

By the time he had left Lily's flat, he had a headache and the sour beginnings of indigestion. He had walked gloomily through the park, irritated with the sunshine and the loafers sprawling on the grass. The newspapers predicted a change in the weather in the next few days, which suited him. He wanted rain. He longed for clouds and cold blustery weather. Eventually he reached the play area and stepped off the path onto springy grass. Then he looked angrily up at Julia's window and saw Kate—the back of her head shining through the glass. In the next second she had disappeared. But it was Kate.

He knew the color of that hair better than he knew the color of his own. For a long moment Magnus forgot to breathe.

He extracted a grinning black girl of two or three from his leg and, gulping air, stepped forward on the grass. His stomach burned. His tongue was a wooden oar lodged in his mouth. He could not have seen Kate. Yet he *had* seen her—that hair shining like the hair of a princess in a fairy story. For a moment Magnus felt one of the strongest and most unselfish emotions of his lifetime, an overriding fear for Julia's safety.

His legs took him over the lawn, racing, to the road out of the park. He ran a few laborious steps into Ilchester Place and then, puffing, began to walk quickly. He scanned the expressionless façade of the house. Impossible to tell what was going on inside. The great moment of the fear had receded, but it lay close enough to bring Magnus up the walk, leaping the three steps, to the door. He pushed the bell. From far within the house Magnus heard the bell's chime, falling away: the house was empty.

He jumped off the doorstep and half circled the house, peering in the windows. The interiors he saw looked motionless, tomblike, immaculately dead. He pounded on the window of the kitchen until its whiteness and sterility repelled him; then he continued around to the back of the house where he tried the handle of the French windows. They were locked. He leaned forward and looked past the parting of the drapes, cupping his hands about his eyes. The stolid furniture bulked on the floor as if it had come from a taxidermist's show window. Before taking out his Access card he glanced at the house next door and saw Julia's kittenish little neighbor staring down at him in horror from an upstairs window.

He shook his fist at her before noticing the tall, weedy man cutting around the corner of Julia's house to come toward him. The expression on his face, that of a policeman about to dress down a tramp, infuriated Magnus, as did everything about the man, his modishly long blond hair and his velvet jacket and glinting ascot.

When the man glanced suspiciously at Magnus' rumpled and stained, tieless exterior, Magnus whirled to face him, balling his fists.

"Just a minute," the blond man began. "Just a minute there, you."

Glowering into his face, Magnus saw, with the sureness of years of sounding witnesses and juries, an essential weakness beneath the bluster. "Piss off," he growled.

The man stopped, as if hesitating, and then approached to within two feet of Magnus. "I don't know what your game is, mister, but you shall be in trouble with the law if you don't leave this house alone. I've seen you here before and I don't like the look of you."

"You utter twit," Magnus said. "Piss off and leave me alone. My name is Lofting. My wife lives here. I don't know who the bloody hell you are and I don't care. Now get going."

Amazement came into the well-cared-for face. "My name is Mullineaux," he blurted. The admission caused him anger and Magnus, seeing it, braced himself. "I live next door to this house you were about to break into. Now I must ask you to leave."

Magnus leaned his forehead against the windowpane, grinning ferociously. "You have a lot of guts for a Golden Wonder," he said. "I'm going inside. I think my wife is in danger." He straightened up and smiled at the man, knowing despairingly that he would have to fight him.

"Your wife isn't here," said Mullineaux. "And I doubt if you could do anything for her, in your condition." He lifted an admonitory finger. "If you will go away this instant, I promise you that against my better judgment I will not speak of this to the police. Now please go."

" 'Now please go,' " Magnus mimicked. "Now *you* will please go, twit, because I'm going inside. You can stand here and watch or you can help me."

"I must say . . ." the man said, advancing and placing a hand on Magnus' arm.

An absolute conviction of his size flashed through

Magnus, and he punched the man on the side of his head, knocking him aside. Because Magnus had used his left hand, the blow was weak, but Mullineaux crumpled to the ground. At that instant Mark's face floated into Magnus' mind. He ground his teeth, enraged, and took a step toward the pale figure now groveling on the grass. He lifted his right boot back, intending to kick Mullineaux on the point of his jaw, but looked upward at the neighboring house and saw the pretty little woman inside shrieking through the glass. "Come and get this idiot inside," he muttered, his fury dissipating, and stalked off back around to the front of the house. He had left his car at Plane Tree House.

Kate? Kate? As he stormed through the park, the slightly hazy, glowing summer air seemed to darken about him.

7

Mark came awake in darkness, the dirty sheet twisted about his hips. He had been dreaming about Julia, a variation on a dream he had been having regularly for the past three or four years. Usually the dream began with his entering a classroom, perching on the desk, and suddenly realizing that he was totally unprepared. Not only had he no lecture or plan for this particular class, he could not even recall which course he was supposed to be teaching. Students from various years and classes regarded him quizzically, already bored: if he could not think of something to say, soon the whole hour, an hour he hadn't the barest idea of how to fill, would be lost. Was this *Working Class Movements in England*, Monday, Wednesday and Friday, 9:30–10:20? *New Trends in Socialist Thought*, Tuesday, Thursday and

Friday, 1:30–2:20? *Crowd Theory*, Monday and Wednesday, 4:00–5:25? He would realize with growing desperation that he did not know what day it was. Last
night, the dream had progressed to this point, and then
Julia had risen from one of the chairs and, pulling a
sheaf of notes from her bag, began to lecture brilliantly
on the London Corresponding Society and its Secretary,
Thomas Hardy. He had resented her usurping his class
at the same time as he had listened dazzled to her initial
summary of information and the cascade of her ideas,
which defined exactly what he had been struggling to
express to this class over the past year. He had been certain he would remember everything she said so that he
could use it in the first chapter of the book he wanted
to write, but all of it had vanished in the first second of
wakefulness. Instead of her ideas, he could remember
how she had looked—dressed in a white blouse and yellow skirt, her hair hanging softly about her shoulders,
she was the Julia he had seen that first morning at Magnus' house. She looked enchanted, like a woman who
conversed with fairies: a woman to whom clung the last
bewitching traces of childhood. Mark stared up at the
low ceiling of his room, realizing that the dream had
caused in him a terrific sexual arousal. He wanted Julia
very badly. She could not consider herself married to
Magnus after his brutal appearance at her home yesterday afternoon; the thought gave him energy to roll
over and punch the light switch beside the mattress.
Magnus seemed to have at last exploded. Both Julia
and Lily had described the incident to him, each of them
advising him to stay away from Magnus for the time
being. Well, when *hadn't* he avoided Magnus? One of
the first utterly clear impressions of Mark's life was that
his adoptive brother detested him.

Maybe loathing was more the word for it, he considered, and giggled.

Still grinning, Mark untangled his legs from the sheet
and stood up beside the mattress, carefully avoiding the
stacks of plates and half-empty tins strewn over the
floor. He had begun eating in bed the previous winter,

when his bed was the warmest place in the flat, and had not yet got out of the habit. A pile of clothing lay atop a chair near the mattress, and Mark extracted from it a shirt and trousers, which he pulled on over his body, taking great care with the zip of the trousers. From the pocket of the shirt he took a pack of Gauloises and a lighter and applied the flame to the tip of the cigarette, relishing the smoke's occupation of his mouth and lungs. Then he felt beside the mattress and found his watch. It was eleven o'clock. He glanced for a moment at his desk, set below the window at the opposite end of the room, and immediately felt the loss of all sexual desire. There lay his typewriter, some pencils in a small bottle, a stack of paper, a few sheets of notes and a dozen books in two piles—all the material for beginning work on his book. They had lain there since the previous summer, when he had deliberately not taken any teaching work so that he could write. But that summer had passed in a series of casual meetings with women, daydreams, grandiose plans which had never come to anything. He had spent an alarming amount of time asleep, as if exhausted by inactivity. After another three terms of teaching, Mark had thought that he could at last get down to the book, but now he could not look at his desk without feeling a panicky fluttering of guilt. He was less sure of his ideas now than when he'd first thought of writing his interpretation of working class social movements. When he could bring himself now to think about the book, he chiefly visualized the reviews it would earn. "The breakthrough in socialist thought achieved by this brilliant young lecturer. . . ." "This classic of Marxist praxis. . . ." He snubbed out the Gauloise on a plate and went down the hallway to the bathroom.

When he returned Mark separated the curtains above his desk and let a drained, weak version of the sunlight enter the room. Well below street level, the little flat required electric lighting at all times of day. Forever gloomy, on overcast days it held large areas of brownish obscurity. The window, like the smaller window in the kitchen—the flat's second room—looked out onto a

wall of concrete which had once been white. Soon his
headache would return. It had first come nearly a month
ago, just after he had awakened. Ever since, he had
been haunted by it, an insistent throbbing behind his
temples and a feeling of constriction over the entire top
of his head. On mornings when he had dreamed of Julia,
it seemed worse. These sensations, never actually painful, had affected his concentration. Even if he were able
to sit at his desk and begin work, he thought, he would
be unable to construct a decent paragraph: he found
himself losing the thread of conversations, of suddenly
being aware, as in his classroom dream, that he was uncertain of what he had planned to do next. Several times
on the street, he had been unable to remember where he
had been going. He often found himself brooding about
Julia and Magnus. A displaced, lost child himself, Mark
had lately begun to see Julia—whom he had for years
thought of as no more than a sweet, moderately pretty
housewife—as his counterpart. Magnus' possession of
her seemed a cruel and blatant injustice. No man as
bastardly and arrogant as Magnus deserved any sort of
wife, certainly not one as sensitive as Julia. And Julia's
money, which he could use to further a thousand worthwhile purposes—the writing of his book only the most
immediate of these—had been squandered on drinks
and bourgeois dinners, and almost certainly funneled off
to Lily. At times, Mark nearly hated Julia for tolerating
so long her brutish parody of a marriage. And the money had come from that old crook, Charles Windsor
Freeman, Julia's great-grandfather, one of the classic
American plunderers and exploiters: Mark could turn
it against that very class and cleanse the money of its
stain.

It was time for his exercises. Mark extended himself
on the carpet, which showed strands of thread beneath
its scruffy greenish tufts, and deliberately emptying his
mind, first lifted one arm and then the other straight upward. He tightened his muscles and pushed upward with
all his strength. He repeated this with his legs.
Loosened, he sat in the lotus position and attempted to

touch his forehead to the ground. He extended his tongue until its roots ached. Then he sat blankly, expectantly. He closed his eyes to a furry darkness.

He stared deeply into the opaque darkness, letting it take shape around him. No movement, no thought. He was a vessel to be filled.

Within ten minutes the chaos of the flat had spun away, leaving him in a vibrant, circling universe. He was a dancing point of light in darkness, a slit of entry for spirit. Stars and worlds moved about him like spheres. The single burning lamp was a glorious golden wheel of consciousness toward which he flew, circling. It breathed and pulsed, trembling with life and knowledge.

His body, no longer tiny, became immense. His whirling encompassed worlds, galaxies. Mark-body became Mark-self, breathing in gusts of spirit. Time cocooned him, light as dust. Everything was holy. He could blow time away and fracture the world, leaving only Mark, only holy light. His hands lay across continents, weightless as the buzzing of a fly. His arms lifted themselves, and extended through vast distances. Wordless chanting filled the glowing space about him. Disembodied peace indistinguishable from tension illuminated and lifted him. Muscles, birds, flight. He was up. Now he was traveling toward a swarm of bright particles which coalesced as he traversed the great distance separating himself from them. He ached for union. He saw first a golden city, then a face he knew to be Julia's even before it came fully into focus. He was creating her from spirit. Space began to hum with energy, to sing. He was dissolving into flames and candles, into sheer brightness. The face he saw was not Julia's, but that of a beautiful child. The brightness unbearably, gloriously intensified.

Outside, far away and to his left, a taxi blared. Mark began to spin downward, heaviness invading his body's vast molecular spaces. He collapsed forward onto the carpet, his thighs cramping. His tongue caught a dusty web of hair. Mrs. Fludd, sitting beside him on a couch in Julia's living room, said to him, "You are being blocked." With the repetition of the taxi's bright, horrid

noise came his headache, settling like night over his
scalp.

"I'm so grateful that you agreed to see me," said
Julia to the pleasant, smiling middle-aged woman who
had opened the door of the large white house at 4 Abbotsbury Close. "It's very important that we talk, important to me—I was so surprised to see your name in
the directory, I thought you would have moved after
your tragedy. Do you remember speaking to me on the
telephone, Mrs. Braden? I'm Julia Lofting. You said I
should come over this morning before lunch. . . ."

The woman opened the door further and admitted
Julia to deep gloom. All of the house she could see appeared to be dark brown; a far wall held a cluster of old
photographs layered with dust. "I am not the one you
spoke to," the woman whispered to Julia. "Mrs. Braden
is upstairs in her room. She is waiting for you. It is
about Geoffrey, yes?" Her German accent sounded like
that of the voice Julia had heard over the telephone
yesterday: but this woman's voice was higher in pitch,
silvery. Julia immediately, irrelevantly thought of it as
the voice of a hypnotist.

"You're not. . . ." Julia glanced up toward the staircase, which ended at a darkened arch.

"I am Mrs. Braden's companion," said the woman,
her voice insinuating, lulling. "I am called Mrs. Huff. I
have known Mrs. Braden only since the tragedy. At first
there were so many, those men from newspapers, the
police, many wicked people coming to pry—the curious. I kept them away from her. Now no one comes
for a long time. She wants to see you."

Mrs. Huff, moving with a stiff efficiency that recalled
Miss Pinner, and which Julia only now recognized as
arthritis, pulled open a door at Julia's left and revealed
a musty parlor. Brown overstuffed chairs faced each
other across a mottled carpet. Beside each rose a hairy
plant. "Please to wait here until I return. It will not be
long."

"Is there a Mr. Braden?" Julia stood uneasily beside one of the fuzzy chairs.

"He died in the war," Mrs. Huff said, and was gone. The door clicked behind her.

Julia did not want to sit in the chairs; they reminded her of some sticky plant that trapped insects and then digested them. She turned in the dark little room and began to pace, too excited to take in the room's furnishings, which seemed to hang in the dusty gloom. Her steps took her to a wooden bookcase; Julia looked at the titles, odd in some way, uniformly stamped in gilt on the thick spines. Then she saw that they were all in German. She ran her hand along the books, and her fingers came away black. Wiping her fingers on a tissue from her bag, Julia walked in small circles on the dark carpet. Surely it was Turkish? Her grandfather had owned a carpet much like it. She became aware of a pressure in her bladder. Where was the bathroom? It was only the excitement, she knew, and it would soon pass away if she could take her mind off it. She began to pace more rapidly; if the pressure increased, she would have to sit cross-legged in one of the awful chairs. Then her steps took her immediately before a small canvas, and she stopped pacing, puzzled by its familiarity. It was not a painting she had seen before, but surely she knew that arrangement of uptilted table, pipe and gash of newsprint. Braque—it was a Braque. She peered at the little painting more closely. It had to be a reproduction; but when she read the signature she saw the buttery raised strokes of paint. Surprise dissipated the urgency in her bladder.

She turned about just as the door opened. Mrs. Huff beckoned stiffly with one hand, smiling. "Mrs. Braden will see you now. Please follow me."

"This painting—I can't believe it!" said Julia.

"Please to come. I know nothing about painting."

Julia hurried from the room, propelled by the silvery, lulling voice. Mrs. Huff gestured toward the staircase, smiling, and then began to ascend. Julia followed. When she had passed through the darkened archway, she saw

Mrs. Huff opening a door halfway down a lightless hall. Julia had time to notice rows of paintings lining the walls, but the obscurity within the corridor effaced them. She went hurriedly through the door Mrs. Huff was holding open for her.

"Please sit down, Mrs. Lofting," said the large gray-haired woman dressed entirely in shining black who had risen at Julia's entrance. "I am Greta Braden and it was I to whom you spoke on the telephone. Please take the chair to your left. I think you will find it comfortable. Thank you, Huff." The door closed softly behind Julia.

She found herself staring at a painting encased in a gold frame from which depended a sliding red velvet drape, now pulled to one side to reveal a fleshy naked woman whose skin seemed to absorb all the room's light. It was, unbelievably, a Rubens. The rest of the bedroom shared with its occupant the atmosphere of elegance gone down in neglect. The flocked wallpaper, once red-gold, had been darkened by grime to a mute shade of brown. Books and newspapers lay over the floor, many of the papers yellowing with age. On the worn black velvety expanse of material covering the massive bed lay a tray holding the ruins of breakfast. Mrs. Braden's large angular face seemed to have caught dust in every fold. The gray hair was stiff with grease. Looking at her, Julia was not sure that Greta Braden was quite sane.

"You wish to talk with me about my son. Why is that, Mrs. Lofting?"

Julia sat on the chair Mrs. Braden had indicated, and felt the cushions slither beneath her weight. Now she was looking at a photograph, hung on the wall above the huge bed, of a small frail-looking boy in spectacles. Beside it hung a second photograph, of a tall, gaunt man wearing pince-nez and a Norfolk jacket.

"That was Geoffrey," said Mrs. Braden. "My husband stands beside him. What is your interest in me, Mrs. Lofting?"

"I saw Heather Rudge two days ago," said Julia, and saw the woman's body stiffen inside the shiny black shell of her clothing. "She was abusive and disturbed, but she did mention that I might speak to you." Overriding a curt, dismissive gesture from Mrs. Braden, Julia hastily added, "I am not working for Heather Rudge, not in any way. You see, I recently bought the Rudges' former house. I was—I was recovering from a long illness. Something about the house demanded that I buy it. Since then I've been looking into the past of the Rudge family—the past of the house. It's been something like a compulsion—I want to know everything I can find out about them. I don't think the truth ever came out about your son's death, Mrs. Braden. There's a lot more, but you might think I was crazy if I said it all. The chief thing is, I have to find out about the Rudges."

Mrs. Braden was looking at her very shrewdly. "And then you will perhaps write about what you find?"

"Well," said Julia, afraid to risk expulsion by uttering the wrong answer, "I'm not sure about that. . . ."

"Twenty-four years ago I would not have talked to you," said Mrs. Braden. "Especially if you mentioned the name Rudge. Now much time has passed, and I have waited for someone to speak the truth about my son's death. Many have gone unpunished. When my tragedy happened, the police would not listen to me. I was a foreigner, a woman, and they thought me suspicious, foolish. They ignored me, Mrs. Lofting. My son's death has gone unavenged. Now do you understand why I am speaking to you?"

"I . . . I think so," said Julia.

"My world is in this room. I have not left my house since twenty years. I have become old in this room. Huff is my eyes and ears. I care for nothing but my husband's collection of paintings, his memory, and my son's memory. Even Huff does not know everything about my son's murder—doesn't that word sound awesome and terrible to you, Mrs. Lofting? Do you know what murder is? That it is the greatest crime against the soul, even the souls of the living? It is an eternal crime."

"Yes . . . I feel that," Julia breathed. "But what I need is proof. Or knowledge more than proof."

"*Proof.*" The older woman expelled the word from her mouth as if it were rotten meat. "I need no proof. That man the police executed was a harmless vagrant. He was a simple man, a child himself. He liked to talk to the children. What proof did the police have when they killed him?"

"So you *are* convinced he was innocent," Julia said.

"Of course, of course! Listen to what I am saying to you. There were no secrets between Geoffrey and myself, Mrs. Lofting. I know what they did to him in that park. Those others tortured him daily. They made his life a hell because he was sensitive and because he had asthma. And because he was partially German. They called my son the Kraut, the Jerry, the Hun. They were all bad children, those others."

"And you knew Mrs. Rudge?"

"That one. She laughed at me. She scorned me. I begged her to help me for Geoffrey's sake, but she was blind and foolish. She could not see what was happening within her own house. She could not see she was defending a monster. I have no doubt about what happened to my son, Mrs. Lofting. The Rudge girl mutilated him and then killed him. And the others helped. Now. Do you think that I am wrong?"

Julia gently touched the sheeny material of Mrs. Braden's sleeve. "What did Olivia look like, Mrs. Braden? Can you describe her?"

The reply destroyed her expectations. "She was just a girl. Her exterior was unimportant. She looked like one of a hundred girls. She has been dead as long as Geoffrey. You must be aware of that."

"I am aware of it, yes, but there are reasons—I have to know what she looked like. Did she have blond hair? How tall was she?"

"Those are foolish details. Blond, yes, she may have been blond. But you couldn't tell she was evil by looking at her, Mrs. Lofting."

"That's the same word her mother said."

Mrs. Braden smiled. "That stupid woman," she said. "That rude common little fool. No, Mrs. Lofting, you must not dwell on the wasted lives of the Rudges. You must find the others. You must make them confess."

"I have to find them," Julia agreed. "I know some of their names. Minnie Leibrook and Francesca Temple and Paul Winter. . . ."

"And John Aycroft and David Swift, yes. And the Reilly boy. You surprise me, Mrs. Lofting. Those were the children who helped Olivia Rudge kill my son. If you want your proof talk to them. And I can help you."

Julia waited tensely, unable to guess what would come.

"Some of them have died. None of them have prospered. As you can imagine, Mrs. Lofting, I have been interested in the lives of this group. I have 'kept up,' as you would say. I can tell you that the Reilly boy disappeared in America, your country, ten years ago—he is lost. John Aycroft killed himself when his business went bankrupt. Minnie Leibrook died in an automobile accident while drunk. Francesca Temple was very wise and became a nun. She now lives in the Slaves of Mary convent in Edinburgh, under a vow of silence. Paul Winter became a professional soldier, as was his father, but was cashiered by his regiment. He lives in a flat in Chelsea. David Swift ruined his family wine business and lost his wife in a freak accident—she was electrocuted. He lives above a pub in Upper Street, Islington. Talk to those two men, Mrs. Lofting. If you can make them talk, you will have your proof."

Julia was stunned. "How did you find out all this?"

Mrs. Braden flexed her shoulders, making the cloth creak. "My eyes and my ears. Huff. I pay Huff very well. She has many talents. I will ask you to leave now, Mrs. Lofting. But first I will give you some advice. Be very thorough. And be careful."

"Well, careful is what you'd better be," Mark said that evening. "I never heard such a tacky idea. You mean you really intend to march up to those two people and grill them about a twenty-four-year-old death? For which a man has already been executed? Look here, have another drink instead and forget all about it. God knows what you'd be getting into."

"I'll have another if you let me pay for it. Please, Mark."

"If you insist, I reluctantly accept." Mark had counted his money a few minutes before in the men's room, and knew that the last round had left him with sixty-three pence. He owed twenty pounds to a colleague, and when he'd paid that, his next check from school would leave him just enough to pay his rent and buy a month's food and drink. Still, he supposed, he could always put off Samuels for another month—maybe he could put him off until the second term. He watched hungrily while Julia withdrew a small purse from her bag and took from it a ten-pound note. With a start of anticipatory pleasure, Mark realized that he already thought of Julia's money as his own. "That's sweet of you, darling," he added. He took the note from her fingers.

When he came back from the bar with the two drinks he put the pile of bills and change on the table between them. He said, "Are you bothered about the change?"

She looked up at him, startled. "Why, do you need money?"

"Just something to tide me over. I've had a tight month."

She pushed the bills at him, her face beautifully focused on his. "Mark, please take it—please. Do you want any more? It's silly of me to have so much when you don't have enough. Really, do you need more?"

"We can talk about that later," he said. In the soft light which filtered through to the back corners of the pub, Julia looked much better, he thought. Her face still seemed milky from lack of sleep, but she was more confident, vibrant, like the Julia of old, before Magnus had sunk his claws into her.

"Are you feeling well, Mark?" she asked.

"Just a headache. It comes and goes." He adjusted his face to put on his most endearing expression, what an old girl friend had called his "sheep in wolf's cloth-

ing face." "I have to say," he went on, "that I think you
should just drop the whole business right now. I don't
think you should have upset yourself by visiting those
two old grotesques. I don't understand your worry
about Kate. You still have Kate, my love. Kate is part
of you. She can't hurt you. I blame Magnus for planting
all that fear in you. I could kill him for what he's doing
to you. You should have let Perry what's-his-name go
to the coppers." His headache had tightened up a notch,
but he kept his face steady, putting, if anything, more
warmth into his eyes.

"You hate Magnus, don't you?" Julia sounded faintly
startled.

"Magnus is a bastard."

"I do think of you as my protection against him. It
was magic, how you appeared that time I fainted. And
you and Lily are the only people I can talk to about
what's been happening to me. If it weren't for poor Mrs.
Fludd, I probably wouldn't be able to talk about it at
all. Did you hear about her?"

Mark nodded, and his headache made the pub swirl.
"Lily told me. Too bad. Funny old girl."

"She saw something, and she knew she was in danger, I think she was killed so she couldn't tell me what
it was. Mark, I'd think I was going crazy if it weren't
for her—I have to make her death mean something."
Julia took a big swallow of her drink. "She was murdered. I'm sure of it."

"She walked in front of a car, didn't she? That's
what, manslaughter, not murder."

"Why did it happen, though? And if it was a straightforward accident, how did she know she was in mortal
danger? Mrs. Fludd said there was a man and a child—
I've been thinking all along that they were Magnus and
Kate, I thought Kate was haunting my house, but there's
another possibility. Of course the man is Magnus, I
know that much—he's completely irrational—but the
girl might be someone else. That girl I saw. And that's
why I have to see those people."

Mark rubbed his temples. "I think you're making a mistake. I think you should forget about the whole business." Julia had got an exalted, excited look which rasped on his nerves.

"What did Mrs. Fludd say to you that night? I have to know, Mark. It might help."

"Nothing. It was nothing. I can't even remember."

"Oh." She seemed chastened. "Really? Please try."

"I can't tell you how much my head hurts. Well, I think she said something like, 'You're being blocked,' and then she said that I should leave your house."

"It's what she told me! Oh, Mark, she wanted to save you too." She reached toward him and stroked his wooly hair. The pain seemed to ebb. He looked at her flushed face and her brimming eyes and saw that some of her exaltation was from the whiskey. "Dear Mark," she said. "Your poor head."

"Maybe she was trying to keep me away from you." That was in fact what he had felt.

"I went to the Tate this week," he heard her say. Her fingers continued to caress his hair. "I looked at that painting. The Burne-Jones. You're in it too. I am so grateful for you."

When he looked up from his cupped hands he saw that Julia was crying. "Finish your drink and let's go," he said. The headache had resumed its normal proportions.

Then they were standing in the squalor of his flat, holding one another. Carefully adjusting his stance to support Julia's weight while avoiding a crusty dish on the floor, Mark stroked her long, rather unkempt hair. He saw a profusion of split ends and wiry single hairs thrust up in a fuzzy corona. "Mark, I don't know what is happening to me," she was saying. Each word floated out into his collar and burst in a haze of whiskey. "Sometimes I'm so frightened. Sometimes it's like I'm not in control of myself. Ever since I read about the Rudge case I've been kind of *dominated* by it—it's all I think about. Because it would mean that Kate. . . ." Her back shook with her sobbing.

"Don't talk about it," he said He slipped his right hand between them and began to stroke her breast. Julia gasped, and then tightened her hold on him.

"Stay with me," he said. "I need you."

"I want to," she uttered into the side of his neck. His back was beginning to ache from supporting her. Julia was heavier than he had thought. "You're the only man I've ever wanted, except for Magnus. But . . ."

"I need you," he repeated. "You're beautiful, beautiful, Julia." He swung her body around, kicking a plate and knocking over an empty, clouded milk bottle, and, grunting a little, lowered her to the mattress. "Please, Julia. Stay with me." He bent and began to unbutton her blouse, brushed his lips on the mound of her belly. In the light from the single lamp beside the mattress, her face looked blotchy and flushed.

"I can't," she moaned.

"You can do anything you want." He peeled her blouse away from her breasts and put his mouth to one of her nipples. Then he leaned sideways, rolled one hip onto the mattress beside her, and kissed her mouth. It was warm and fleshy, with the feeling of crushed fruit.

"Mark. . . ."

"Shh."

"Mark, I can't." But still she did not move. "Just stay beside me," she said.

Mark pulled the blouse over her shoulders and slipped it down her arms, then tossed it aside. He rapidly stripped off his own shirt, and gave her another long kiss. Julia lay inert, her eyes glazed and bloodshot, out of focus, in the light of the lamp. After undoing his belt and pulling off his boots, Mark shed his trousers. "I will," he said. "I'll just stay beside you."

"Promise. Please."

"Yes."

He discarded his underwear as she distractedly, uneasily, removed the rest of her clothing. "Your house is a mess," she said, laying her skirt atop the blouse.

"Touch me." He guided her hand.

"You're soft." She smiled into his face. "Sweet. Big soft Mark."

"I still have my headache," he confessed. "This doesn't usually happen to me." Julia's hand warmly cradled his penis, holding it hesitantly. "No. Keep your hand there." Now he was beginning to feel a fractional urgency, and he stiffened a little. Her hand jerked him awake. He tongued her nipples, sliding his hand between her legs. Julia's body seemed an immense, fruitful meadow of warmth.

"My God," he said. "What happened to your thighs?" They bore enormous purple bruises.

"I hurt myself crawling in a window one night when I lost my key."

"Damn it," Mark said. He had lost the small erection he had just gained. His headache throbbed. He lowered his head to the place beside hers on the pillow and reached down to pull the sheet up over them. He touched a warm knee, the curve of a calf, then looked down to see that the sheet lay tangled at their feet. He closed his eyes again and felt her hands pulsing warmth into his back. He slid one hand between her thighs and caressed a bush of long coarse hair.

"Don't," she said, suddenly gripping him tight. "Don't. Just stay with me."

But Mark was incapable of anything else. His head seemed to have grown to twice its size. There was a whirling vacuum between his legs. He punched the button on the lamp and held to Julia's warm body because it anchored him in the room. His head found the cushion of her breast. Everything spun about him. He tried to create an erection by willpower, but his brain could not retain the necessary images. His body felt as though it were traveling—traveling great distances toward a cluster of lights. Julia's voice brought him closer to his real size, but he could not focus upon that either.

". . . keep seeing grotesques. Did you see that man in the pub? He had a red stump instead of a hand— just scar tissue—and his mouth. . . ." He forced himself to think: he had not seen a man with one hand in the pub. ". . . a roomful of blank, flabby people reaching for me . . . that old woman at Breadlands . . . swearing. . . ." Her voice slipped away altogether.

In the morning she was gone, and his body stretched uselessly, achingly, into air. Beside his head on the pillow he found a note which read *You're a darling. I'm off to do my detecting. Love.* Beneath it was a check for a hundred pounds.

8

The spirit did not like her leaving the house for an entire night. When Julia entered her home, wanting to wash and change clothes before looking for Paul Winter and David Swift, she saw with little surprise that some of the furniture had been tumbled about, chairs overturned and cushions flung to the corners of the living room. From upstairs came an angry knocking and banging that she knew would disappear when she set foot on the staircase. In the midst of the din, she could hear a radio playing some vapid forties dance tune, and that noise too would vanish. The odd, fumbling night with Mark—he had lain against her unmoving all night, as unconscious as if drugged—slipped away. As much as tenderness for Mark, she had felt all during the long hours after the alcohol had worn off an acute awareness that she was not in the *real* place, the place where the important things happened. Mark's inability to make love had been a relief; apart from her house, deflected from her quest, she wished only for comfort from the desolation. Back in her house and close again to the source of the mystery, she felt that desolation as her familiar element—it was the gray commanding sea in

which she swam. What was happening to her was necessary; she was at home.

Julia went into the kitchen and experimentally turned
the tap. A pipe clamored in the wall like a trapped owl.
A viscous brown jelly plopped at the mouth of the
faucet, and she hurriedly twisted the knob of the tap.
Into the air she softly said, "You're angry with me." The
hullabaloo upstairs quieted for a moment. When she
had poured three bottles of Malvern water into a pot for
heating, she quickly went through the living room, up-
righting chairs and replacing the cushions.

"You're not Kate," she said, tilting her head back.
"You're Olivia. I'm going to prove it. I'm going to find
out, I'm going to *find out*—it's what I'm here for, isn't
it?"

The toby jug lamp crashed to the floor and shattered.

"I'm going to help you," Julia whispered. The house
seemed to get warmer with each word. "You are very
powerful, but you need my help. And when I find out,
I'll find out everything. I'll know why you are torturing
Magnus. And then I'll be free too."

She waited for another bang from upstairs, but the
house seemed to hover about her, expectant.

"I'm going to free us," Julia repeated softly. "You
want Magnus to hurt me, but I'm going to set you free.
That's why I came, isn't it? You needed me. You had to
have me live here."

A heavy painting thudded to the floor, cracking the
glass with a sharp noise like a pistol shot.

"I'm not afraid," Julia said, and then added, "I don't
have to be afraid until I know." She was lying—at any
moment she expected something to fly at her head—but
it was a lie which contained a glowing corner of the
truth. Fear could not keep her from the hot center of
the truth: fear was only personal.

After she had washed at the sink, scrubbing herself
in armpits and private parts with a sponge, Julia
ascended to the throbbing heat of the upstairs. Her bedroom door gaped open. An elbow of noise seemed to
pulse from the walls. The heat from her room gusted out

in a breeze which lifted her hair and dried her skin as she entered the bedroom. The paint on the storage heater had blistered, leaving brown ulcerlike disks on its surface, curling upward in serrations. Julia heard rustling footsteps in the hall where she had just been. The closet door hung open. She went toward it, pulled it fully open and looked inside, her throat clenched. Some of her clothes had been pulled from their hangers and lay tumbled and twisted on the closet floor, mixed up with her shoes. Then she saw the box of dolls. It had been burst open, and the dolls scattered all over the back of the closet. Their floppy, uncomplicated bodies were torn and slashed. Ancient gray wool foamed from their chests. The terror poured back into her, and she fell gasping to her knees. Her certainty blurred with her vision. Kate had treasured the dolls; a malevolent Kate would destroy them. For a moment she was sick with yearning to be back in the hospital.

When she dashed into the bathroom, she first noticed that the figure in the black mirror—*her?*—looked haggard and old, her hair a mess and her eyes big with shock. Then she saw that the large untinted mirror over the marble sink had been heavily scored with soap. She stared at the lines and slashes until they coalesced into a list of obscenities. All the details of lying next to Mark flamed in her mind, dirtied by the words glaring at her from the mirror. The spirit knew, and hated her for what she had done. The last word jumped out at her: MURDERESS. *"Liar,"* she snarled, bone-jolted, and seized the nearest heavy object—a large ovoid rose-veined stone, polished to glassy smoothness—and with it shattered the mirror. Her heart froze, contracted. Magnus seemed all about her, wrapping her in a chill, despairing blanket of deception. That accusing word still burned in her sight. After a few minutes she breathed deeply and began pushing together the long silvery shards of the mirror. Her mind skittered away from her as her hands mechanically brushed at the smaller pieces of glass. Had she written those words herself? Had she

mutilated the dolls? For a moment she was certain that
she had.

   Winter, Capt. Paul S. 2B Stadium St. SW10. Both of
the men had been in the directory. Stadium Street occupied the seedy lower end of Chelsea, near the four
wharves and World's End: Julia drove the Rover down
the crowded carnival of King's Road from Sloan
Square, and after inching through the packs of young
people parading in costume from one boutique to
another, crossed Beaufort Street and found herself in a
different world. The brilliant, nervous crowds had
vanished, the restaurants and boutiques replaced by
factory walls and the peeling façades of bed-sitters.
Here, the few clothing stores hung their wares from their
awnings; bent old women with shopping carts trudged
along the pavements, mumbling to themselves. When
she turned the corner of Cremorne Road she fleetingly
saw through the side window a grossly fat man in a
ripped topcoat bunched at the waist by string struggling
to force a terrified spaniel into a paper bag. He was
gripping the dog by the throat, working the bag around
the dog's frantically kicking legs . . . *murderess* in letters
of crusty soap appeared in Julia's mind.
   The bright red side panel of a bread van blocked her
windscreen, and she wrenched the wheel to avoid a
collision. The letters MOTHER'S PRIDE wheeled off; the
Rover fishtailed to the right, ticking a parked car, and
then swung back in its lane. Car horns and shouts
erupted about her. She sped away.
   On desolate Stadium Street she left her car and immediately caught the smell of the Thames. Its sunless,
oily odor seemed to settle on her fingers and hair. She
felt as though she were inhaling damp cobwebs impregnated with the smell of fish. Julia peered at the door
nearest her, and made out through encrustrations of
paint Number 15. She moved slowly down the block,
hearing blinds rattle as she passed the row of mean,
dwarfed houses. The rusted frame of a bicycle lay beside
the curb like the corpse of a monstrous insect. 10, 8, 6.

Number 5 had been painted in swarmy patches of red and blue and yellow across which had been written in large black letters REVOLUTION IS THE RIGHT OF ALL and HENDRIX; the front door was fixed by a big gray padlock. Julia crossed the street and pushed open the small stiff gate to Number 2. At the end of the line of cracked paving stones, the front door was festooned with a rank of bells beside nameplates. She went up the walk and read the names scrawled on the plates—Voynow, a blank, Mertz & Polo, Gandee, Moore, Gilette, Johnson. No Winter was listed, and she felt unable to ring any of the unidentified bells. Her confidence sinking, Julia stepped back and saw on the pitted concrete facing a glossy black letter *B* above an arrow. In relief, she looked upward and truly noticed for the first time that the weather had changed. The sky held a shifting mass of clouds, obscuring the sun and piling toward a top layer of hard, thin gray.

B was a narrow door set into the rear of the house. Through it seeped a trace of some tinny music. When Julia knocked the door almost immediately opened upon a thin figure dressed in black turtleneck and black trousers. The music, swelling past him, resolved into Ravi Shankar. Julia first took in the man's prominent, bitter cheekbones and then that he wore an obvious wig several shades lighter than his hair.

"Captain Winter?" she asked, unsure.

"It's been ages since anyone called me that, dear," the man said. "I suppose you're Roger's outraged sister. Well, you'd better come in."

Julia stepped across the threshold into a heavy musk of incense. "I'd better explain," she said. "I'm not who you think I am. My name is Julia Lofting, Captain Winter—"

The man groaned. "*Please* don't. Call me anything, but don't call me Captain."

"Mr. Winter."

"Paul."

"Paul. Thank you." Looking at Winter's alert, essentially dishonest face, Julia was surprised to see that the

man was roughly her own age. She realized that he must
have been about thirty when he had been forced to
leave his regiment; though, looking at his crowded,
exotic little room crammed with paisley cushions and
African wall hangings interspersed with reproductions of
paintings and bright Druze rugs, she could not see Paul
Winter as a member of any sort of army. But she permitted herself the disloyal thought that Winter had
solved the problem of how to live in a single room
better than had Mark. Except, she saw, that this was the
kind of room which implied that it was forever night
beyond its door: it was a room which denied daylight.

"You can't be Roger's sister," he said behind her.
"She'd never take such a time appreciating my little
collection of things. You like my chambers, don't you?"

"Yes, I do," she answered simply.

"When I close my door," he said, "I close out the
world and exist here in a world I've created. It's my
oasis, my haven. In fact, I rarely leave it. It contains all
my needs—beauty, peace, art, refined sensation. And it
does have a Chelsea address, which is important, don't
you think? I wouldn't live anywhere else, and I've lived
all around the world. The army, you know." He was
preening himself before her, and Julia caught an odd
mixture of failure and arrogance in the man; he saw
himself as an Oscar Wilde, but the absurd vanity of the
toupee made him pathetic. In a minute, she sensed, he'd
begin inventing weak epigrams. "But of course you
know," he said. "My distinguished military history,"
and his cheekbones seemed to sharpen into points. "All
in the past. Would you care for a cigarette? They're
Turkish."

"No thank you," Julia said. "I'm sorry to bother you
like this, Capt—Paul, but for personal reasons I am interested in something in your past."

"Oh, God," he groaned theatrically. "The past
doesn't exist." He considered that a moment, and re-
vised it. "No intelligent man believes in the past."
Finally he satisfied himself. "Those who believe in the
past are condemned to live in it."

Julia seemed to catch a justified suspicion in the man's glance. "Well, the past has everything to do with my present," she said. "It's very difficult to explain." For a second, she saw before her the box of ripped dolls and the accusing words soaped across the mirror, and her blood swung heavily downward.

"Say, you look about to faint," Winter said, alarmed, and pushed a chair toward her. When she sat, he moved to one of the cushions and perched on it. "What's the matter?" he asked.

"I'm being haunted," she blurted out.

"My *dear*," he cooed. "Turn yourself into a tourist attraction and charge admission."

She smiled at him.

"Am I to understand that this delicious condition has something to do with me?"

Julia nodded. "Yes. . . ."

"How fascinating. Ask away. I have no secrets any more, my dear. I simply *am*, and people must accept me or reject me, for it's not worth the trouble to conceal one's inner nature. One's truth always wins out in the end. I only joined the army because my father wouldn't hear of anything else, you know, and I found it simply rife with hypocrisy. That was why they got rid of me, I must tell you, because I could no longer tolerate their petty restrictions and poses. I had to be myself. It made it pretty awkward for them, I can tell you, my being a general's son. Like Rimbaud, was it? The French poet. I say, you're not taking some sort of survey, are you? I couldn't bear that. Or doing research for a book?"

"No, this is personal," repeated Julia. "I've become involved with something you can help me with, if you would be so kind."

"I've always been so interested in the spiritual side of things—I'm Virgo with Aries rising."

"I want to ask you about some people you might remember."

"Fascinating." He scrunched down further into the cushions. "Ask away. I'm *so* glad you're not Roger's sister."

"I don't know how to begin. Do you remember, um, Francesca Temple? Or Freddy Reilly?"

He blinked. "Good heavens, you are going back. I used to play with them."

"You do remember."

It was too intense for him, and he backed away from a definite statement. "Barely. Just faintly . . . one catches the outlines, as it were. One isn't oneself in childhood. Childhood is a lie adults tell themselves. The man fathers his own childhood, if you see what I mean. Now let me see. Francesca Temple. A very modest little girl, with the loveliest brown curls. Yes, I can"—he pivoted a hand in the air—"catch her now. She was a follower. *She* was a soldier, if you will. Do anything you told her to. Freddy Reilly was a bit butch, if you understand me. A great one for games. Don't tell me you're being haunted by Freddy Reilly!" He silently clapped his hands together and revealed an even row of small, slightly discolored teeth.

She took up all her courage. "Can you tell me anything about any of the others? For instance, do you remember Olivia Rudge?"

He gaped at her, then toyed with the fringe of the cushion. "Can't remember her very well, I'm afraid. Rather a strange little girl, I seem to recall." He suddenly stood up and straightened the crease of his trousers. "Would you like a cup of anything? Tea? I make an excellent cuppa—half China, half India. Exquisite."

"No, please," said Julia. "What can you tell me about her? Olivia?"

"I think," he said, "I think you're beginning to be just the tiniest bit boring." He radiated an emotion it took Julia a second to recognize as fear. "Childhood is our least interesting period, I've always thought. I don't think I wish to answer any more questions about mine."

"I have to plead with you," said Julia. "You won't be in any trouble—there are just some things I have to know."

He ostentatiously examined his watch. "I don't think I have time for any more of this fascinating reminiscence. That woman was supposed to be here at two, and I can't tell you what a bother she'll be—now *there's* trouble for you."

"Mr. Winter—Paul—how did Geoffrey Braden die?"

He went nearly white with shock. Or was it shame? "I'll have to retract my invitation to tea, darling. I must ask you to kindly push off before my visitor arrives. Can't say I really heard your last question. Did you have a jacket?" He was prodding her shoulder with the tips of his fingers. "Really, dear. It's a waste of time asking me about ancient history. That was always my worst subject." Julia reluctantly stood.

"Could you just describe Olivia . . ." she began.

"I know I'm an old fool for being in such a flap," he said, urging her toward the door, "but that is one subject on which I do not propose to expound. The book is closed, my dear."

She was standing outside the narrow door, looking at his painfully contracting face beneath the cheap blond wig. The Indian music built to a frantic climax behind him.

"She wants me," she said. "Olivia."

"I believe it," he said. "Don't come back, please. Leave me alone, whoever you are."

"Julia Lofting," she said, but the door was closed.

The two of them sat on the terrace at the beginning of the evening, watching the rain pelt down onto the park, bending the leaves and tormenting the small bushes outside the walls. When a gust scattered drops onto the floor of the terrace, she delicately hitched her chair back out of the rain's territory; he ignored the spattering of drops and allowed it to dampen his shoes. They were, Lily noticed, already caked with mud and webbed with cracks. Magnus' whole being seemed in disrepair, and she experienced a moment of sheer distaste for Julia, who had done this to him, and for her brother, who had allowed it to be done.

"So it was *that* house," she said. "This is a fine time to discover it."

"I didn't think it was any of your business."

"Magnus," she said in exasperation, "how do you expect me to help if you conceal things from me? Concealment amounts to a lie. Is there anything else you've been hiding from me which might affect Julia?"

"An impossible question," he grunted. He stared dully at the rain. "I like this weather. It's more English than all that sunshine."

"Oh, you're simply maddening. Don't you realize that she has been looking into that wretched old case? I don't think she even bothers to eat anymore. She's convinced it's got something to do with Kate. In fact, she told me she was being haunted. Haunted! In her condition, every detail becomes exaggerated and blown up and inflated—Magnus, you must tell me if there is anything else she is likely to discover."

"I don't know. What *has* she discovered?"

"I'm not sure she would tell me."

"She'd tell that bloody psychotic Mark."

Lily tactfully ignored this remark while silently agreeing with it. "If you want your wife back, and I can only assume that is the motive behind your extraordinary performance this past week, you must tell me whatever you know so that I can use it for your benefit."

"You mean that you want to use Julia for *your* benefit."

"I will ignore that remark." She glanced at him before saying, "If you don't move out of the wet you'll catch pneumonia."

Sighing, Magnus shoved himself backward in his chair.

"Is there any way you can be connected to that house? That would push her right over the edge, you know. Well. At least then we could put her in hospital, where she belongs."

"Is that what you want?" Magnus stared at his sister in genuine surprise. "She's coming home with me, not back into hospital. But no, I don't think there's anything. All of that was so long ago."

"What about the daughter? Did you know her well?"

"Never met the little lady."

"You're sure."

Magnus winced. "Of course I'm sure. Now stop grilling me. Have you anything left to drink?"

"It was drink almost put you in jail, remember. That and your temper. But help yourself, if you want something."

He said, "I don't want it, I need it," and went across the terrace and into the kitchen. A few moments later he returned with a tumbler half filled with amber liquid.

Lily waited until he was settled again in his chair before saying, "Well, what did you do this last time? Leave notes about?"

"I threw some of the chairs around. That's all. She'll know it was me." He drank with visible satisfaction.

"And I suppose you think that will help. Magnus, there are two things that I regret. One is allowing her to keep her fantasy about Kate's death. She needs to be shocked out of it. I'd tell her now if she were here. The other thing is introducing her to poor Mrs. Fludd. Those two together got her started on this ghost business."

"Mrs. Fludd? Oh. Your guru."

"Before her death she stirred Julia up with all sorts of dark hints. Rosa had the gift, but she could never resist playing to her audience. And she died at the most unfortunate time."

Magnus was clearly not interested in the fate of Mrs. Fludd. "I think Julia needs a psychotherapist," he said. "Maybe I do too. I don't know what's been happening to me lately. I have funny blackouts. I see things. One day I saw Kate."

"Poor baby," said Lily. "So you agree with me that we must get her back into hospital?"

"Maybe I do," Magnus mused. He looked at Lily for a moment with perfect complicity.

"Tell me something," Lily said, now that was settled.

"What did you feel when you went back inside that house again? Did you feel no shame?"

"No," he said. "It was simpler. I felt fear. I was scared out of my wits. It made me want to murder someone."

"You should have married someone your own age," said Lily.

"Someone like you, you mean."

"We do have a marriage of a kind," said Lily. "We understand each other."

Mark Berkeley stood beneath the awning of the package store, watching the rain spill down the gutters and gradually form a black slick pool which would cover all that part of the street. He still had in his pocket about seventy pounds, after cashing Julia's check and buying some tins of food, a pair of boots and a snake-skin belt—and just now, the two bottles of whiskey. He could remember deciding to put Samuels off until next term, for the sake of the boots; he could remember shopping and dialing Julia's number several times that afternoon; but he could not remember leaving his room in the rain to walk to the package store. He stared down at the blocked drain by the side of the curb—the street-lamp revealed on the surface of the water the shifting, mesmeric pattern of an oil slick—and tried to reconstruct the walk from his building. His shoulders and hair were soaked with rain. Maybe, he thought, these lapses were somehow derived from his exercises, lately far more successful than ever before. He was more than slightly fearful of where these long, otherworldly sessions might take him; but weren't they proof of what the old woman had said about his "receptivity"? This, he was certain, lay behind his headaches—proof of a power he hadn't known he possessed. He was Mark, he was special, he was the child of luck.

A tall girl whose name he could not remember stepped out of the rain and stood beside him. She shook her hair and smiled, and he knew the shape and taste of her mouth.

"Going to a party?" she asked. "Good night for it."

"What?"

"A party. The bottles, Mark. Are you going to a party?"

He looked at the bottles in the white bag. "I couldn't tell you what I was going to," he said. "I sort of don't remember."

She looked at him bristlingly. "I suppose you're on something."

"No. No. I've been meditating. I'm doing it a couple of hours a day."

"Well, it's too late to meditate now," she said firmly. What was her name? "Do you want to come back to my place? We could have our own party."

Then he remembered: Annis. Annis was one of last summer's girls. Looking at her wide, greedy black eyes and hair in which drops of rain sparkled, he felt a spasm of sexual interest, but then Julia's face superimposed on hers. His mind seemed to waver. "Annis, I can't tonight," he said. "There's someone I have to see."

"Well, do me a favor and fuck yourself," Annis cheerfully said, and ran off through the rain.

Swift, David N 337 Upper Street N1. Julia stirred restlessly on the passenger side of the Rover's front seat, trying to find a comfortable position while still looking directly at the inconspicuous door immediately beside The Beautiful and Damned. She had already tried to fill in the time by trying to remember how many other pubs in London were named after novels, but could only recall The Cruel Sea in Hampstead, which Lily had entered once and decreed "puerile, like its namesake." Julia had come to Swift's address at eight, driven aimlessly around Islington before returning at nine, had again found him not at home and driven on impulse over to Gayton Road, where all the lights burned and open drapes revealed empty rooms, and then returned to wait for Swift's return. Now it was just past eleven, and her back was beginning to hurt. From time to time she thumped her feet on the floor of the car to keep her

legs from falling asleep. When a man in a shabby overcoat and tweed cap loitered before the door beside the
pub, Julia switched on the windshield wipers and
leaned forward, tense. The man turned his back to the
street. Not daring to breathe, Julia waited for him to
open the door. But the man merely hunched his back
against the rain and stood spread-legged beside the door.
Finally Julia understood what he was doing, and she
looked away in exasperation.

More people slouched past the pub, and Julia idly
watched them until they had gone into the Wimpy bar
down the block. At eleven fifteen the pub disgorged a
group of young men who hung, half in and half out of
the rain, beneath the small canopy, wrangling and stuffing their hands into the pockets of their jackets. They
obscured Swift's door, and Julia groaned, silently praying for them to break up and go home. More young
men left the pub. They formed a desultory, nearly unmoving mass all along the side of the building. If Swift
were to come home now, she could easily miss him.
"Please," Julia whispered. David Swift was her last
chance.

As she watched, one of the men began to shout. A
friend gripped his arm, but the man violently pushed
him away, sending him sprawling off the street. In a
second, half of the crowd had vanished; a third man
circled the first, who still shouted, and then they were
brawling. Julia watched them slipping on the wet pavement, clutching at each other's wrists and shoulders before separating to begin punching again. The street had
become wholly quiet around them, except for the rain's
spatter. One of the men—Julia was not sure which—
gave a solid, thunking blow to the face of the other, who
went down in the heap of his clothes. His attacker
kicked him savagely once, then again. Julia, terrified,
put her hand to her mouth. The attacker picked the man
up from the pavement and began to strike him again
and again in the face. *He's a Magnus,* Julia thought, and
in desperation stabbed at the switch for her headlights.
The attacker turned his head into the glare of the lights

—Julia saw a bearded chin and a prominent nose—and then pushed the bleeding face away. He turned and ran slap-slapping along Upper Street. His victim lay alone on the pavement, his clothing soaking in the rain. All the others had scattered. As Julia watched, the man's body trembled, and then inched across the pavement like the hulk of a wounded boar. The man rolled against the side of the pub and sat up. His face was a gash of red.

Julia pushed down the lever in the door and leaned out. She had to call for an ambulance—she looked frantically about for a phone booth, but rain, flying directly into her face, blurred her vision. She wiped her eyes and saw, far up the block, a red booth outside a darkened cinema. She crossed the empty road and began to run toward the booth. A burly coatless man cradling a dark clanking bag passed her, but she scarcely noticed the man until she was within the kiosk. Then, looking through the streaked glass, she saw the man set down his bag before Swift's entrance and dig out a key from his pocket. She hung in the booth for a moment, deliberating, and then slammed down the receiver just as the man disappeared from the street.

She pounded down Upper Street to the pub. The beaten man now crouched over the pavement, his elbows planted in his own blood. He was moaning incoherently, perhaps drunkenly. She pressed Swift's bell rapidly several times, then held it down. The man against the pub rolled over on his side and clamped his hands to his face.

Heavy footsteps thumped down a staircase. When the door jerked open, Julia saw a man's bulky frame in the shadow of the tiny hallway. Far above, a single light burned, illuminating the top of the dingy staircase. "Mr. Swift?" she asked.

"That's me," the man said. Julia caught a pungent whiff of whiskey. "What is it?"

His upper-middle-class accent both surprised and comforted her. It was the accent of Magnus and his friends—the accent Mark had consciously discarded.

"I have to talk to you. And there's been a fight. This man's been hurt. We must telephone for an ambulance."

"I don't clean up after drunks," Swift said. He thrust his head out the door, revealing in the reddish light from the pub a broad, pinkish face and close, rather curly black hair. His jacket looked oily and frayed. "Let him rot. You said you wanted to talk to me?" He looked at her appraisingly, and Julia nodded. "I'm willing. Come on into the fleapit."

As Julia stepped into the hallway, again catching the clear, biting odor of whiskey, she promised herself to telephone for an ambulance no matter what Swift said. He was already moving a bit unsteadily up the stairs. "Come on and talk, if that's what you want," he called down.

At the top of the stairs he was holding open the door to a shabby sitting room. Blotchy yellow wallpaper, a stained green carpet as threadbare as Mark's, battered furniture she recognized as coming from a discount warehouse—it was like the furniture in her Camden Town flat, years before. Swift was standing at a low table, pulling bottles out of the paper bag. Grunting, he broke the seal on one of them. "Drink?"

"May I?"

"I asked you."

"Then yes, please."

Swift removed two glasses from a wall shelf and poured several inches of whiskey into each. He gave Julia her glass, and she saw above the line of the whiskey fingerprints, water spots, smears. She set it down on the table.

"Can I telephone first? That man downstairs. . . ."

"No," Swift said. In the electric light, his pink face was scrubbed with hot reddish spots, as if scoured. "Fuck him. What did you want? Who are you, anyhow? A solicitor?"

Julia moved to one of the unsafe-looking chairs and sat. She wiped some of the rain off her face. "My name is Julia Lofting, Mr. Swift."

"You must be a solicitor."

"No, I'm not, I promise you. I'm interested in—involved in something you can help me with, if you would."

"Don't tell me it's a business deal." Swift snorted. He was still standing, holding his glass in one hand and the bottle in the other. "I'm afraid Swift and Company is no longer. Three generations of sharp practice end in the wreck you see before you. Do you want some sort of towel?" He gulped down whiskey as she shook her head. "Well, don't just sit there looking all confused and sexy and helpless."

"It's about your childhood," Julia quickly said. "I have to know about something that happened then. I promise you that I won't divulge anything you say to me to anyone else—that I'm interested for purely personal reasons." I won't tell this man I think I'm haunted, she vowed, he'd throw me out. She had to avoid the mistakes she had made with Winter. "I'm not a writer or anything like that," she said. "Or the police."

He rolled his eyes up toward the ceiling. "I'd better sit down." He moved heavily to the couch and fell into it facing her, still holding the glass and bottle. "My childhood. I suppose I had one. Now what the devil do you want to know about my childhood?"

Julia knitted her hands together, stared at the filthy carpet, and then looked directly at Swift. He had a froggish, unlined, well-brought-up face. She could easily see him in an expensive suit, ordering secretaries about. That she disliked him on sight somehow made it easier to talk to him.

"I live at Twenty-five Ilchester Place," she said. "Olivia Rudge's old house. I want to find out all about her."

Swift was momentarily shaken. His head bobbed toward his drink; but he made no move to throw her out. "God," he said. "That wicked little bitch. She's been dead over twenty years." He gazed at the liquid in his glass, clearly not intending to offer more information.

"This afternoon I spoke to Paul Winter."

Swift brightened. "That poof. I bet *he* wouldn't say anything."

"You're the only one left," Julia said. "The Aycroft boy killed himself and Minnie Leibrook died in an accident. One of you disappeared in America. Another girl is in a convent. And Paul Winter made me leave his house."

The man facing her snorted. "I don't suppose he liked the idea of having a woman in his room. I relish it, I can tell you. He was probably expecting one of his chums. That's why they pitched him out of his regiment, you know. He fell in love with his driver, but the driver wouldn't reciprocate. Paulie got a little too passionate, the driver kicked up a fuss, and they rubbed Paulie out as if he were a little foul spot on the rug. Bang. Finish." He took another swallow and repeated, "Finish. General's son in disgrace. As for Aycroft, he put paid to himself when he was found embezzling money from his firm. Excuse me, bank. His bank. Good-bye, Aycroft. And Minnie Leibrook. . . ." He caught himself short. "What do you want to know about all this for, anyway? So you live in the old Rudge house. Congratulations. What's that got to do with me?"

"It's personal," said Julia. "I just want to know about Olivia."

"You're fascinated." He poured more whiskey into his glass. "You've been looking into her short and nasty life and now you're keen on her. How do I know that you won't use whatever I say against me?"

"I promise," said Julia, and inspiration came to her. She dug in her bag and withdrew two ten-pound notes and put them on the table. Swift's eyes gleamed at her. She put down another note. Her heart fluttered. "I want to buy information from you."

He snaffled up the notes. "I guess you do. A woman like you doesn't come up here every day and offer me money." He leered at her. "I'll talk to you if you come over here and sit beside me."

Julia hesitated, and then went around the little table

to the couch. Cautiously she sat beside him. "Now you have a drink," he said. "You're behind." Julia sipped from the bleary glass. "More." She did as he commanded.

"Tell me about Olivia," she said. "Please." She allowed his hand to rest negligently on her knee.

"You'd never forget her if you ever met her. She was really wicked. It was the most impressive thing about her. It was the reason all of us, the kids you know about, followed after her. We had a club. Do you want to know the rules?" He squeezed her knee, and Julia nodded. "Have another drink." He poured more whiskey into her glass, and she sipped at it. "The first rule was you had to kill an animal. Aycroft killed his dog. He brought it to her and she ripped it open with her knife and made him drink some of its blood. Proper little ceremony. We all did it. I brought a neighbor's cat. Same folderol. I was clever—just touched my tongue in the blood. Then we had to light fires. We had to burn a house or a shed, something in that line. We did that together. She watched us and told us what to do."

"You did it?" Julia asked.

"We tried. She stole a can of petrol from somewhere and we soaked the porch of a wooden house behind the High Street. The bugger wouldn't burn. Olivia was madder than a hen—she looked just like a witch. Maybe she was a witch. We all thought she was. Anyhow we burned most of the porch, but the firemen came before the rest of the building went. Then we had to do lots of thieving and give it all over to her. You see, we had to see her every day—we had to spend all day with her in the holidays. We all had a crush on her, I suppose, even the girls, and she had us scared out of our wits. We knew there wasn't anything she was afraid to do. We learned all about sex from her, in her bent little games. If you didn't do what she wanted, she'd tell your parents about everything else. She had ways. If you told anyone in authority, she'd kill you."

"Yes," said Julia.

"She would, too. She would have. She was evil. She made the Temple girl—who did everything Olivia wanted—lick her. You know what I mean, lick her?" He stroked Julia's knee. "She could beat up any of us."

"And she killed Geoffrey Braden," Julia softly said. The hand tightened and released on her knee. "A man was found guilty of that and executed."

"A harmless vagrant," said Julia. "He liked the children. He used to talk to them. You know he didn't do it."

Swift turned his pink face toward Julia and drained his glass. "You were a fool to give me that money," he said. "You were a fool. Nobody's thought about Geoffrey Braden in twenty-five years. Nobody's going to do anything about it now."

"That's not why I have to know."

"I don't care," he said, and her heart sank. Then he added, "I was going to tell you anyhow. You were stupid to give me that money. I was innocent. I didn't do anything."

"You just watched," Julia guessed. She could feel her pulse thrumming in her neck.

He grinned at her. "I watched."

"So she *did* do it," Julia whispered.

"Of course." He looked at her with an expression like triumph. "She covered his head with a pillow. She tried it twice before, but an attendant heard his yelping and ran over. She hid the pillow just in time. Then one afternoon she did do it. Three of the bigger kids held him down and stuffed things in his mouth. Then she put the pillow on his head and sat on it. It was what she always wanted to do. To kill someone. You could see that. It was what she was all about. I'll bet the little bitch had an orgasm."

"What did she look like? Was she blond?"

"Sure. Blond. A color anyone else would have to get out of a bottle. It was the most beautiful hair I ever saw. And a sweet little face. Oh, she was charming.

Sometimes I think about the way she'd look if she were still alive—Christ, that bitch would have changed the world." His hand slid over her leg. "I like talking about this, you know. If I weren't drunk, I'd probably chuck you out, but I like telling you about it. It was funny. She made us feel that we were all in a war. Soldiers."

"Her tooth," Julia said. "Didn't she . . . ?"

"How did you know about that? The first day she tried to do little Braden, he hit her mouth with the top of his head—broke one of her front teeth. He didn't have a chance after that. She had to have him. But he never really did have a chance, the little bugger. Do you know what happened afterward? With Paulie? Your poof friend?"

He was gripping the underside of her thigh, and she put a hand on his wrist. It was feverishly hot. She shook her head.

"Paulie was bent even then. She liked that. She made him bite him after he was dead."

"Bite him?"

"Bite him. Bite his cock. She made him bite his cock."

He leaned over and snared her wrist. His mouth slurred on her cheek. "She said if he didn't do it, she'd do it to him."

Julia twisted away and stood up. She broke her hand away from his grip and tottered backward toward the door.

"You're not leaving," Swift growled. "You're going to stay with me." He struggled to stand.

"I have to talk to Olivia," she said, facing him.

It stopped him long enough for her to seize the doorknob and pull it open.

"You're crazy," he shouted, half-crouching before the table. His trousers bulged at the fly.

When she fled down the stairs she heard him yelling above her. "Cock-teaser! Remember—nobody cares anymore, you bitch. You can't do anything."

She slammed the street door. The beaten man no longer lay beside the pub, but still some blood re-

mained, tinting the puddles of rain. Julia ran toward
her car. She knew, she knew. It had been Olivia Rudge
all along: Kate was safe. Once in the car she began to
sob, whether from horror or relief she could not tell.

YOU KNOW. The words had been smeared in soap on
the black mirror above the bathtub. From the atmosphere of tense quiet within the house—for the first time
in two weeks, Julia had not heard the rustling noises
from upstairs—she had expected some atrocity, and had
been fearful of leaving the ground floor of her house.
She had no idea of what Olivia intended to do with her
now that she had discovered the truth. Julia mounted
the stairs, looking for signs of triumph or outrage. In
her throbbingly hot bedroom, all lay undisturbed from
the morning: the burst dolls sprawled at the back of the
closet, sprouting gray curls of wool, their power to
frighten her gone. Every time she looked over her shoulder, she expected to see Olivia Rudge. That adult, challenging smile. Or she feared to see Magnus, controlled
by her. But all she found were the two words of confirmation. YOU KNOW. She scraped them off with a
table knife, and wiped the remaining flecks and smears
with a towel until the black mirror held only a foot-long
blur which translated her reflection into cloud. There
would be more, much more. This lull, this truce, and the
two words were more frightening than Olivia's displays
of power.
    Julia gazed out of her bedroom window into night
and rain. Out there, everything had disappeared into
darkness. Reality lay within.
    She snapped off the light, undressed in the dark and
felt her way to the bed. Then she lay beneath the burning sheet and watched the darkness move. A black plane
composed of millions of particles sifted down toward
her, withdrew, and sifted down again. Perspiration trick-
led into the hair above her ears.
    She stabbed the reading light on in sudden fear and
the plane of darkness disappeared. There was nothing.

There was no giant pillow of dark. She switched off the light, and saw it return.

When the first touch of small hands came, she went rigid, aware that she had somehow fallen asleep. A cool hand slid up her inner thigh, and she rolled over, twisting in the sheet. The hand returned on her buttocks, caressing, probing. Julia gasped at the violation and spun around, rolling to the other side of the bed. Arms braced her shoulders to the bed. They held her immobilized; her legs, trapped in the twisted sheet, were as if pinned to the mattress. The cool small hand found her pubic hair, then her cleft. It began, delicately, to rub. Her body felt naked to the dark air, though the sheet bound her. Julia groaned as the hand pressed toward her clitoris and stroked. Feathery: feathers, tongues. She was a fly caught in a sticky cocoon, ministered to by the spider. Against her will, with horror, she felt her body build up a rhythmic tension. The relentless hand stroked, rubbed, as if dipped in oil; it circled, insinuated into her. Her back arched. She felt her nipples harden. Sweat broke out on her chest. Julia inhaled a gulp of burning air. She seemed to be falling into a deep well. Her knees twitched. The tight sheet, wrapping her like a shroud, was itself the lightest of caresses, palms on her taut nipples. The pressure, arching her back, subtly increased and began to beat outward in circles. Suddenly she saw Mark before her, his body taut with longing. The oiled rubbing hands were the huge tip of his penis. The embracing arms were his. Her legs moved wide apart and his shaft slid deep within her. She bared her teeth. Arms, legs, hands, deep velvet held her. She saw, felt him stiffen and plunge and a sound died in her throat as everything burst.

And the next morning when Julia tottered sick with nausea into the bathroom, Olivia showed herself within the house for the first time. She did not jump out of sight at the last second; she did not flicker away. She stood, a small blond smiling child, behind Julia as Julia looked into the black mirror opposite her. Julia placed a protective hand over her abraded, sore cleft and whirled around. Again, the child appeared behind her in the facing mirror.

As Julia watched, Olivia gave her asymmetric, challenging smile and slowly drew an index finger across her pale throat. Her other hand gripped the pulped, still trembling body of a headless bird.

A Thames gull slapped into the window late at night, making a noise like a train wreck, and startling into wakefulness the man who reclined on a fluffy Indian cushion. Uneasy—he had been close to fear for the past twenty-four hours—and not as yet quite certain where he was, the man extended one hand and knocked over the bottle of Calvados. His room, crowded with details of his life, reassuringly came together about him; the needle of the record player crackled and hissed in the final grooves. He righted the bottle, shaking his head. None had spilled, for he had consumed most of what was left during the night, after his guest had left. His mind seemed thickened, syrupy; the aftertaste of his heavy cigarettes coated his mouth.

From beyond the door, his name quietly sounded. He sat up straight, pulling his legs under him, and listened to the sound of the voice. It uttered his name over and over, beseechingly, in a voice neither male nor female. "Foolish little scut," the man muttered, and for several seconds considered his promise not to open the door again. But that too was foolish. Both had had far too much to drink. The man bent forward and stood in one motion, feeling the muscles in his thighs protesting. Upright, he patted his hairpiece and straightened his pullover. He moved to the door as slowly as he could, relishing the sound of his name, half whispered, urgent, full of need.

He opened the door to a stranger—a stranger? The voice was a voice he knew. The visitor smiled, and he knew the contours of that smile.

Too late, he saw the knife slide from beneath the coat. His mind fluttered with bright, hopeless panic and he stepped backward as the visitor moved through the doorway, still voicing his name.

Part Three

The Closing: Olivia

9

Julia moved hesitantly up Kensington High Street at the end of day, buffeted by the crowds returning home late from work, unsure of where she was going. Confused, she had taken the wrong way, and was dimly aware of this. Her left wrist was still oozing blood, and she dabbed at the deep cut with a wrinkled yellow tissue, hoping it would stop; but the cuff of the blouse was stained and smeared with blood, as her sheet had been. Because of the pills, her mind had difficulty in retaining images, and she looked at the sky twice before being certain that it had stopped raining. All of the sky was a vast dark undifferentiated gray. *No holes,* she thought, *no air spaces,* and saw herself beating at the undersurface of gray cloud as if it were a thick layer of ice trapping her in arctic water; the pavements and street were still filmed with black rain. Ascent, escape, ascent, escape, revolved in her brain. But she could think of no escape. Olivia held her fast.

She thought of the beggar maid's king, Cophetua, his face immobilized by love. Mark. Was he safe? He had rung immediately after the grinning specter of the girl had vanished from the mirror.

—Take some pills and go to sleep, he'd said. Do you have anything?

—Yes. Pills? Yes.

—You need rest. Take a couple of pills and get a really good rest.

—I have to see you. I'm in danger. Like Mrs. Fludd said. I am, Mark.

—Listen to me. Ghosts don't kill. Your danger is entirely from Magnus, and you're staying away from him. Julia, love, you're overtired. Lock your door and knock yourself out for the rest of the day.

—I need you, Mark. She wants me.

—Not half as much as I do, he had laughed. I'll see you this evening, sometime tonight.

—Save me.

Had she said that, *save me?* Perhaps she had imagined the entire conversation. All that was clear, besides gulping down two pills—memories of the hospital making her shudder—was running back upstairs and heaving the polished, rose-veined stone at the walls of the bathroom. Heaving it, again and again, until the black mirrors had showered down, leaping off the walls and shivering past her face. Then she had slipped on a large panel of glass and gone down into the mess, gashing her wrist. She had barely felt the pain. *Now she can't come in here,* Julia had thought, uncaring of the blood which welled out of the gash and down across the palm of her hand. The walls were unreflecting gray-white plaster marked like a graph with small black studs, to a few of which adhered an inch of mirror. Broken glass, some of it catching muted light from the ceiling, was strewn over the bathroom carpet, tumbled in long snaky shapes in the sink and tub. She felt warm blood falling onto her bare feet and snatched a towel from the rack and wound it about her wrist. Pebbles of glass snagged at her cut. Then she had swallowed the two pills. And staggered across twelve feet of broken glass to her bedroom.

(Thus she did not hear the bell seven hours later

when Lily and Magnus came together to her front door.)

As in the hospital, she was visited by long fluent dreams. Those had been of turning the knife on herself, of sacrificing herself for Kate, that Kate's vibrant little life could be restored: her blood for her daughter's, a barter. She had felt Kate's forgiving approach at such times. But now her dreams all had the same flavor; they were as ashy as failure and loss. Even as she began to slip steeply into them, she resisted, sensing the approach of that hopeless territory. She was again walking through the gritty streets, carrying her daughter's corpse. The child she knew to be Olivia lurked ahead, unseen, and it was her duty to find her. The sky above the blackened roofs of tenements was lurid, red and orange shot with black streaks. Again, her long, burdened wandering took her to a mean courtyard. She moved across the filthy cobblestones and past abandoned, bricked-up warehouses and passed through the arch of the yard. A hunched leering man in a tattered coat winked at her, summoning from a doorway a small black girl with a curly ruff of hair. Julia ascended broken stairs and came out, as she knew she would, on a flat rooftop. A little woman in a large brown coat sat alone on the rooftop, her weight supported by a rickety chair. The woman was Mrs. Fludd. Seeing her, Julia felt tears welling in her eyes.

—I'm sorry, she said. I put you here. And I still need your help.

I cannot help you.

Kate's body was taken from her; it had been needed to bring her here, and now it could vanish.

—You called her up.

—Yes, said Julia.

—You invoked her. She needed someone to call her back, you see, and you were chosen. This happened because of your daughter.

—What do I have to know?

—She won't like you knowing her secrets.

Mrs. Fludd turned sideways in her chair, refusing to speak further.

—Talk to me.

The old woman's face, heavy and washed of color, turned again toward Julia.

—She will have your friends.

Then she had been running into a long tunnel, noticing even as she ran that the tunnel led nowhere, that it narrowed the further and deeper she went. At the end was Mark, the New Hampshire valley, peace . . . but she knew that at the end of all her running would be only a black narrow hole. About her rang Heather Rudge's coarse, wheezing laughter.

She had awoken with this laughter still reverberating above her, joining the other noises of the house. The towel had been dragged off her arm, and the left side of the bed was stained by irregular red blots. For a moment she sensed that, as in her dream, Olivia Rudge hung nearby, just out of sight, waiting to appear. It would not be long. Mrs. Fludd's final words had then come back to her. Struggling to impose firmness and direction on her dream-tattered mind, Julia had wrapped her wrist in the top sheet and groggily sat up. She looked out the window across the room and saw rain drizzling down from a ghost-gray sky. A scarf of cool wind reached her from the open window and instantly vaporized in the heat. For the first time, Julia was consciously aware of the hot, feral smell pervading the bedroom, the reek of a lion's cage.

Throwing aside the ruined sheet, Julia had risen and looked at her watch: now it was eight, and she had slept through the entire day. *Your friends.* Mark, her truest friend, was in danger. Her mouth filled with dust. When she had glanced into the closet and seen again the ripped, scattered dolls, she staggered away from the bed and felt blood begin to move sluggishly down her wrist. She tore several sheets of Kleenex from the box near her bed and clamped them over the slash, which had begun to pulse and complain. When she struggled into her robe, she buttoned the left sleeve to fasten the Kleenex to the wound and went down the echoing stairs to telephone Mark.

Olivia was abroad; Olivia would have anyone she wanted. *It can't be got rid of. It wants revenge,* Heather Rudge had said. *It wants revenge.*

Mark's telephone had shrilled a dozen times. She would have to go to his room.

So now she walked blearily along Kensington High Street, the wad of sodden Kleenex dropped somewhere behind her and blood seeping into the cuff of her shirt. Between the flat gray sky and the rain-blackened streets, the streetlamps had already switched on, and cast an acid yellow light over the crowds through which she pushed. From time to time, a wave of oblivious men carried her back a few paces, making her stagger as she was thrown, almost unseen, from one comfortless shoulder to the next. She looked in all their faces for Mark, and found instead—it seemed to her—only sneers and laughter. Julia realized that the men thought she was drunk. Sleeping pills had never affected her so strongly before. Maybe it was due to lack of food. But the image of food—a greasy pile of pinkish-gray meat—made her stomach lurch and tighten.

A heavy curtain of dark appeared before her vision, blotting out the bunched, jostling crowds and the snarling jungle of traffic beyond them. Julia tottered, blind, and fell sideways against the rough facing of a building. For a moment, as the people sweeping past brushed her elbows and knees and trod on her feet, she lost all awareness of her identity and surroundings. The wave of nausea and dizziness was nearly a relief, sucking responsibility from her, and she gave herself over to it, forgetting why she was out on the street and where she was going. Her mind fled back to the image of the drained Mrs. Fludd, seated on a rickety chair alone on a rooftop. *Your friends.* Then the long, long flight down a narrowing tunnel. Kate had been her nearest friend. Her thought bucked like a rearing horse.

She opened her eyes to a dark burned with acid yellow. I'm in her world now, she thought. Soon I will

meet her again. I nearly know it all. The two impris-
oned women, the two ruined men had nearly brought
her to the full knowledge she sought, and she had to
make her way through Olivia Rudge's world to find the
rest. Men like beasts rutted past her, each eyeing the
stricken woman leaning against the brick wall of a
bank. A high thin red line—a scream—traced the sky.

Men followed her with their eyes. Before her, as she
watched them quicken with lust or amusement (*What
in the world can I look like?* she wondered), they drew
their faces into the masks of beasts, boars, bulls, wild
dogs. Bristles jutted from their snouts, their feet were
hooves tearing the ground. Their skin burned in the
yellow light, unhealthy and sallow. In the babble of
voices, she thought she discerned Magnus' low growl,
and started, her mind a fluttering rag.

Her hands brushed her thighs: cotton. She was wearing cotton trousers. She could not remember dressing.
Looking down, she saw that she wore a pale shirt, a
short tan jacket. She touched her hair and felt oil. The
voice was not Magnus', merely that of a man shouting
to another man in the street.

Four young men passed before her, their hair languorously curled; as they turned to stare, she saw their
faces inflamed with pustules, death in the pouches of
their cheeks, their eyes like razors cutting pieces from
her body. In the high, curved, bald forehead of a man
thrusting past she saw death, the skin tightening on his
skull; and she saw in a woman's colorless lips death, as
they parted over her teeth. And she saw they were all
dead, sweeping past her in the noise of raised voices
and automobiles. The dark gained on them all.

Bone-shining foreheads, skeletal umbrellas against
the dark, now nearly invisible sky and the wash of yellow from the lamps and headlights. It was the world of
her dream life.

Julia fought to right herself steadily on her feet.
Simple movement would cure this dreadful trick of vision. The boys, now further down the block, were only
boys; the men and women merely weary from work and

the journey home. She felt a familiar pang—an echo
from her old personality—as she realized that the little
tan jacket would probably cost two weeks' wages for
any of the men crowding past. Magnus had persuaded
her to buy it: or had he bought it, using her money?
After so many years, it made little difference, but she
wanted him to have bought it. Possessions were shame-
ful. Then why had she bought the house?

She had been chosen. In that was the last mystery.

One step, another; she tugged at the hem of the jacket
and straightened her back. No one was looking at her,
in all the sweeping flood passing by. Julia began to walk
more steadily, and recognized she had come over half
the way to Kensington Church Street. It was one way
of getting to Notting Hill, though roundabout. She hung
unmoving on the crowded pavement for a second, debating whether to go back and take the walk along the
side of the park which went directly north and ended
at Holland Park Avenue, but then decided, in the cool
gauzy air, to continue on the long way. The unaccus-
tomed coolness would clear her head. She moved on
again, passing W. H. Smith's, a package store, a clothing
shop where mannequins flung out their arms as if wailing.

Then she caught sight of herself in a shop window
and hurried past, unable to look away. Her face was a
formless white puddle, with discolored blots beneath
her eyes—it was the face of one of the women in the
Breadlands Clinic, the face of a dazed animal fleeing
experience. For a moment she saw how she would look
when old, and she turned wildly away and rushed down
the street, her bag bumping at her side.

A known face at a queue at a bus stop across the
street from Biba's made her shorten her stride. The old
woman in the long black dress hadn't yet seen her;
Julia turned her back to the line of people at the edge
of the pavement, feeling an instinctive desire to escape. . . . Still, she might have been mistaken. She edged
sideways and back, and dared to turn around. The long
narrow face now in profile, the dogmatic chin, tendrils

of white hair escaping from beneath a black hat: it was Miss Pinner.

Her first response had been panic: perhaps she did not want to know what the old woman had seen in the mirror that disastrous night. Perhaps she already did know.

But her curiosity about that evening was too great to be dismissed; she could not flee from Miss Pinner too. Julia's decision seemed to help her dispel Olivia's world, for the tired people at the bus stop all appeared reassuringly ordinary, and she waited until two or three men had walked between them and then crossed the blackly shining pavement to tap the old woman on the shoulder. She pronounced her name, and heard her voice emerging levelly, distinctly.

"Yes? Yes?" The old woman started out of her reverie and turned her headmistress' blue eyes on Julia.

She doesn't recognize me, Julia thought. "Excuse me," she began, and saw the old woman purse her mouth expectantly, as if she were about to be asked for directions. "I'm surprised to see you here, Miss Pinner," she said.

Fear jumped for a second in the woman's eyes, and she stepped out of the queue. "Mrs. Lofting?" she said. "I'm sorry, I didn't recognize you at first, you see . . . you look ill, my dear. Yes, you are quite right, I am not here often . . . and I am afraid that I shall have to be getting off home." She lifted a small brown parcel. "We used to enjoy shopping here, and since Miss Tooth's birthday is approaching soon, I wanted to see if I could find anything for her at Derry and Tom's—but I found that they had been replaced by that very curious store across the street, and the little restaurant on the roof was shut, so I bought her something elsewhere." As she chattered, she glanced down the street obviously looking for her bus. "I'm late already. I must be home in time to prepare our dinner. Heavens, it's past eight."

"Do you have time to talk to me before your bus comes, Miss Pinner?"

"I can't say, I'm sure." Then the little flicker of fear

was replaced by something like cunning. "I'm sorry that I was taken ill at your charming house, Mrs. Lofting. It was a very distressing evening for all of us, I'm sure . . . and then poor Mrs. Fludd's sudden demise . . . her niece forbade any of us to attend the funeral . . . but I was remiss in not writing to thank you for your hospitality. Miss Tooth and I were entertained in many grand houses years ago, when Miss Tooth could still follow her career, as you know, and we never sinned against hospitality in that way. I do hope you can forgive me."

"You were taken ill?" said Julia, focusing on the one sentence she had been able to follow.

"A spell of faintness," said Miss Pinner, showing the faint but detectable embarrassment honest people bring to their untruths. "I've been kept very busy these past months, going through all our old scrapbooks." She hitched up her shoulders painfully, in the movement of one adjusting to the twinges of a long-standing arthritis. "I can't do it in the mornings anymore, so my afternoons are very tiring. But Miss Tooth"—here the dogmatic face forgot all embarrassment—"Miss Tooth can still do her exercises."

"Can she?" said Julia, wondering if the drug were still clouding her perceptions.

"She can still work at the barre," said Miss Pinner with great satisfaction. "Miss Tooth is very supple yet."

"At the bar?" said Julia, trying to visualize little Miss Tooth serving up pints of bitter in a public house.

"Oh, yes. Of course she hasn't the stamina she had when she was younger, but she has all of her grace. We are preparing a book from the scrapbooks. Many people still remember her, as I see you do yourself. Of course, you would only have heard of her. You're too young to have seen her dance."

"Unfortunately, I was too young, yes," said Julia, seeing it at last. She remembered how, during the séance, Miss Tooth had seemingly floated to the floor in one effortless motion. "But she was very famous, wasn't she?" Julia guessed.

"How kind of you to remember," said Miss Pinner,

and now her manner was entirely friendly. "Rosamund was a great artist. I was her dresser for twenty-five years and we retired together. After working for Rosamund Tooth it was impossible to work for anyone else. And I wouldn't touch any of the young lot. All technique and no poetry."

"Did Miss Tooth see anything in the mirror after you'd fainted that night?" Julia said brutally.

Miss Pinner's face trembled into an utter blankness of expression.

"I thought I saw something when I followed her in," Julia added. "And I know what it was."

Miss Pinner looked aghast, and Julia felt a twisting of guilt for making the old woman confront her lie. "Perhaps you saw it too."

"No—no—Mrs. Lofting, you should not be asking me about that night. I was tired from the long ride down from our home and from putting the scrapbooks in order. I don't know what I saw." She stepped nervously back into her place in the queue, and Julia followed her.

"Was it a little girl? A blond child? She is, she was, a wicked person, Miss Pinner. Please tell me, Miss Pinner." But she was already confused by the expression of mixed astonishment and relief on Miss Pinner's angular face. "Wasn't it the blond girl?"

"I am afraid to tell you, Mrs. Lofting," said Miss Pinner. "Oh. There's my bus down the road. Please don't detain me. It'll soon be here."

Julia, afraid that she would never know, gently touched the thick black stuff of Miss Pinner's coat with her right hand. "Wasn't it the little girl? She does horrible things. She once made me faint too."

Miss Pinner shook her head. "I don't think . . ." she began. Down the block, the bus swerved into traffic and came toward them, its headlamps beaming yellow through gathering dark.

Julia suddenly felt a sick certainty that her assumptions had been wrong; she was again at the edge of the abyss, afraid to look down. The bus swung heavily toward the curb, a wing of yellow light flashing below the upper deck. In his cage behind rain-streaked glass the driver looked totemic.

"I must get on now or wait another twenty minutes," said Miss Pinner. The queue moved forward slowly, a crippled insect laden with parcels and umbrellas. "I would not have said so much except that you knew about Rosamund." She was nearly at the steps of the bus, kept from them by only a fat woman struggling with two small dogs and a little girl with the face of a pampered pig.

"I have to know," said Julia as the woman swung the pig-child up onto the steps and gruntingly lifted herself and the dogs into the bus. "I have to know." She raised her hands, as if praying.

Miss Pinner looked in shock at Julia's left hand and shirt cuff, and then gazed straight into her face with a tense compassion. "I saw you," she blurted, and the conductor raised her up onto the platform and the bus was gone.

Earlier that day, brother and sister were sitting across from each other at Lily's table, two empty wine bottles and soup bowls and plates littered with bones between them. Magnus sat slumped in his chair, staring at the unappetizing remains of his lunch. He looked flushed and puffy, but he had changed into a clean suit and shirt, and wore immaculately polished shoes. He was impressive. Locked into his face, at a complicated level beneath the features but informing them, was a combination of authority and power and malice which she had seen in him all her life.

She said, "Magnus, you are a beautiful man."

"What!" His head jerked up and she saw his blood-shot eyes. "For God's sake, Lily. I am fifty-three years old, I'm nearly three stone overweight, and I have not been sleeping well. I am tired."

She wanted to reply, but he cut her off. "And I'm not sure about this. I think you're rushing it."

Enjoying this moment as she did each of those rare occasions when she was stronger than he, Lily said, "Yesterday you agreed with me. We both know that she must be put back into professional care as quickly as possible. Magnus, your wife is in danger—she may do permanent harm to herself. Not to mention the damage she is doing to you."

"Humph." Magnus shook his head.

"I trust you wish to keep her from Mark," she said slyly.

"Mark is a wretch. He is a failure. There has always been something wrong with him. You know that."

"You are what is wrong with him, and of course I know it. Does Julia? Magnus, she scarcely knows him at all."

"Yes, I do want to keep her from him."

"Have you ever told her about his breakdowns?"

He shook his head. "They were a long time ago."

"Well, you see my point," she said, "she really only knows Mark's surface. And that is very seductive."

Magnus was not ignoring her now.

"You do take my point, and you needn't pretend that it hasn't been preying on you as it has on me. If we can get her back into the hospital, we shall have taken care of *that* problem. Now. As I see it, we must first persuade her to leave that house, by whatever means, and to move into my spare bedroom. It's possible to—I mean to say that the door locks from the outside."

"Yes," he said. "Are you certain—are you absolutely certain there couldn't be anything in that story of hers? I saw Kate in the window of her bedroom one afternoon. That afternoon I struck that ninny. I'm certain it was Kate. I couldn't be wrong about her. I know it was Kate. It knocked the breath out of me. And I have felt —things—in that miserable house. I don't know how to describe it. All I know is that I want her out of there. That place upsets me."

"You upset yourself," Lily said calmly. "You see your daughter, whom you miss terribly; Julia is ob-

sessed with a case a quarter of a century old in which
a mother stabs her daughter to death. You haven't been
eating or sleeping regularly, and Julia is burning herself
up. Of course the two of you see things. But as far as
Julia actually being in touch with spiritual manifesta-
tions, any such thought is absurd."

"How can you be so certain? I was certain too, until
I saw Kate."

"Experience," she said dismissively. "Ghosts are seen
all over this country by people who are upset, or have
had too much to eat or drink. Magnus, this is my field
as the law is yours. I assure you, if a spirit were to appear to anyone in this family, it would appear to me.
An untrained, inexperienced person like Julia would
simply not have the faintest idea of how to interpret an
authentic sighting. Magnus, with respect, do let me tell
you that when an untrained person gets it into her head
that she is in contact with a spirit, a sort of hypnosis
begins to take effect—the untrained person has all sorts
of fancies—wild thoughts—and she can easily persuade
others to share them. I'll confess that I had a small trace
of this myself."

"Lately?" Magnus said with interest.

"Yes."

"So you saw Kate too." His big face was suffusing
with blood.

"No, but if I listened long enough to you and Julia
I very well might. I saw—I supposed myself to see—
something far more mundane."

"*What?*" Magnus seemed to be increasing in size, and
Lily felt a thrilled, appreciative trace of her fear of him.

"Actually, I imagined that I saw Mrs. Fludd," she
said, and Magnus slumped back into his chair. "Which
simply proves how careful we must be not to be swayed
by Julia's delusions."

"But what if she *is* right? What if I was right, and
not merely overtired?" But even in his tone of voice,
Lily heard that he did not want to believe it.

"Then I expect that we should *all* be endangered.
Any truly vengeful, destructive spirit, once set free,

draws strength from its own evil. It might even control any mind weak enough to be open to it. But such cases occur very infrequently. There isn't one in a century. Genuine evil is as rare as that. Most of what we call evil is merely lack of imagination."

"Most murderers are an unhappy lot," Magnus agreed. "I've defended several who didn't so much commit murder as fall over it."

"Precisely," Lily said. "So I think we can dismiss the possibility of this being a case of genuine manifestation."

"What did I see in the window, then? And what did I feel in that house?"

"You saw and felt your own fear. If that can happen to my commanding brother, then I think this has gone far enough. I should never have introduced Julia to Mrs. Fludd. Neither of us should have permitted Julia to indulge her ill fantasies about Kate's death."

"That's enough of that," Magnus said warningly, and pushed himself away from the table.

"Except for this," said Lily. "We—you and I—must accept the truth. We are going to institutionalize Julia. For her own good and for ours. Do you think that she might be suicidal?"

"I don't know," Magnus said.

"There you have it. We don't know. You can't afford to have her divorce you, and you don't want her to die. She must be put back into the hospital, and kept there until she is docile. And I suggest that you take whatever steps are appropriate to ensure that her money is accessible. You must be able to control her money. You must be able to control *her*."

Magnus was leaning forward, his elbows on his knees, staring directly at her. "You are being very frank, Lily."

"It is too late to be anything else," she said straight to him. "In truth, Magnus, we all desire to own her. That is what we wish. You, I—and Mark. We wish to possess her."

"I wish to save her," he flatly said.

"Did I say differently?"

"Fine, then," Magnus said.

"I adore you when you're reasonable," Lily half sang, "and there'll never be a time when I don't. I think we should go over there now. We can walk across the park."

"I'll begin to look into things tomorrow," Magnus said, and shrugged; he stood up and dropped his napkin beside his plate.

When Julia had numbly watched the bus disappear around the corner and up Kensington Church Street, exhaustion seemed to invade her with every breath, weighting the marrow of her bones. Her body seemed very heavy; she no longer felt able to trudge up to Notting Hill; she wanted to lean on Mark's arm. She thought with longing of her bed, of long sleep, of reading a book propped against the blanket while a light kept her safe from the dark. She saw me dead, she thought. Or had Miss Pinner seen—an idea fragile as a moth's wing, but freighted with all of Olivia's darkness, flickered for a half second at the borders of her consciousness and was then tamped down, forgotten, and her mind veered away, not recognizing what it had done.

And with it she veered, turning to her side, blinking, knowing only that she wished to be at home.

She got halfway back up the street before her burning feet could carry her no farther. A few steps away was a bench, and she limped toward it and collapsed onto it, sighing. A man in a black raincoat with the collar turned up sat beside her and brushed her legs with his. Very lightly, he brushed her leg again. Julia peeked at him, hoping he would leave, and saw—thought she saw—that the man had no lips. His face seemed to be chopped off below the nose, and to begin again at the chin. Between was a white scream of teeth, a permanent snarl of rigid teeth and blackened gums. She was afraid to look again and was too tired to move on, so sat hunched within herself, staring directly ahead of her, seeing nothing. He too hunched in his black raincoat, the collar turned up, and stared ahead. His leg

hung against hers, with almost no pressure save that of
the thin black cloth of his trousers. After what seemed
an hour the man shifted, and she glanced quickly at him
and saw that his face was, after all, utterly normal,
rather pudgy and full-lipped. She realized that she had
been holding her breath, and noisily inhaled. The man
pressed his leg to Julia's but now he was just an ordinary man, and she moved down the bench, pretending
to look for something on the wet sidewalk, so that she
would not offend him. After a time he moved away,
leaving behind a copy of the *Evening Standard*. Julia
unthinkingly picked up the newspaper and numbly
walked home. Noises and screams drifted across from
Holland Park.

The house pulsed with heat and expectant, waiting
quiet, its lights flaming. Julia walked through rooms
which seemed alien and dead, utterly apart from her.
She heard none of the by now familiar noises of the
trapped echoes and spirits of the Rudges. Julia thought,
as she sat wearily on the McClintocks' ugly couch, that
Olivia might have withdrawn, leaving Julia in her world
forever: that was the strength of evil, she saw, its ab-
sence of hope, its stink of moral failure. For a moment
she saw the tramp on Cremorne Road savagely stuffing
a dog into a bag; from an accumulation of these sordid,
hopeless moments evil was condensed.

She bent her neck backward and closed her eyes and
suppressed a half-formed image which threatened to
flood into her mind.

To distract herself, Julia took up the newspaper she
had taken from the bench. In time she would have the
energy to face the stairs and her bedroom. Then she remembered the carnage she had made of the upstairs
bathroom—bare white-gray walls like dead skin and
skeletal shards of black mirror over everything. That
mess: Olivia seemed alive and present in its midst. She
could not bear to look at it now.

Julia skimmed the news on the front page—it seemed
remote and irrelevant. She read the names of politicians,
looked at their photographs, and scarcely remembered

who they were. They had nothing to do with her, nothing to do with Olivia Rudge. Why was she reading this? It was the first current newspaper she had looked at in weeks. She felt the atmosphere of the house intensify around her, and turned the page.

At the bottom of page four she saw the little headline. Paul Winter had not been judged worthy of much space. The headline read GENERAL'S SON FOUND DEAD IN CHELSEA FLAT.

Captain Paul Winter, 36, son of General Martin Somill Winter, second in command to Montgomery at Alamein, was found dead this morning by a friend in his small flat in Stadium St. SW 10. Captain Winter, who had left the army several years ago, suffered multiple stab wounds. General Winter was informed of his son's death soon after discovery of the body. The General and his son are said to have not been on speaking terms for many years. Captain Winter was unmarried.

Julia's first thought was of David Swift: he had to be warned. As she began to move dazedly across the room to the telephone, she heard the sound of chattering, high-pitched laughter—gleeful hiccuping childish laughter. "Damn you, damn you, damn you," Julia screamed, at the same time recognizing with a part of her mind that Olivia Rudge could never produce a sound so innocent. It was the delighted laughter of a young child.

Where was it? For a moment it seemed to ring all about her and pervade the house. She forced herself to be still and quiet, and then heard that it came from beyond the kitchen. She knew where. If she had not shattered the black mirrors, it would come from upstairs. Julia ran through the rooms, her warning to David Swift forgotten, and rushed down the hall to the bathroom.

Some figure lurked in the mirror, pouring out that delighted laughter. When she banged open the door she saw its shape crouched on the side of the tub, darkly reflected in the rose mirrors. She stabbed on the light.

The little black girl, Mona, perched on the side of the mirrored tub, rocking with glee. From her upturned throat poured gasping high trills which bounced off the shining walls, redoubling. Mona saw her and raised a short pointing finger and continued to screech.

"What . . ." Julia uttered, and spun around. Olivia Rudge passed the bathroom door and was proceeding calmly, her back to Julia, into the kitchen.

"*Stop*," Julia shouted. She sprinted out of the bathroom, Mona's screams of glee locked in her inner ear, and saw Olivia, in jeans and a red shirt, going out the side door of the kitchen into the dining room. As Julia reached the door Olivia twisted the handle of the French windows and disappeared out into the garden. Rage flashed through Julia's entire nervous system, and she followed.

She went around the side of the house and saw the blond child moving easily and swiftly, well ahead of her, down the street. You won't get away from me, Julia thought, not with that highly visible hair, and began to walk quickly down the street after her in the direction of Kensington High Street. Olivia's hair shimmered in the dark air like a beacon, drifting twenty or thirty yards ahead of Julia. The child turned left on the High Street and was lost from sight.

Alone in the darkness, Julia ran to the corner, hearing her shoes clapping on the pavement. At the corner she looked to the left and saw Olivia moving resolutely up the street, two blocks ahead. A cocoon of silence seemed to have descended over the two of them. Julia was unconscious of the babble of voices and traffic sounds which had so penetrated her earlier; the other people on the street, now merely evening strollers, were insubstantial specters between herself and the girl's flickering hair. She crossed an intervening street and came up onto a long block, following Olivia. Anger and determination were joined presences, thin, high and sweet, thrumming in her blood.

The girl drifted ahead of her, slowing whenever Julia was detained by a knot of people or by traffic at an intersection. When Julia tried to gain on the girl and ran for the length of a block, Olivia effortlessly and without seeming to increase her pace quickened her movement and maintained the distance between them. Around Julia, the cool gauzy air, still smelling of recent rainfall, seemed to congeal into a glowing envelope which contained only herself and Olivia Rudge. Energy—Julia's energy—burned within this envelope, beating at the pulse of her blood.

After a time Julia ceased to be aware of the stream of traffic, to see the other people on the pavement. When her view of her quarry was blocked, she crossed to the other side of the walk and saw her moving easily and determinedly up the street, jeans and red shirt beneath the pale flame of her hair. There was no one else in the world, there was no other movement in the world.

At the long terrace of the Commonwealth Institute Olivia paused and turned. A block away, Julia saw her unsmiling, intent face and for the first time did not find in it a challenge. It was nervous and blank, waiting for her to come closer, almost fearful. Julia pushed off a curb to give leverage to her running and nearly went headlong into an oncoming car. "Look here," came a man's outraged voice, but Julia barely recorded the protest. Olivia was leading her somewhere; Olivia seemed almost to be pleading to her.

From her right she heard the clang of gates and knew that the attendants were locking the park. It was nine o'clock. As if it were a signal for her, Olivia turned her face from Julia and scampered up the steps to the terrace, passed through a line of columns and began to move quickly up the lane running north alongside the park. A few stragglers emerged just as Julia reached the path and blocked her view of Olivia; and then they were alone again, walking rapidly up the long dark path. The girl's hair shone.

"Olivia!" she shouted as the girl slipped into the darkness between the rows of trees. Again she followed, trying to lessen the distance between them, and began to jog, feeling her muscles catch like gears. Olivia was now far ahead, lost in the dark.

Then she appeared in the flaring circle of a lamp, still moving effortlessly between the twin rows of trees. Julia passed the lower portion of the silent green length of park and reached the gate to the youth hostel just within the grounds. Olivia had vanished again. She shouted her name; silence. Making a frantic guess, Julia pushed through the wooden gate and ran up another smaller, twisting path: far ahead, confirmingly, she thought she heard the sound of Olivia's footsteps.

At the bar of the metal gate pulled across the path she hesitated for only a moment, and then swung her trunk over, awkwardly lifting her legs, and half tumbled into the locked park. Her body was a weapon, an arrow for Olivia. Before her, the path wound darkly past the side of Holland House and the wooded hostel. It went far up into the area of the park Julia did not know, a woods traced with many small unpaved paths. Olivia was moving resolutely, unhesitatingly up the narrow way toward the woods.

"Olivia! Olivia!" Julia screamed, but the child did not turn. Julia went after her.

After a few minutes she had left the path and was running across soft grass. Olivia's shining hair appeared flickering between the trees, moving steadily forward. Julia's cuff snagged on a low branch, and then ripped away. Her shoes sank in loamy earth, and admitted chill moisture. In the sparse wood she lost her quarry, then saw a gleaming flash of white up to her right, cutting through bushes and across a barren dark space. They went deeper into the wood, Olivia floating over the low wooden fences and Julia tripping over them, staying on her feet by sheer momentum. In this way, Olivia seemed to lead her for nearly a mile, tricking her into loops to one side or the other, disappearing behind trees and surfacing in wide clearings, tracking back to the right.

Where the wood ended Julia saw the girl racing through low bushes to a wire fence, and ran after. When she reached the fence Olivia was already beyond it, going slowly down a pitted asphalt walk. In the darkness Julia saw only a shimmer of white, pale as breath, to mark her going.

She would have to get over the fence, which was chin-high. Pulling at the top bar with her hands, she lifted herself up to place a toe between the links of chain, then her other foot, and pushed on straining leg muscles so that her torso was above the top bar, where sharp twisted strands of wire prevented her from rolling over. She tremblingly balanced herself, leaned out across the bar, and raised her right leg over the top. Down the sloping path she would find Olivia: this conviction allowed her to swing her other leg over the top, catching the ripped cuff on one of the strands of wire. She tore it impatiently away, and pushed herself off the fence onto the lightless path.

From ahead of her came the sound of running. With all of the breath left in her, Julia forced her body into a trot; the downward slope of the path carried her into a run she was unable to control. It was as if she were running down a mountain, her legs flying out to keep her body upright. Gravity brought her forward, falling like a boulder, toward the sound of Olivia's movement.

Light, noise, astonished faces met her as she tumbled out onto the street below the path. Still ahead of her, she heard Olivia's noise, and she bounced off and around a metal containing fence and raced out into the middle of Holland Park Avenue. Headlights fixed her like a pinned butterfly; her upper body, head, arms and shoulders were still traveling faster than her legs. When she fell, a car squealed to a stop, horn blaring, only inches from her body.

10

Olivia had murdered Geoffrey Braden; she had murdered Paul Winter; she had murdered Mrs. Fludd; and she had tried now to kill Julia. She had been called up from whatever rank, resentful obscurity she had inhabited; Julia's appearance on Ilchester Place had clothed her in flesh, and now she was a bodily presence in the house. Or so Julia had felt: she could not enter a room without imagining that her tormentor had just quit it. When alone in her bedroom, she locked the door, knowing that Olivia could reach her at any time she wished. The long run through the park had been something like playfulness. Olivia had been toying with her, trying to reproduce Rosa Fludd's "accident."

They were in a new configuration: the screw had tightened, and Olivia wanted her blood. Julia stood on weak, aching legs in the kitchen, waiting for her coffee to boil. It was as dark beyond the windows as if it were still night; the sky, a patch of which Julia could see above the wet brown boards of a fence, hung motionless and woolly, looking as if it might snag in the trees. A few small drops dashed against the window.

Paul Winter. Someone had visited his room and butchered him. Someone under Olivia's control, some man driven by hate so that Olivia could enter him; a man whom absurd, touching little Paul Winter trusted. Someone who was his Magnus. Whoever it was would not know that he had killed a man for talking to a woman named Julia Lofting. Maybe he wouldn't even remember committing the murder—maybe Olivia could sweep into a mind and then flow out again, leaving no real memory of her occupation. This thought weakened

Julia's legs, and she leaned against the counter on shaking knees, perspiring.

The disturbed, reclusive woman in Abbotsbury Close would read the newspaper item or hear of it from Huff, and be savagely glad. She too was Olivia's victim.

And David Swift would be the next, if she understood what Olivia was doing. Julia immediately left the kitchen and went into the living room. She had to check in the directory to find Swift's number. Would her story convince him of his danger? He had seen Olivia at work, but Swift was a stupid and arrogant man. She had no choice, she had to persuade him. She dialed the number and listened intently as the telephone shrilled at the other end. She prayed for him to answer it, but the telephone continued to ring. He might be outside, she thought, or in his bed, sleeping off a hangover.

Julia did not want to look at the third possibility, but neither did she evade it. In the A-D directory she found the listings for police departments, and rang the Islington police. "A man may be dead," she intoned. "Look at Three Thirty-seven Upper Street, the flat just above a pub called The Beautiful and Damned. His name is Swift. This is in connection with the murder of Captain Paul Winter. Hurry."

"What is your relationship to Mr. Swift, madam?" inquired the policeman's drawling voice.

"I'm afraid for him," Julia said, and hurriedly hung up. Relieved that she had at least done something, she went back into the kitchen, where the kettle full of Malvern water was emitting its high shriek. She promised herself to telephone Swift later.

She drank her coffee standing at the white counter, trying to decide how to act, what to do to meet Olivia's challenge. Olivia would try again to kill her. All the previous night, after she had been aided by the puzzled, half-solicitous, half-furious man who had nearly hit her, she had lain atop her sheet in the steaming bedroom, afraid to close her eyes. Then, she had vowed to leave Ilchester Place; Olivia's secret was known, there was nothing left to find; she had to defend herself. Yet in the morning she had realized that Olivia could reach her anywhere. No house was any safer than her own. She had cleaned up the bathroom, filling pails and bags with sections of black glass, with that certainty lodged in her mind.

She thought of it just as she finished her coffee: if freedom from Olivia were anywhere, it would be in America. It was time to return. Her marriage was finished. She did not want Magnus or need him. She was closer to Heather and Olivia Rudge than to anyone else in England—save Mark. But she and Mark had almost never had even so much as a serious conversation. Would he like to live in New Hampshire? She realized with dismay how little she knew about him.

But the thought of him gave her courage to answer her telephone when it began to ring in the living room. She braced herself, thinking that she might hear for the first time the voice of Olivia Rudge. But it was Lily's voice she heard.

"Julia, I hope you don't mind my asking you how you are?"

Julia found that she could speak to Lily only in the coolest, most detached manner. Lily seemed to have emerged from another era.

"Good morning, Lily. How am I? I don't know. I feel sort of suspended. I feel very odd. A lot's happened. I know how Mrs. Fludd was killed. Olivia almost did the same to me. I think it was her idea of a joke."

"My darling, if you are saying . . ."

"That Olivia tried to kill me. That's right. Next time, she won't be so playful. What would you do if your life were in danger?"

"I'd go to Magnus," Lily said simply.

"Well, so you would. But I can't. The next time, it might be Magnus trying to run me over. So I can't do that, Lily, can I? No."

She could almost hear Lily's patience snapping.

"I understand that you're overtired, darling," said Lily. "But you should realize that you're being almost absurdly unrealistic. Magnus loves you, Julia. Magnus

wants you for his wife. He wants to begin rebuilding
your marriage. We—Magnus and I—went to see you
yesterday, just past lunchtime. I wish you had been at
home, so you could have seen how pathetically distressed he is."

"I was at home, I was asleep. I'd taken two sleeping
pills. Olivia had just given me a message. Do you believe me, Lily? And last night she tried to put it into
effect—she lured me outside and ran me into traffic. I
was almost killed. It was like being hypnotized. It's what
she did to Mrs. Fludd. Would you have called it an accident, Lily?"

"Have you ever wondered why it is to you that all
these things are happening? Why is it you?"

"You're clever, Lily. That's all I have left to find
out."

"You have been very active and you have been
through a great deal, my dear. How long has it been
since you've been out of the hospital?"

"I don't know," said Julia, feeling her artificial de-
tachment begin to recede. "What difference does it
make? A month, maybe."

"Not as long as that, I shouldn't think. My dear,
darling Julia. You've had such a rotten time of it.
Don't you think you really deserve another rest? Don't
say anything now, but I do want you to think about it.
And I want you to consider moving in with me for the
time being. All alone over there, you might be hurt, or
injure yourself in some way, and no one would know
anything about it. That's what Magnus and I wanted to
talk about with you yesterday afternoon. We wanted to
beg you to move in with me for the time being."

"You and Magnus," Julia said. "You and Magnus
wanted, you and Magnus thought, you and Magnus this
and that. So you're afraid I'll hurt myself. What do you
mean by that, Lily?"

"Nothing, darling, we were simply . . ."

"I want you to know something, Lily. I was just
thinking, this morning, right before you called, that I
would like to go back to America. There's nothing here

for me any more, unless it's Mark Berkeley. I want to
divorce Magnus. He seems impossibly remote to me. If
I live through this siege, I'm going to divorce him.
There. What do you think of that, Lily?"

"I think it's calamitous," said Lily. "It's psychic disaster. You still blame Magnus for what happened, and
you should not be permitted to do that."

"I see," said Julia coldly. "I think you'd like to have
me back in the hospital, Lily."

"I just want you, darling, to *think,*" wailed Lily.
"How much sleep do you get? How well do you eat?
Can you take care of yourself? Why, why, why do you
think this Olivia person wants to kill you? You—out of
all the people she might have chosen."

Julia listened, her mouth open, almost thinking that
Lily would tell her.

"We're not making any progress," Lily said finally.
"Please think about staying in my guestroom, darling.
You don't truly want to return to your troubled country
and leave dear old England and Magnus. You need
Magnus. You need help. Julia, none of us shall be
happy, none of us shall be what we were until you accept some basic truths. The truth about Kate—"

Julia shouted into the telephone, "You don't know
the truth about Kate, you don't know the truth about
Magnus!" Then she hung up.

Lily rang back several seconds later. "Julia, you are
still heroic, I respect you in every way, darling, but you
are also a bit erratic. Did you ring off on me?"

"Give up, Lily," said Julia. "Give up on me. I'm not
in your world anymore. I'm in hers. Ask Miss Pinner."

"You'd better begin thinking very quickly and very
well," Lily said five minutes later to Magnus, having
roused him from sleep with her telephone call. "She
wants to divorce you. And she mentioned that she is
thinking of returning to America."

"Good God," Magnus managed to utter. "Is she
mad? She can't divorce me."

"I should imagine, brother dear, that she has grounds

sufficient to divorce you fifty times, should that be necessary. But, yes, I think she is mad. This Rudge affair has utterly unhinged her. She has snapped, Magnus. There is surely some way that you can have her put away in the hospital. Put away for good, if necessary. Or at least until she is capable of listening to reason."

"Lily," Magnus wheezed, his voice foggy and menacing, "what the devil did you say to her? Did you wave Kate in front of her again?"

"No," Lily said, "at least not directly. She is much too full of this Rudge matter to consider Kate. Will you go to your chambers and look up in your musty old books whatever law you can invoke to get her safely put away? Because if you do not, you will not have a wife at this time next year. She could go to Reno, or wherever it is Americans go to be especially vulgar."

"I'll see what I can find," Magnus growled. "I'll look up what's needed for an involuntary commitment."

"You might have done that when she left you," Lily offered in her sweetest tone.

"I needed you to suggest it, Lily."

One question of Lily's stayed with Julia. *Why is it you?* She could have answered, because it was I who bought the house, but that merely pushed the question back a step. She was not satisfied with what she already knew; it seemed to her that the force which had taken her out to Breadlands and had led her to Olivia's group had not yet released her.

What she most wished to do was to take two more pills and sleep out the rest of the day. But there had been something, some idea she had not followed up. . . . Her mind traced the flicker of memory back, almost catching it. A magazine. Then she had it: *The Tatler*. She had been going to look for pictures of Heather Rudge's parties in *The Tatler* on the day she saw the Burne-Jones painting.

Well, she thought, why not? Since making the discovery of Olivia's role in the Braden boy's death, she had felt occupationless. Now it seemed that she was

only to wait—wait for Olivia to decide in what way she
would move. Leafing through magazines in Colindale
was far more attractive. Let Olivia appear in the reading room, let her wave her knife over bound stacks of
John O'London's and *Punch*. The image was so bizarre
that Julia, for the second time, caught at the fluttering
tails of her sanity. Was it possible that she *had* ripped
the dolls and written on the mirrors? Turned on the
heaters? Perhaps she had imagined seeing Olivia. Her
doubting mind bent back on itself.

Yet someone had killed Paul Winter. She had not invented that. Olivia was no delusion. Aware that she was
on the verge of feeling grateful for Winter's horrible
death, Julia dressed in her hot silent room, went out to
her car, and drove through drizzle and glittering streets
to Colindale and the periodical collection.

Her reader's card was inspected with almost insulting
thoroughness by a uniformed guard; as she walked
down the symmetrical rows of desks she obliquely saw
two young men seated behind a large heap of Victorian
magazines smirk at each other as she passed. Julia supposed that she looked more than ever like an actual
beggar maid. Her shoes were mud-stained from the
chase through Holland Park, her tights were ripped,
and she hadn't washed her hair in a week.

The desk she was accustomed to using was occupied
by a large black man wearing gold spectacles which
seemed to emit fierce light. His long flat cheeks bore
triple raised scars, purplish black. He glanced aggressively at Julia, a bear defending his territory, and she
wandered to the other side of the room, looking for a
vacant desk. Two or three men tracked her with their
eyes, looking benignly amused.

At last she found a desk near the wall and dropped
her spattered raincoat over the top of the chair. After
filling in a request slip for all the copies of *The Tatler*
from 1930 to 1941, she took it to the desk and gave it
to a new librarian, a dark-haired young woman with
large tinted glasses. Julia watched the young librarian
take her card to one of the runners, and realized that,

two weeks ago, she had seen her outside the French
restaurant on Abingdon Road. It was the girl with
whom she had felt a sympathy, the girl who had smiled
at her. They had been members of the same species.
Now she felt nothing of the kind. She had nothing in
common with this pretty young librarian.

With her hair a reddish mass of tangles, in her ripped
black tights and muddy shoes, dark circles beneath her
eyes, Julia sat behind her blond desk, her mood lifting.
She would not feel sorry for herself. A boy set half a
dozen fat black volumes on the desk before her. "They'll
send up the others when you have finished with these,"
he said, nearly apologizing, as if he expected this strange
woman to shout at him.

She knew that she would find something. She felt
morally renewed. Julia pulled the top volume off the
stack and began to leaf through it, staring hungrily at the
pictures of men and women in evening dress, remembering her childhood. Almost, she could hear them speak.

The first hour she found nothing, nor the second; it
was slightly before noon when she had even a faint suc-
cess. She had flipped halfway through the volume for
1933–34 when a picture, a face, on an earlier page
burned back to her, and she tore backward in the book
to November, 1933. There on the right-hand side of the
book, grinning up at her, was Heather Rudge, holding a
cigarette and a champagne glass, her shoulders gleaming; the sexuality of the woman scalded Julia's bowels.
On both sides of her dangled young men. Julia rushed
to the caption. "The well-known American hostess Mrs.
Heather Rudge at Lord Kilross' party, here seen with
Mr. Maxwell Davies, Mr. Jeremy Reynolds, Lord Panton, the Hon. Frederick Mason, and Viscount Gregory."
That was all. None of the young men, who glittered with
an identical infatuation, were familiar to Julia, and she
saw no other photographs of Heather at the party.

She went slowly through the remainder of the volume,
but Heather did not reappear. Nor did she for another
forty-five minutes, when Julia saw her oval, challenging,
vain, sensual face again rising up from her dazzling

shoulders on a fluted neck. More young men surrounded her—Mr. Maxwell Davies, Viscount Gregory and the Hon. Frederick Mason among them. They looked unchanged. The occasion, Julia read, was a party given by Lord Panton, who appeared beside a frilly little blonde, the Hon. Someone-Someone, all teeth and curls. These were her young men, undoubtedly: Julia wondered which of them had owned the honor of siring Olivia.

Thrice more, in the volumes leading up to 1936, Julia found photographs of Heather. She seemed to travel usually in the company of the same young men, with a slight mixture of mustached older gentlemen with straining bellies and popping eyes. Oliver Blankenship, Nigel Ramsay, David Addison. But every time one of these older men appeared, he was shadowed closely by several of Heather's younger set. Heather was always "the well-known (or popular, or famous) American hostess" in these photographs, but there were no pictures taken of her parties.

Julia signaled to the runner to take the six heavy volumes and return with the later set. Her face was warm and hectic, flushed, and she began to drum her fingers on her desk and look wildly around the quiet room, where men bent their heads over books as though drinking from them. Her watch said three thirty. She'd had nothing to eat or drink since morning coffee.

One wing of the library contained a small cafeteria. Julia wondered if she should get a sandwich before going on. The impulse grew out of her rising mood, the optimism she had begun to feel, and she decided to follow it, even though she felt no hunger. She scrawled a note for the boy and went quickly down the aisles and out of the reading room, giving a bright, unfocused smile to the guard at the door.

Julia flew down the long lightless hall to the cafeteria, selected a tray from beneath the gaze of a bored Indian woman wearing a hairnet, and looked over the available food. "Too late for hot lunch," the Indian woman announced from her stool. Julia nodded, examining the sandwiches. "No hot lunch now, only sameges," the woman insisted.

"Fine," Julia said. She took from the rack a cheese and tomato sandwich wrapped in thin cellophane; touching the whispery layer of cellophane, Julia instantly imagined it plastered across her face, adhering there, stuck to her nostrils and mouth. She dropped the sandwich on the tray.

"Coffee?" Julia said, standing before the shining coffee machine.

The woman shook her head. "No coffee. Too late, coffee again at half four."

"Fine," Julia said, and plucked a container of orange drink from a carton.

When she reached the cash desk, the Indian woman left her stool and moved slowly past the racks of food, audibly sighing. At last she reached the register and rang up Julia's purchases.

"Two pounds."

"That can't be right—one sandwich?"

The woman stared deeply into Julia's face, then looked with great boredom back at the tray. She punched more buttons on the register. "Thirty-two pence."

Julia took the tray to a clean table, and looked back at the waitress, half expecting to be ordered to one of the uncleaned side tables. The woman was shuffling back to her stool, conspicuously not taking notice of Julia.

The orange drink felt cool and sweet on her tongue, and it opened a channel all the way down into her stomach. She chewed experimentally at the dry sandwich; its bread seemed poreless, synthetic, and the cheese did not separate between her teeth. For a few moments she continued to chew distractedly at the stale sandwich, lubricating it with orange drink.

When her insides contracted, she quickly left the table and rushed across the room to the door marked LADIES. Inside one of the metal cubicles she vomited neatly into the bowl, and tasted the heavy sweetness of orange drink; when her stomach contracted again, only a thin yellowish drool came up.

She went to a sink and wiped water across her mouth. The mirror showed a drugged-looking, raddled harridan of indeterminate age; gray showed clearly in the frizzy hair at the sides of her head. Her lips were cracked, and beside her right eye was a small bruise she'd got when she had fallen down in Holland Park Avenue. Julia tried to comb her hair with her hands, and managed to coax it back into mere disorder before she left the washroom and returned to the reading room.

The five fat volumes sat atop her desk. Within minutes, Julia was lost in the first, examining all the photographs on a page and then flipping it over. By four o'clock she had seen two more pictures of "the famous American hostess," once in company with Mr. Jeremy Reynolds and the other on the arm of Viscount Gregory. Heather was unchanged, but the young men, five years older, were visibly coarser and meatier, beginning to show double chins and jowls.

In the volume for 1937–38, Julia found a photograph of Heather standing beside a wheelchair. Strapped in the chair, incredibly shrunken and frail, was David Addison, one of the portly, pop-eyed older men who had customarily accompanied her; on the other side of the wheelchair stood Mr. Maxwell Davies, his earlier slender and dark handsomeness now softened and blurred by fat. Davies' face was opened in a thoughtless, greedy maw of a smile—it made Julia shudder. It seemed to her that she could smell his breath, taste the thin flavor of the man's mouth. Heather Rudge glinted, smiling a cool winner's smile, between the two ruined men.

There were no further pictures of Heather in that volume, and none in the next. Some of the young men, Lord Panton and Viscount Gregory and others, appeared at balls and dances, grown fatter, gross of face, with the ruddy look of once-athletic alcoholics. She closed this volume at five o'clock. The library closed at five thirty, and Julia debated whether or not it was worthwhile to leaf through the remaining two big volumes.

She decided to skim through them in the half hour left to her, and then to telephone David Swift again. Julia hefted the volume for 1939–40 and turned to the first number and began to flip through the issues more quickly than she had before. When she reached the issue for May 19 she glanced down at a page of Cambridge photographs and gasped aloud. A young Magnus Lofting, standing erect in a dinner jacket, beamed out at the world from the page; beside him stood Mr. Maxwell Davies. "Two Cambridge men discuss the Blues," read the caption and gave their names.

From that moment Julia burrowed into the last two volumes, looking for the picture she knew she would eventually find. Even isolated shots of Heather, or of Heather with her familiar retinue, did not long delay her; Julia flipped through, scanning the pages for one inevitable photograph.

The photograph appeared at the end of the 1939–40 volume, in an issue for February, 1940: the year before Olivia's birth, Julia remembered. "Wartime Spirits Kept High in Kensington," the article was headed. One of the pictures showed, unmistakably, a corner of the living room at 25 Ilchester Place. The wallpaper looked gaudy, and instead of the McClintocks' heavy furniture, graceful small chairs and lounges stood against the walls. Men of various ages seemed to fill the room, many of them in uniform. Heather, looking as young and sensual as she had in 1930, appeared in over half of the photographs. She danced with Lieutenant Frederick Mason and Captain Maxwell Davies, and was seen in ardent conversation with Colonel Nigel Ramsay; but the photograph at which Julia stared until the bell clamored throughout the reading room was on the second page of the set, and showed an elderly couple, wildly out of place at the party, smiling somewhat tremulously into the camera. They were identified as Lord and Lady Selhurst. Behind them, in one of the

corners of the room, twenty-one-year-old Magnus Lofting had his right arm about Heather Rudge's bare
shoulder.

She looked up as the African at her old seat was
rising from his chair and gave his ferocious countenance
a glance of such peculiarity that he dropped a sheaf of
paper. She thrust the volumes to the back of the desk
and stood up—only she and the African were in the
reading room, apart from the pretty librarian and the
last two or three stragglers already passing the guard.
Her heart seemed to blaze. Now she knew how to
answer Lily's question, *Why is it you?*

"Because," she thought, "Magnus is Olivia's father.
Because both of his children were stabbed to death. Because Olivia wants revenge. Because the patterns are
clear."

Light-headed, she left the library and entered a steady
gray falling of rain. Chains of black clouds printed the
dark sky. Julia absently searched her bag for her keys,
unlocked the car door, and bent in behind the wheel.
Her face felt chilly and slick with rain, and her hands
were cold, wet. These sensations, like the bitterness at
the base of her tongue, skidded off the reflective surface
of her mind; at that moment, if asked, she would have
hesitated before answering in what country she was. All
of the puzzle had finally been connected, it had clicked
into place, and the answer to Lily's question had been
found, as it must have been, in the past. Julia did not
need Magnus to confirm or deny her knowledge: she
knew that she was right. Magnus was Olivia's father;
he'd had a youthful affair with Heather Rudge and then
deserted her. It explained everything. And it clarified
Heather Rudge's conduct when Julia had met her at the
clinic. Now she knew why the old woman had thrice
asked her, *Is that your real name?* Julia leaned back in
the car seat and looked up at the black chain mail of
the sky, seeing each of the pieces fall into place. What
could make more sense than that Olivia Rudge would
seek to kill her deserting father's second wife, Olivia

being what she was? That she would make a deadly
rhyme of her own murder?

There was a place she had to go. One area of her
mind knew this with utter clarity, even while all the rest
still floated, stunned by Olivia's symmetries. Ordinarily
she would not have trusted herself to drive—she felt as
though she'd had half a bottle of whiskey—but there
was no other way of getting where she had to go. She
pulled the key over in its slot and heard the Rover's
engine kick into life. She slammed the car into gear and
shot forward across the parking lot. Rain blurred across
the windshield, and Julia flicked on the wipers at the
same moment as she turned out into the street. The map
in her head would lead her where she had to go, though
she did not know how to get there.

Olivia, Magnus.

Olivia, Magnus. She had known from the night of her
meeting with Mrs. Fludd, but only now did she see
how the connection worked, how she was a part of
Olivia's web as she was of Magnus'. Olivia could have
been Kate, she thought, and the Rover rocketed forward, just scraping past a yellow Volkswagen. She
meant, Olivia could have been her daughter. She and
Heather Rudge were interchangeable.

"*No,*" she said aloud, and swerved her car out into
the passing lane, stepping on the accelerator.

Sisterhood. They were sisters. Women of the same
man. Mothers of murdered daughters.

Julia brought the car to a squealing stop when she
finally saw the red light, and ignored the curious glances
from beneath umbrellas on the sidewalk. She sat, her
mouth slightly open and moistureless, behind the wheel,
looking upward, waiting for the light to change. Magnus
seemed more incalculable than ever, a sea of possibilities and surprises: she could never encompass him nor
dismiss him. The poison which was Olivia came from a
level deep within him, from some power stunted and
sent awry in his childhood. (Like Mark, said a disloyal
cell in her mind.)

Horns erupted behind her, and she threw the car into

gear and shot across the intersection. She knew where
she was going. The sky's darkness leaked down, staining
her hands on the wheel.

Had she hit a dog? She could not remember: indeed,
she could not remember most of the drive. There had
been a dog, in the vicinity of Golders Green and the
Finchley Road, a rust-colored dog bounding out into the
road; Julia had cramped the wheel immediately, in-
stinctively to the side, and had sent the Rover into the
side of a parked car, crumpling one of its doors; but she
thought that when the Rover had ground its way out of
the parked car, a second thudding sensation had come
from the left front tire. Speeding away, she had been
afraid to look in the mirror.

Now she stood beside her car in Upper Street, a
steady rain dripping into her hair, thinking about how
terrible it was to kill a dog. She could not look at the
Rover. Magnus' present to her (bought with her
money), it had been importantly clean and sleek, feline:
an exemplar. It was like Magnus to buy something for
her with her own money and then use it against her.
From the side of her eye she caught an impression of a
wrinkled rear end and a back bumper curled in like a
ram's horn. She hunched her shoulders against the rain.
Where was her coat? Not in the car. She had left it
slung over her chair in the periodical library. She hoped
that she had not hit the dog. It would leave no marks,
but still be dead.

Across the street the lights of the pub burned softly
red through the windows; glasses hung upside down,
bat-fashion, gleamed like Christmas, points and blurs of
red. Rain jumped in the street and ran in rivulets
toward the drain. The streetlamps produced a shining
streak along the pavement, a harsh acid yellow, a color
which eats the skin. Water caught in Julia's eyebrows
and lashes. She looked above the pub and saw no lights
in the windows.

She had to go up to the flat; she had to see.

There were no police, what did that mean, no police?

Julia moved across the street, forgetting to turn off the lights of her car or to remove the key, pausing to let half-seen cars splash by before her. She came up on the pavement before David Swift's door, and knocked twice. Then, her head and neck streaming with water, she found the bell and pushed it down.

When no one came, her insides seemed to freeze. What had happened to the police? Hadn't they understood her message? Julia pushed at the door. It held against her. Numbly, in baffled frustration, she turned her head and saw the Rover's headlights shining at her from across the street; she was pinned within them. They were all of the car she could see.

Frantic, she turned again to the door. Something Magnus had once described to her came back to her in miraculous detail: he'd been defending a housebreaker, and he had told her how the man had used a plastic card to slip the catches on locks. He had used her check card to demonstrate. She dug in her bag for her wallet and pulled the card out, spilling loose papers and bills into the bottom of her bag, and inserted the top edge of the card between the door and the jamb. She pushed it up and in. A hard sloping edge floated back; she heard a loud click. When she pushed at the door-knob, the peeling door swung in. She slipped inside, escaping the beams of her lights.

It was the dingy staircase where he had called to her, shouting. From the top she heard a muffled noise. Julia's heart clenched, and then released her, though fear poured through her like cold water, and she went up the filthy stairs. She had dreamed of doing this, though she could not remember when. Her fingers shook on the wood of the door at the top; muttering came from the other side, a meaningless series of syllables. She pressed her trembling fingers to the wood, and pushed the door gently in. Her fingers left small dark stains on the wood.

She was conscious of Olivia: that tense, webbed atmosphere of waiting tension. Olivia's air seemed to

fill the room. Her lion's smell. She was here, or had just
left. Julia saw the knife first. Wonderingly, she picked
it up from the floor, feeling her palm adhere to the handle. She remembered—as though it too were dreamed
—the penknife she had uncovered in the sand on her
first day in her house. Holding the knife, she could feel
sand in her palms, grinding at her skin. Olivia.

She whirled about, certain she had heard Olivia calling. But it had been a noise from the couch, the repetition of that whiffling noise she had heard on the staircase. As if truly in a dream, Julia walked smoothly
across the bare carpet to the couch and saw David Swift
lying on his back, his eyes open and his mouth working.
Broken syllables came from him. He was sleeping, Julia
thought, talking in his sleep.

As she looked, his head snapped to one side and his
chest seemed to bloom. A red slot opened up from his
breastbone to his belt, and redness spurted out, foam-
ing over his shirt. It was as though a flower had opened,
revealing a sudden configuration of great complexity
and intricacy. More blood flowed from beneath his chin
and sheeted across his neck. He stared up into Julia's
eyes and tried to speak. Blood filled his throat, and it
welled from his mouth, garbling his words.

"She . . ."

"She's just left," Julia finished for him. He had already lost an appalling amount of blood; Julia took up a
cloth from the little table and pressed it over the long
wound on the man's midriff. She must have seen it
wrong, she thought, her mind surprisingly calm; he had
been dying when she had come in. As Julia held the
useless cloth over the long wound, David Swift thrashed
on the couch and sent a wave of blood over her hand
and then fell back. Julia dropped the knife into the
sticky fluid beside the couch. She stood up, blinking.
Olivia had got here first and had killed him while he
slept. Her stink was in the room.

She washed hands at the sink, her back to the dead
Swift. When she was free of blood, she fled down the
stairs and left the street door ajar, so that a policeman

would look within. Through increasing rain she ran in
the beam of the Rover's headlights toward her car.
Laughter and music from the pub followed her.

The horror of what she had seen broke over her when
she sat again in the car, rain sliding down her collar
from her hair, and she shook back and forth, slamming
from the seat to the steering column, yanking and pushing back with her arms, her hands locked on the circle
of wood. She had been too late; even the police had
been powerless against Olivia. Julia slammed the
Rover's door and cowered within, shaking and freezing.
Her mind cleared long before she was able to control
her body. Images of America, of valleys and green distances, invaded her.

11

She drove through dark, rain-slicked streets, her window wipers thumping, on what she knew was the wrong
side of the road. She should have been on the right, because she was driving through the back reaches of a city
like Boston, which was familiar to her in a surrealist,
dreamlike fashion; yet all the other traffic was on the
left, and that too was dreamily familiar. Julia went with
it, driftingly, faintly pleased by her knowledge of this
strange city, and faintly annoyed that she could not get
her bearings properly. She saw a spot of blood on her
thumbnail, and in reflex wiped it on the seam of her
trousers.

Her turnoff, the access road to the expressway, lay
somewhere nearby; from there it was only a couple of
hours' drive to New Hampshire. She knew that because
she had never in her life been more than a couple of
hours' drive from her family's valley: Julia could visual-

ize all the roads, the highways and expressways and turnpikes and seal-coated county roads and gravelly tracks used by farmers, which formed a lacy web of connections between where she was and the valley. And she could visualize with a perfect wholeness the last turning before the valley, the sweep of the exit ramp from the freeway down through dark hills, a few mysterious lights shining in deep vales, far off the glow of a town. She could see every inch of that dark access to the valley, and she knew where the river was, though you couldn't see it. She wanted to see it now, before her.

She was driving through an American city, a city like Boston, bearing generally south. Nineteenth-century houses, built of red brick, now a grimy brown, stood on either side of narrow streets. Cold rain rattled on the top of the car.

Driving through an American city, driving through America. London was a furry patch in her memory, London did not exist. She was in Boston, and there was no London. Soon she would find the Berkshires, and that lovely long highway through banks of trees. Tanglewood. Julia pressed hard on the accelerator and her car slewed on wet Pentonville Road, fishtailing in its lane. Except for all these cars, it looked like the outer edges of Boston. She knew that people drove on the wrong side of the road here. It was habit with her by now. Why should that be? She pushed the question down.

She was of no age, she was going home, nothing had happened to her. Her father waited, dressed in an elegant dark gray suit; her grandfather had just died, and that was why she was going home from Smith. Boston was a mistake, she should not be in Boston; but she knew the way to go.

Now she was near the Fens, she thought. It would look much different, for everything had changed, and she had not been at Smith for years. She wheeled the car around a corner, blindly, her mind fluttering. A vision of a man's chest gouting fluid. . . . It meant nothing, though her feet had slipped on red blood. Nothing. Julia forced herself to smile at a young man striding across the road, walking on broad white stripes, and he returned the smile. He had an American face, round beneath floppy hair. Wet with rain. A slippery face, a face which left no traces.

The Rover jolted forward past the boy. Soon she would find the way, and then she would be sailing, with no mental effort at all, down the turnpike, leaving the city behind, moving toward the sloping bank of the exit, turning down between hills, passing small ghostly lights deep in a vale where the winding of the road shone under the trees.

At the same time, she knew where she was going, though her mind seemed to detach itself at times and go floating through Boston. As she drove down Marylebone Road, she noticed on the back of her left wrist another smear of blood, and hurriedly, disgustedly, wiped her wrist on the car seat.

But she could not rid herself of the feeling of being in Massachusetts until she had left her car parked outside a house in Notting Hill, rushed up the path in the rain, gone down six steps at the side of the house. Her mind seemed to be flying apart, a wispy cloth tugged by birds. She pounded at the bell. A basement, a valley. Breath caught and tore, chugging, in her throat. Her mouth open and cottony. Finally the door opened, and she rushed against the man who stood within, touching his wet face with her hands. He held her tightly while he struggled to remove his coat. Raindrops coursed down her face, and she butted against his chest, shaken by what she recognized as crying only after what seemed a long time of it.

Mark stood just within his door, letting her sob. His damp coat hung uncomfortably on his shoulders, and while he cradled Julia he shrugged first one arm out of its sleeve and then the other. He allowed the coat to fall squashily to the floor and hugged Julia tighter. She trembled against him like a trapped bird, her elbows and forearms whipping at his chest.

"Oh, thank God you're home," she finally uttered. "I

was so afraid I wouldn't find you and then I'd have to . . ." Her voice became too damaged and soft to continue.

"I just got home, just this minute," he said down into the wet hair on the crown of her head, plastered down on either side of a natural part. "Good Lord," he said, "I never thanked you for that money. I really shouldn't have taken it, but it came just when I was short, and—"

Julia's distorted face tilted back to look at him confusedly. She had obviously forgotten all about the check.

"Never mind," he quickly said, and hugged her to him again. "What's happened to you?"

She rested her cheek on his shoulder, and breathed heavily for a moment. "Everything's happened," she finally said. "She's going to kill me. I saw—I saw—" Julia stared at him with blurred eyes, her face looking directly into his without recording it.

"You saw?" Mark stroked her cheek, but she made no response.

"I thought I was in America all the way here. I thought I was driving through Boston. I was looking for the turnpike, so I could get to New Hampshire. I was going to my grandfather's place, in the valley. Isn't that funny?"

"You're under strain," Mark said.

"I'm going to be killed," she said again. "Nobody can stop her. I don't want to die. Can I stay with you tonight? You're all wet." She touched his face. "Why are you wet?"

"I was out," Mark said. "I was having a chat with Lily. About you." He smiled at Julia. "I got in just before you came crashing in. Come in."

He led her into his room and helped her to sit on a cushion and removed her shoes. Then he dried her feet with a towel and wiped her hands. He finished by dabbing at her face.

"You have another bruise."

"I fell down. In the street. She was playing with me then."

"And what's this on your wrist?" He stared at the thick dirty bandage under the cuff of her blouse.

"I cut myself. Not on purpose. It was after I saw her. I called you." Julia was looking straight before her, as if now that she had come to him, he could offer no further help. "She wanted me to be hit by a car. Like Mrs. Fludd. She doesn't care about murder. She likes it. She makes other people like it too."

"Hold on," he said, taking her hands and chafing them. Mark was squatting down before her, looking at her unfocused eyes. "Who's this 'she'? That girl you were talking about earlier? Olivia Rudge?"

Her eyes snapped into clarity. "I didn't tell you her name," she said, staring at him and beginning to snatch back her hands.

"Lily did," he said. "Just now."

"Lily doesn't believe me. She can't. It's because of Magnus."

"Don't worry about Lily. What about this girl?"

Julia watched in fascination as an ant crawled out of Mark's shirt and traversed one of the wings of his collar. The ant, small, red and very quick, sped down the collar and across his chest and fled again into the interior of Mark's shirt.

"She wants to murder you."

"Yes."

"She knows that you found out about that child, whoever it was, twenty years ago."

"Geoffrey Braden." Julia thought of the ant struggling through the hair on Mark's chest. She felt astonishingly light-headed.

"And now she wants to kill you."

"She's killed two other men, Paul Winter and David Swift. I just came from Swift's flat." Julia spoke in a level voice, looking straight at his shirt front. "May I lie down on your mattress?"

"You'd better," he said, and lifted her up and helped her across the room to the mattress. Sheets and blankets lay rumpled at its foot, and Mark pulled them up over her legs. Then he sat on the floor beside her, shoving clothing and plates to one side.

"I'm going to find you some sleeping pills," he said. "They'll help you relax, Julia."

"I don't need sleep," she said.

"You need to rest," Mark said. He lifted her head and pulled the grimy pillow across the mattress to place beneath it. Then he left her staring up at the ceiling and went to his kitchen for a vial of pills and a glass of water. "It's just Valium," he said.

"Take too many pills," Julia mumbled, but swallowed one anyhow. Then she focused her gaze on his eyes—he could see her pupils contract—and said, "I found out that Magnus is her father. That's why it's me. That's why she wanted me from the start."

"Just close your eyes, Julia," he said, "and we'll talk about it all in the morning. We have a lot to talk about. You'll see."

She obediently closed her eyes. "I washed my hands because I had blood on them." She turned her head toward Mark and opened her eyes to look at him. "I want you to protect me. Just tonight. Please."

Against his will, Mark was looking at the outline of Julia's thighs beneath her trousers. He noticed a smear of some dark, brownish substance along the seam of the wool, and felt everything with him leap as though touched by a live electrical wire.

"I think I might be sick," he heard Julia say. "I feel so funny. I don't want to die. I don't want to die, Mark."

After Mark had switched off the light, he threw off his clothes in the darkness, unsure of where to sleep. Julia lay unconscious and fully dressed across his mattress. He did not dare to move her—Julia's condition seemed dangerous to him, fully bearing out everything Lily had said. It was as though she could spin off into outright lunacy if she were as much as touched. And her suggestion about Magnus had upset him, reminding him again that she was his adoptive brother's wife, despite the events of the past week or two. Mark knew all too well that Magnus was stronger than he, and would not hesitate to beat him senseless if he suspected him of sleeping with Julia. Magnus had beaten him twice during his youth, and Mark shied away from the memory of these experiences. He pulled a patterned Indian rug, given him long ago by a girl whose name he could no longer remember, from the closet and arranged the stiff scratchy thing over his body as he lay back in a chair.

Magnus seemed to be everywhere, behind every rock and round every corner: Magnus' virility, according to Julia, had spawned Olivia Rudge, Julia's fantastic wraith. Though they were approximately the same height, Mark invariably thought of Magnus as much taller than he, twice as massive, twice as serious a presence. Was it really possible that Lily could control him? Her offer had been a neat instance of payment for services rendered, but it would be a valid offer only if Magnus agreed that his efforts to persuade Julia were worthy of recompense. Mark knew that Magnus considered him an incapable, nearly insignificant man, but he did not think that Magnus would cheat him. Certainly none of them could permit Julia to leave England.

Mark lay back in the chair, his head lolling and the blanket scratching his skin as if it were sandpaper. Julia still lay motionless beneath the sheet. Magnus and Lily were right about her needing a long rest, under supervision. All he had been doing was humoring her along any direction that seemed to lead away from Magnus, but perhaps it was now time to be more thoughtful. His academic career, in truth, was at its nadir; Mark could not imagine enduring much longer the boredom of teaching. His book was a phantasm, a dead thing which had lived only in illusion. Teaching was his only income, apart from the beggarly amount Greville Lofting had bequeathed him. There had been no nonsense about equal division of wealth in that old bastard's head. Not that, in comparison to Julia, he'd had much anyhow.

She groaned from the mattress, and muttered something.

He had expected his headache, which had descended on him when he was leaving Plane Tree House and had not left for four hours, to return with Julia's arrival, but he was surprisingly free of it. It was, he thought, because of her condition: a Julia so weak, so dependent, could not pull whatever trigger it was that launched his headache. (For in these past few days, it felt like that, as though a bullet, a red-hot foreign substance, had tumbled into his brain.)

He heard Julia's voice: "Mark?"

"Here," he grunted. "In the chair."

"Why aren't you with me?"

"I was thinking."

"Uh-huh," Julia offered, already half asleep again.

Had she used to talk in the night, half muttering, to Magnus? Wanting him to come to her bed? This thought stirred Mark, and he sat up in the chair and examined Julia's sprawl beneath his sheet. Her face was dug deep into the pillow, her hair bursting out around it. With her hair disarranged and uncombed, she looked far more like most of the other women whose heads had rested on that pillow.

She pronounced his name, very clearly, in her sleep.

Involuntarily, Mark suddenly imagined Magnus' heavy, serious body straddling hers, Magnus' belly pressing on Julia, Magnus opening her legs, Magnus' confidence taking her. She was his. Mark could see Magnus' arms circling her, her legs bent at his hips. His penis surged forward against the roughness of the cloth, and he threw the blanket off and crossed the room to climb onto the mattress beside Julia. A little later that night, after a quick struggle with buttons and elastic, he felt his mind traveling over enormous distances as he plunged atop his brother's wife. It was like making love on LSD, but even that had been a pedestrian experience beside this, for during all of the night remaining, hallucinations and visions lifted and inspired him: he was a gorgeously sexual bird, fertilizing the air. Innocence irradiated the air, canceling odors of sweat and old cooking.

In the morning Mark left the flat to shop for eggs, bacon and bread, and Julia, alone in the squalor of his room, began to weep. She felt abandoned and helpless, beached on a gray shore. Even Mark could not restore her to the ordinary human world or save her from the bleakness. She cried for a few minutes, and then arranged the sheets atop the mattress. They bore ridges of dirt and crusty stains, which Julia rather consciously overlooked. She was wondering if the police had discovered the body of David Swift; and if they had, if the papers would carry a story about the death. Swift was not a general's son. Someone had to be told what had happened. Mark had only pretended to believe her; and she had been too weary and shocked to fully explain the events of the night. She realized that she knew only one person she could telephone.

Lily picked up the receiver on the first ring, thinking that Magnus had discovered what had to be done to have his wife safely hospitalized.

"Yes," she said, and looked dartingly around the room at her Stubbs horse, her vases, the Persian screen. Julia's voice came to her, tired and faint, making each of her possessions seem locked in its place.

"Lily? Lily, I have to tell you some things. Listen to me."

"Where in the world are you?" Lily swiftly said. "Magnus and I tried to talk to you last night. You weren't at home."

"Well, now I am," Julia lied. "I was out last night."

"Do you think that's wise, darling? All of us feel that you should get as much rest as possible. I'd be happy to help you move some of your things over here, so you wouldn't be alone. . . ."

"It's too late for that, Lily," came Julia's faint voice.

"Darling, speak more directly into the mouthpiece."

"You must believe me, Lily. No one else will. I can't

talk to anyone else." She sounded far-off and desperate,
and Lily for a moment visualized her sailing off west-
ward, a figure in an airplane getting smaller and smaller
in the sky.

"You've been fretting again," she said. "Why don't
you come over and tell me about it?"

"Lily, Magnus is Olivia's father. I know it. He used
to meet Heather Rudge—in my house. There's a picture
of them together here. Taken less than a year before
Olivia's birth. He's Olivia's father, Lily. That's why she
picked me. I saw her kill someone last night. David
Swift. He knew her, and he talked too much, like Paul
Winter. She made someone kill them. I came in just
after, and he was dying. I'm next, Lily, there's no one
left but me. I'm next."

Lily scarcely heard the latter half of this announcement. When Julia had said that Magnus was the girl's
father, Lily had immediately felt that she was speaking
the truth. Rage at Magnus' deception and lies flashed
through her like an electrical explosion. She felt completely betrayed. "You're certain about Magnus," she
managed to say.

"I'm sure," came Julia's bruised voice. "That's why it
was me she wanted. It's the pattern."

"My God," said Lily, immediately seeing another
pattern. "Do you see what you are saying? Julia, if
what you are saying is true, there *is* a reason why you
were chosen by Olivia. Magnus . . ."

"Magnus and Kate," Julia whispered. "Magnus and
Olivia. The difference is that Olivia was evil. And she
can work in people's minds."

"Julia, this is important," said Lily, her mind spinning among possibilities.

"Look for that man's name in the newspapers," Julia
said, not listening to her. "Swift. He was one of her
gang. He told me about Geoffrey Braden's murder. She
had him killed. I saw his body—I saw his blood, all
over him."

"Ju—"

But Julia had hung up. Lily dialed her number and,

her mind still whirling, listened to the phone ringing in
Julia's house. "Pick it up," she urged, "pick it up, pick
it up." Eventually she depressed the button with a finger
and after hearing the dial tone again, tried Magnus'
number at Gayton Road.

"Lily," he said. "I can't just flick a switch, you know.
There are a couple of options. It'll all happen. I'll let
you know tonight."

"That's not what I rang you about," she said angrily.
"I want to ask you something, and I want you to tell me
the truth, Magnus."

"What now?" The boredom in his voice made her
furious.

"Were you the father of that wretched child? The
Rudge girl? I've just spoken to Julia, and she says she
has proof you were her father."

"Syntax, Lily," Magnus said. "Did you say proof?"
His voice came through with an amused incredulity that
was as good as a confession.

"She knows that you were—I think those were her
words. I want you to tell me the truth, Magnus."

He said, "I don't know the truth."

"Meaning?"

"I don't know if I was her father. I could have been.
So could two or three others. She bled us all for money. Perhaps the child was a committee effort. Some
weekends, one nearly had to punch a clock."

"You are a fool, Magnus. You could have told me
that a week ago, and perhaps done a deal of good. Now
I expect that you shall be lucky ever to see Julia again."

"Can't you do *anything* while I find out about the
paperwork? I can't do it all myself."

"You petulant fool," she snarled at him. "At the moment, I am going to see if I can find anything in the
morning papers about a fellow named Swift. Your wife
says she saw him killed."

"For God's sake, now you're going mad too."

"Good-bye." Lily delicately put the phone back in its
cradle and went to the couch, where the morning's
Times and *Daily Telegraph* had been folded over one

of the arms. She ripped the two papers off the couch and spread them on the carpet. She flipped through the *Times,* scanning the headlines on each page. When she had reached the sports news, she went through it backwards, making sure. No mention of a David Swift, no unexplained deaths at all.

With great relief, she turned to the *Daily Telegraph.* It was a hallucination of Julia's, another reason for locking her away. Nothing, of course, on the first page, and nothing on the second. Lily scanned the third page with a growing certainty that she had been rushed into a foolish panic; she would have to find a face-saving formula for apologizing to Magnus. A headline on the fifth page, two inches up from the bottom, put an end to these thoughts. KNIFE DEATH, it read.

The body of David Swift, 37, was discovered by police in his Islington flat during the early hours of Thursday morning. Police were investigating the open doorway to the flat when they found the body of Mr. Swift, who appeared to have died from multiple stab wounds. Witnesses located by Islington police say that an unidentified woman was seen leaving Mr. Swift's flat approximately one hour before discovery of the body.

Lily hastily read the short paragraph again, and then stood and dropped the paper to the floor. It was true: Julia had been seen running from that man's flat. Magnus was Olivia's father. The pattern she had seen while talking to Julia became clearer and clearer to her. Julia was unable to see it, and so had invented another pattern to suit the facts she could acknowledge. All along, Lily had dismissed Julia's stories because there had been no compelling reason for her to have been the object of a genuine manifestation. Now the reason seemed so obvious—so glaring—she could not think how she had failed to guess it. (But she shamefully knew how much her dismissal of Julia's story had to do with pride.) Blood rushed to her face. Lily walked to her window and looked down at the empty park. Rain leaked from a dark sky.

Now more than ever it was important to get Julia out of that house. Suppose Olivia Rudge were to appear there . . . Lily shuddered, and returned to the telephone. She was afraid, she recognized, for all of them. If Julia were right, none of them was safe. Suppose Rosa really *had* seen something, and had died for it? Lily groaned, and picked up the telephone to ring Mark.

Julia knew that Lily would call her back at the wrong number. Then what would she do? Look in the paper, she hoped. Surely a man could not meet a violent death in London and not have a paragraph written about him. Someone has to believe me, Julia thought, and now there's only Lily. Mark's attitude, whenever he wasn't in bed, was distant, doctorly, calming; she had seen that he hadn't believed her, and had been surprised that, even in shock as she had been, she was not more wounded by his disbelief. It was confirmation of her isolation: what was Olivia's atmosphere if not that? The atmosphere of the rooftop dream.

She sat on the edge of the mattress, her mind vague, uncertain of what to do. Eggs and bacon had been Mark's idea. For Julia, the thought of food was almost anthropological in its remoteness. What she wanted, though her vagina throbbed, was to cling to Mark again, to put her arms about him and nest beside him without thought, in a deep blankness.

She allowed her eyes to rove over his incredible flat. The floor was crowded with articles of clothing and plates and cloudy milk bottles. Books were heaped in odd places. Underlying the general odor of Gaulois cigarettes was an odd grainy smell like that of an uncleaned birdcage.

She unsteadily stood up, having decided to do something about the floor. When she bent to pick up several plates stacked together, blood pounded into her head and she saw moving blots of red and black, and sat heavily on the mattress again until her vision cleared.

The room seemed to wobble about her. She touched the plates. Brown stuff had hardened on the top surface, and glued all the plates into a single unit. Julia held them in her lap until the room ceased to vibrate and then carried them into the kitchen. The sink was already jammed with china and glasses submerged in cold greasy water, so Julia set the plates on top of the little fridge and returned to the other room to pick up more things. When she came back to the kitchen with two glasses and two milk bottles, she found two dozen webby milk bottles ranked on a ledge behind the sink. Complex green spidery growths and furry tendrils linked the bottles. Julia rattled them backward and squeezed in her two bottles.

The telephone shrilled from the other room and Julia hesitated before she left the kitchen to stand over it. Perhaps Lily had guessed where she was: did she care to hide it any longer? Indifferent, she lifted the telephone. A rich breathy female voice floated into her ear. "Mark, what *have* you been up to lately? Annis said you were positively rude to her, and garbled something about meditation; well, *we* think you've got some Great Love taking up all your time, it's just not like you, why don't we all meet sometime at the Rising Sun to—"

"He's not home," Julia said and hung up on a whoop of startled laughter which caused her to drop the telephone. When it hit the floor, the plastic base cracked apart like the shell of a snail.

Julia wandered across the room to Mark's desk. She sat in his chair and pulled the drapes to one side. Rain fell into the gray well before the window, flattening the few spears of grass which had struggled up through the concrete. A wedge of gray sky hung in the upper corner of the window, seeming out of perspective, crazily tilted. Julia touched Mark's typewriter and then licked the dust off her finger. She could not make sense of the telephone call. Now, behind her, the broken phone began to buzz periodically like an angry bee. Great Love? Annis? Was that a girl's name? Julia could not make her mind understand the words of the girl on the telephone.

She felt as though she had been jeered at, made fun of,
by the whoop of laughter. Even that had been in a
Knightsbridge accent. She put her head down on the
cool keys of the typewriter.

His desk, his books, his papers. He was working on
something. She felt intense gratitude for his working, for
his being part of that comfortable line of men who did
things, who made bridges and books and decisions. She
caressed the stack of paper beside the typewriter. Mark.
His name seemed to heat in her chest. He could not be
blamed for his inability to accept her mad story. Later
in the day she could show him a newspaper and prove
that she had not invented the death of David Swift.

The afternoon seemed an impossible distance away;
even thinking seemed to require an unreasonable
amount of effort. She was sure that the breathy woman
on the telephone had laughed at her. Again, she thought
of leaving for America.

She rolled down onto the mattress, hoping that Mark
would soon return. The door of a wardrobe gaped open
beside the mattress, and Julia idly looked at Mark's few
clothes hanging on wire hangers. He seemed to possess
only one necktie, nearly six inches wide, silvery in color,
with a sunburst painted on it in orange. Julia thought
of Magnus' neat rows of striped ties, hundreds of them,
and managed to smile. Mark owned a green tweed suit
which clearly derived from the late fifties and looked as
though it had not been worn since then. Magnus had
seemed not to care for clothes, but he had owned a lot
of them. He had, for instance, owned seven pairs of
shoes, all exactly alike and made by the same bootmaker
on Cork Street who had made his father's shoes. Mark
appeared to own only boots, no shoes at all. Black and
brown boots, one pair of each, with zips up the side.
One pair of sandals. Something brown and partially
hidden by a bag at the back of the wardrobe caught her
eye, and she looked closely at it. The particular woody
shade of brown was familiar, and even as she registered
its familiarity, she felt the beginnings of alarm, as if a
bell had begun to ring.

She reached from the edge of the mattress into the closet and twitched the bag aside with her fingers. She was looking at the backs of a pair of shoes with chunky low heels and a benchmark stamped discreetly into the leather just at the bottom of the back seam. It was a small letter *D,* and stood for David Day, who had made the shoes. She had purchased them four years ago, and even now she could remember how much they cost. They were the shoes she had lost climbing in her window on her first night in Ilchester Place.

Julia stared at the backs of the shoes for a moment, panting slightly, her mind unable to reckon with what she was seeing. She reached into the wardrobe as though it contained a rattlesnake and extracted the shoes. Their uppers were waterstained and scruffy from their two days outdoors. It was Mark, not Magnus, who had taken them.

"Wait," she told herself, touching the brown shoes. Her heart had begun to thrum. She looked at her right wrist where she wore the little green bracelet Mark had given her. Something taken, something given, Mrs. Fludd had said. Julia tugged off the bracelet and dropped it onto the dirty sheet. Mark had appeared in Olivia's wake several times; sympathetic magic, she had once thought it was. But he had appeared every time, every time.

Could he have just found her shoes? Then why would he hide them in the wardrobe?

Receptive, Mrs. Fludd had said. *He wants to be filled, like a bottle.*

Julia became aware she was making a noise in her throat, but found she could not control or stop it. Her heart seemed to thunder, banging her rib cage like a noisy drum. She plucked at her bandage and tore it off her wrist. She could feel herself breaking, as though she were a thin bone. The long wound on her wrist pouted, a ragged weal along the skin, and she tore it apart with the fingers of her right hand, separating the lips of the wound. A bright surprising ribbon of blood appeared in the gash.

He'll know, her mind said. She tore at the wound
and the ribbon of blood bannered out across her hand
and onto Mark's bed. She rubbed the shoes in her blood
and left them on the bed. Her arm began to throb. She
realized that the noise in her throat had subsided to a
choked gurging noise, half a snarl. She printed the mark
of her wound on Mark's sheets.

When she stood from the mess she had made, she
wound the bandage around her wrist again, ignoring the
fresh stains on her trousers, and then ran toward the
door. She had to get out before Mark's return. Her
vagina throbbed in the same rhythm as her wrist.
Wounds. She gasped, realizing that five minutes before,
she'd been thinking about safety. There was no safety,
only its illusion.

Julia opened the door and looked fearfully up the
steps, as if she expected to see Mark Berkeley smiling
down at her. Rain filtered gauzily down onto her face.
Julia went up the six steps to the street. Within seconds,
the thin material of her blouse had adhered coldly to
her skin. She ran down the block, pursued by Olivia's
taunting smile and the thought of Mark. Only one
escape, only one safety, existed. Kate was there before
her. In her haste and fright, she forgot the Rover until
she had reached the end of the block.

Her house seemed as hot as Ecuador. Julia slammed
the front door and bolted it, knowing that Hazel Mullineaux had seen her come limping up from the sidewalk, her hair streaming and her clothing soaked. Her
neighbor had been standing at the side door of her
home, her face white and gleaming beneath the cover
of a wide black umbrella. She had looked like an ad-
vertisement for skin cream. Breathing hard, Julia waited
behind the door for what she knew would happen. Before thirty seconds were out, the bell rang down the
hall. "Go away," Julia whispered.

Hazel Mullineaux knocked on the door, then rang the
bell again.

"I'm all right," Julia said, a little louder.

After knocking again, Hazel Mullineaux bent to lift the flap of the mail slot and called, "Mrs. Lofting? Do you need any help?"

"Go away," Julia said. "I don't need your help."

"Oh!" Julia could tell that Hazel was kneeling outside the door. She probably looks adorable doing that, Julia thought.

"I thought you looked . . . well, upset," came the low voice through the slot.

"Leave me alone," Julia said. "Get away from my house."

"I don't mean to intrude."

"I'm glad to hear it. Please go." Julia remained leaning against the door until she heard her neighbor's footsteps go reluctantly down to the pavement. Then she went into the dark living room and yanked the cord of the telephone out of the wall. Holding the severed telephone in her hands, Julia noticed that the weeks of abnormal heat had effected some chemical change in the walls of the house, for the wallpaper had buckled in places; one strip curled down from the ceiling like a dog's tongue. The whole room seemed to have aged during the weeks of heat, to have become wrinkled and shabby. The McClintocks' furniture had lost its solid fat Victorian look, and now appeared to be peeling, like sunburned skin. The glue had cracked in one of the dining room chairs. The carpet lapped up at one end of the room.

Julia dropped the useless telephone to the floor. Her wounded wrist, the muscles in her calves, and her vagina all ached. The flesh on her face felt as though it were blubber, puffing out from the bones. She could trust no one.

Upstairs, she sat on the edge of her bed, waiting. The house hung emptily about her. No one could telephone now, and she would not answer the door. The others knew what they needed to know. It was Mark or Magnus, one of them. One of them had been used by Olivia Rudge, and Mrs. Fludd had seen it weeks before.

She had been tricked by Mark. It was Mark. It could be Mark.

Julia got up and moved to her desk and pulled a sheet of paper and a pencil from a drawer. Someone would have to know, or Olivia would never be stopped, she would keep on filling people's minds, using them, going from one to another like a disease.

If I am found dead, she wrote rapidly, *it will be no accident. If I am found dead in this room or anywhere else, whatever the cause of death may appear to be, I shall have been murdered. The murderer will be either my husband or his brother, Mark Berkeley. One of these two is planning to kill me. This same person will have been the cause of the death of Rosa Fludd, and will probably have killed Captain Paul Winter and David Swift. (But maybe not.) This is because—This has to do with a dead child named Olivia Rudge, who died in the same way as my own child. My husband Magnus was also the father of Olivia Rudge. Look her up in the newspapers for the year 1950. But leaving the supernatural aside—since it may prejudice the opinion of whoever reads this, I beg you to know that I am not suicidal, and that my death will in no way be an accident. PLEASE KNOW THIS.*

Without rereading what she was written, Julia folded the paper and inserted it into the pages of her address book, and then slid the book between two sweaters in a drawer. Then she lay down on her bed and stared up into the heat and watched paterns move across the surface of the ceiling. She waited. Gleeful noises seemed to well up from other parts of the house. Hot air and a feral stink blew about her. Eventually she swallowed three of her sleeping pills.

12

Once, everything had been different. There had been
a pretty, rather placid young woman named Julia Lofting, who had lived in North London with her successful
husband and their beautiful daughter, and all three of
them had unthinkingly led happy, contented lives, each
devoted to the unity they made, each devoted to the
other . . . once there had been a girl with a great deal
of money named Julia Freeman, and she had married
an older man, an Englishman named Magnus Lofting,
and lived with him in London, tolerating his infidelities
and his angers for the sake of their daughter (her
daughter) . . . once a confused, uncertain American
woman named Julia lived in a house with her daughter,
seeing her husband late in the evenings when he came
home from one of his drinking clubs . . . there had once
been a beautiful and imaginative child named Kate
Lofting . . . but she was dead . . . once there had been
a couple, Magnus and Julia, with a nice house but not
as nice a house as they could afford because they (she)
hated extravagance, and with two cars and one daughter, and they'd had few friends outside the family because many people did not like Magnus and because
Julia was a bit shy and their daughter was all they
needed, really . . . once an American girl had thrown
herself at a man named Magnus and made a daughter
with him, she used her money to make him sleep with
her (marry her) . . . once there had been a girl everybody liked. Julia looked up at the cracked ceiling of
her bedroom, thinking of the girl she had been, her
father's darling (her hair was her best feature). She
waited. Her best and truest self was in the past which
had sent her Olivia Rudge. Whose father she had mar-

ried. She was too tired to move from her bed, and her mind spun from version to version.

From downstairs came the noise of a rampage—she could hear glass breaking, a series of popping, hollow explosions, and ripping noises, fabric being torn. The noises had started in the kitchen and then moved into the dining room. It sounded now like chairs being thrown up against the wall. I wanted to set you free, Julia thought, meaning that I wanted to send you away in peace. But you don't want peace. You want control. You hate all of us, and you hate this house. I did set you free, but in the wrong way. Wood splintered somewhere in the house, and this sharp sound was immediately followed by another series of popping explosions. The cups in the dining room. Then the broader, flatter sound of the china plates being broken. A bottle of some kind smashed against a wall? Wine? Whiskey? Julia, half in a daze, sniffed at the air but caught only a faint odor of excrement.

"It's settled."

"In what way?"

"We need a certificate signed by her physician and one other. Two doctors at the hospital, Dr. Whatever and another one, will agree to sign it. Then she goes in for a period of examination. It's a temporary order, but it gives me time to look into ways of keeping her there out of trouble. Does that satisfy you?"

"I don't know what would satisfy me now."

"Lily, don't go soft on me. This was really your idea, you know."

"My idea for your good, brother."

"For ours. And hers."

"Chiefly yours."

Magnus looked across the room to where Lily sat on her delicate little couch beside the Persian screen. She was staring at him oddly. Her eyes seem slightly larger than usual, and the hazel irises appeared to swim in the surrounding white. Lily's whole face was pale. "For God's sake, Lily," he said, "are you still angry with me about that wretched child? You're making it all up, you know, I did not lie to you. I never did see the child. Anyone could have been her father."

"Anyone wasn't."

"It's a trifle late for a blood test, Lily."

"I wish you weren't so obtuse at times."

He looked at her in complete puzzlement. "Lily, let me explain our position. Julia can be put into the hospital as soon as I have the doctors' signatures. That should be no later than Tuesday. I have control over all monies, whether held jointly or separately, in case of Julia's hospitalization or death. I mention the latter only as the extreme case. The legal point in question is mental incapacity—which shall be proven by the doctors' authorization of our request that she be involuntarily hospitalized. It is very simple."

"Try to ring her," Lily ordered. "Right now."

"What? Do you want to bring her here? There's really no need for that now, since the doctors—"

"Try to ring her."

"Lily, what in the world is going on?"

"I'm terrified, you idiot," she said. "She has been telling us the truth all along, and I was too stupid and vain to recognize it. She is in mortal danger."

"What in the world . . ." Magnus stared at her in disbelief. "Are you telling me that you believe in that cod's wallop now? Didn't you just assure me, two days ago, that it was all fantasy? Didn't you say that?"

"Yes," she admitted. "But I was wrong. We have to try to save her life. Please ring her, Magnus. I want to know that she is still safe."

Magnus reluctantly lifted himself heavily from his chair and padded across the room to the telephone. He dialed Julia's number and listened silently for some time. "No answer," he said. "What's this all about, Lily?"

"Revenge," she answered. "Olivia Rudge's revenge."

That was it, Julia thought, listening to the savage noises from downstairs. It was revenge. She hated being thwarted, and Heather had cut off her career: so Heather was part of her revenge, Mrs. Braden immured in her bedroom was part of her revenge, and all of her gang had shared in it too, seeing their lives disintegrate or grind to powder, nothing accomplished except by the severest penance.

She had been meant to buy the house. Olivia had reached out and found her, the only woman who could release her into the world again.

If only Kate had not tried to swallow that piece of meat . . . if only she and Magnus had waited longer for the ambulance. Julia seemed not to be lying on her bed, but to be suspended above a thrashing seacoast, sharp upthrust rocks and seething water. Her skin was boiling, as with fever. She imagined holding Kate in her arms. But Kate was in that small deep hole, in that small box in the deep, deep hole. In wretched Hampstead cemetery. She wanted to carry Kate away from here. To float with her, far above the sea and the rocks.

Then she saw Kate with her back turned to her. It was what she had seen before Mrs. Fludd stopped the séance. *I am responsible,* she thought, without knowing what she meant.

A black bird zipped past Mark's head and muttered some message to him, as it would to another bird. It was a single word. *Brief,* perhaps, or *free.* Or *be.* He watched the bird whirl off into the glowing area above the tops of the trees, where the sky was unnaturally pink. The cottony undersides of the thick clouds, which had just ceased to release their drizzle of rain, seemed to reveal some incandescent color laid across their upper surfaces. They looked as though they had been painted by Turner, and Mark, thinking this, was moved to the edge of tears. His scalp tingled. Birds spoke to him, he walked beneath Turner clouds. Since completing his last meditation, he had felt almost unbearably, uncomfortably happy—he had reached ecstasy. Colors of the grass and trees boomed out at him, as if they

were shouted through loud-speakers: so many different
greens! He felt that he had never truly seen any of these
shades before, how they rippled next to each other,
jumped forward or receded in space. Color was a stu-
pendous bounty.

Julia had bled on his sheets. That too seemed a sign
of grace. Blood after making love. He felt as though
Julia were his other half, as though they shared the
same limbs, or the same heart. She had dug the shoes
out of his closet, knowing in what love he had spirited
them away from her garden after finding them one
morning. He'd had to look at her house, he'd walked
all round it, passing his hands over the rough brick, almost swooning. Even his headache had not diminished
his joy. Julia had left Magnus, and she would be his.

She was his. He moved dazedly through Holland
Park, nearly alone on the paths, chiming with this
knowledge. He had flown deep into her; he knew her
bones and joints. Julia was light and vision. And a
creature of blood, a furnace of it. *Be,* the bird had said
to him. Traveling toward Julia, he was traveling toward
blessedness. A pure greedy joy smashed drunkenly at
him. Queenly, she was waiting. *Be.* He staggered under
the impact of it.

A girl walking slowly in front of him lowered her
umbrella with a motion of such grace that he nearly
sobbed aloud. He recognized the back of her head and
neck, where black hair fell down over a brown leather
jacket. Mark quickly crossed the ground between himself and the girl and linked his arm into hers, laughing.
When she twisted toward him, startled and a little frightened, he kissed her familiar mouth and felt his soul ex-
panding with a scream of happiness.

"I can't believe this," Magnus said, still holding the
telephone. "I tried to persuade you that there might be
something to Julia's story, recall that? And you were
certain that it was all a delusion. You convinced me. I
cannot be convinced back again, Lily." He set the

receiver back in its cradle, very gently, a sign Lily knew quite well: he was rapidly reaching the demarcation between annoyance and outright irritation.

"Perhaps not," she said. "It makes little difference whether or not you are persuaded. But do think back, Magnus—what did you see on that day you thought you saw Kate?"

"How can I answer that? I don't know what I saw. The reflection of a cloud, a flash of sun on the window. . . ."

"No. I mean, what did you think you saw?"

He looked at her in disgust. "I am not going to be made a fool of, Lily."

"Tell me. Just tell me what you saw."

'Kate. Standing in the window of Julia's bedroom."

"How do you know it was Kate? Was she facing you?"

"She needn't to. In fact, the girl I thought I saw was facing the other way, and I saw only the back of her head."

"It might not have been Kate! It might have been the other one!" Lily half-started from her chair. "Magnus, that's it. You saw Olivia Rudge. She wanted you to see her, and to think that she was Kate. She wanted to hurt and confuse you."

"Lily," Magnus said slowly, "I have never interfered with your enthusiasms, and I have never jeered at them. But if you are telling me that I saw an apparition in that window—"

"What did you feel when you went into her house that day? Didn't you tell me that you were terrified?"

"I was spooked. You told me that yourself. I was also drunk."

"No, Magnus. You felt her. You felt her evil. She hates you too."

"My God," Magnus said. "This is a nest of ninnies. What reasoning is behind all of this? Why should this little demon out of the past suddenly appear again?"

"Because of Julia," she said. "She needed Julia to

free her. Both of your daughters were stabbed to death
by their mothers. Julia was what she needed."

First I gave birth to Kate, Julia thought, and then I
gave birth to Olivia. But part of Olivia is still in me. I
complete her. The sleeping pills and lack of food made
her mind swim about a general focus, which was her
awareness of the noises from the ground floor. Things
were still being smashed. The suffocating heat that dried
her throat and burned her eyes seemed to carry her
some inches above her bed and leave her floating above
a vast, undefined space into which she could be spilled
at any moment. Julia knew that this was due to a warp,
a wrinkle in her mind that was a part of Olivia. She
wished to read, to bring herself back into gravity, but
she was too weak to pick up any of the books on the
bedside table. A wind seemed to blow through the
house, hot and African. The glass across one of
the McClintocks' paintings shattered, accompanied by
screams of laughter. Then she heard the thunking noise
of the painting's being kicked in.

Maybe all this is just in my head, she thought. *Would
that make it less true?* Indeed, everything in the world
seemed crowded into her head. The smell of beasts and
burned skin settled about her.

"A rape, Mark? Not in your style, I should have
thought." Annis stood before him, breathing a little
heavily, her face flushed. He could see the place on her
full lower lip where he'd bitten it. "I thought I was
being sent away, anyhow," she said.

"Lovely, sweet Annis," Mark said, holding her again,
"darling, lovely, gorgeous, sexy Annis, how could I
send you away?" He laughed at both her absurdity and
his own, bubbling up within him.

"Is meditation responsible for these moods? I think
I'd advise a little rest. Are you up on something?"

"On you, Annis, on you," he chanted, and swung her
around.

She pushed at his arms. "Mark, put me down. Mark, I don't like this."

He whooped with laughter, seeing himself from both within and without, and nearly fell down. "Are you going somewhere? Let's go to a pub. Let's go to a pub and hold hands. I was just noticing how the sky looks like a Turner. Don't you think?"

She looked at the sky half with genuine interest, half with bemusement. "It looks like a slate roof, if you want my opinion. You know, you don't have to act like this with me. I'm perfectly willing to start seeing you again. But I thought you had some new interest in your life."

"On the contrary, dear Annis, I am shedding some of the old interests. I decided to quit teaching. I'm just going to travel for a while. Travel with me, Annis. You'd look lovely on a boat." He began to laugh uncontrollably, and fell onto a bench. Annis and Julia shared one substance, and Mark giddily witnessed Julia's features shining through the other's face. When she turned away from him in irritation, he caught her wrist and pulled her down beside him. "I'm serious, let's have a drink and talk about it." He looked into her wide, beautiful, hungry face and felt himself turn on all the voltage he possessed. Annis' face broke over him like a wave.

"Well," she said. "I'm going somewhere now. How about lunch at one?"

"Lunch at one, what fun," he sang. "Only an hour away." Joy seemed to smash at his ribs again, and he gripped her hand. "Name two places you want to go to, Annis."

"Well, I've never seen California," she said. "I can't think of any other place I'd like to go."

"Europe?"

"Europe is boring. I'd settle for California."

"You'll have it."

"Doesn't it take a lot of money to get there?"

"Doesn't everything come through meditation? Lord Buddha provides, Annis, Lord Buddha provides."

"We're going to have everything," Magnus said, having by now passed firmly into outright anger, "we're going to have the lot, and you decide to get mysterious and orphic. Aren't we going to have everything you wanted? I have a mad wife who's going to be locked away for God knows how long, but you'll have the bleeding lot, Lily. What do you think you're trying to do to me?"

"Self-pity isn't your most attractive trait," she said. "What I think I am trying to do, as you put it, is to tell the truth at last. Look, Magnus. Suppose that Julia came to you with some idea about a point of law that you'd been thinking about for months? Suppose she said something about it at breakfast?"

"Bugger the analogies," he said, even angrier, and causing her more fear than she knew she could afford to reveal.

"I'll tell you what you'd do. You'd ignore her, and resent her incursion on your special territory. That's the way I felt."

"The law is not a ridiculous bundle of lies and fantasies!" he shouted.

She merely looked at him, not daring to speak further.

When he turned away and slammed his fist into the counter top, she waited for him to settle down again —she could see his shoulders sinking back to their normal level, and his neck lose its swelling, as if it were shedding layers of tissue—she said, "Try to ring her again. I am afraid for her, Magnus."

"Damn you," he said, but said it quietly.

She said to his back, "Someone killed those two men. Julia knew about it before they were in the papers."

"Are you sure? She's no fortune-teller."

Lily thought back to her last conversation with Julia. "I *think* so. She told me about the second one, certainly. The Swift man. She was in his flat."

"Then I'm glad he's dead."

"She was there to warm him about Olivia Rudge—I think that's what she said. Or I may have gathered it."

"That's two things you're vague on. You're not terribly persuasive."

"And Mrs. Fludd was killed because she saw Olivia."

"Nonsense. Wait. Did you imply that Julia was in the Swift man's flat when he was killed?"

"That's what she told me."

"She told you that she saw him—what? Die? Be killed? What did she say?"

"I can't remember. She said that she was there."

"*Damn,*" Magnus said loudly. "Didn't she inform the police?"

"I shouldn't imagine that she thought they had much chance against a ghost."

"Ghosts don't murder people," Magnus said and went quickly back to the telephone. After dialing and listening intently, his lips working in and out, he said, "Still no answer."

"Then she has either drugged herself to sleep or she's gone out," Lily said. "We must do something quickly, Magnus. Olivia is after her. I know it. She's already tried to kill her once."

"I wonder if Julia is actually madder than you. You should both be put away." He considered a second, containing his anger, and said, "Think about this, Lily. If Julia was right, then aren't we all endangered? You and I as well as Julia? After all, we know about Olivia too."

"We're all touched by it, we're all soiled," she answered him. "Mark too, I should imagine. We may be in as much danger as she is."

"Rubbish."

"Remember how you felt inside that house," she said. "She hates you too, Magnus. She's enjoyed torturing you."

Julia was carrying Kate, a bundle no heavier than an armful of leaves and twigs, to the hospital. Kate was injured, and it was urgent that Julia find the hospital immediately: she could feel some warm fluid soaking into the sleeves of her blouse. Down grimy, vacant streets she was wandering, looking up at barred doorways for the name of the hospital. It was her fault that she could not find the hospital, that instead she was trudging through these gritty hopeless streets, looking exhaustedly into one filthy sunless court after another, dirty cobblestones . . . she had failed, and she knew that Kate had already died, that the merest breeze would lift away the feather of her body. Soon she would be on the bare rooftop, surrounded by failure and loss, carrying them within her. She saw herself turning the knife from Kate's body and turning it toward herself.

Footsteps ran through the house, raising the smells of heat and lions.

She wandered through these hopeless streets, looking for the hospital that could undo what already had been done.

"Where are you going?" She watched tensely as he rushed around her flat, gathering up his raincoat and umbrella.

"I have to get out of this room," he said as calmly as he could. "Before I deliberately break something, I am going to take a short walk. *You* ring her."

"Will you be back? Magnus, please. . . ."

"I'll be back," he said harshly, almost barking the final word. As she watched, half-cowering by the door to the kitchen, he turned away from her and thundered across the floor like a bison. When he left he banged the door with such force that he split a section of the jamb.

Julia moved fractionally toward consciousness, her heart thudding, aware that the hand she had turned toward herself had not been Magnus'. It was a woman's hand, like hers. It was hers. Her mouth flooded with pain and a residue like tar, and she realized moments later that she had bitten halfway through her tongue. She had recognized her hand from the dream. She swallowed a trickle of blood, not really feeling the pain for longer than the time that lay between the vision of the woman's hand with the steak knife in its fingers and the recognition that it was hers. Instead of pain, there was a drumming sensation through her tongue. Her entire body seemed as dry as a cracked riverbed. Kate's twig-light, leaf-light body lifted out of her arms. Her lips went numb.

In the next instant she had fled back into the condition of the drugs, and was walking up filthy stairs to the bleak rooftop. She knew every discoloration and stain on the walls, every warp of the stairs.

Mark lay sprawled on wet grass, feeling the ground damply claim his shoulders and buttocks. He was dimly aware of the burnished tips of his new boots, gleaming a dark rich brownish gold all the way down the length of his body. His head was filled with birds. That he had just met and spoken to someone appeared miraculous to him, an unbelievable effort of coherence and will.

But I've seen her too, thought Lily, still facing the door and listening to Magnus go noisily down the stairs. It was the day I saw Rosa Fludd sitting on the park bench. She led me across the park. Was Rosa really there, or did she conjure her? She wanted me to see Magnus breaking into Julia's house. She wanted me to feel that sick disappointment. Perhaps Rosa came to me as a warning. She had warned Julia, and that day she was warning me. Lily sagged against the counter, felt the metal strip along the top of the wood dig into her hip.

Mark was moving at the center of a golden, glowing haze, a bowl which had settled down over him as he lay on the wet grass. He knew that this humming golden aura was the outward form of his headache, given him by his most successful meditations, and that it was transformingly beautiful proved the rarity, the absolute value of his mind. It proved also the absolute value of his exercises, even of the headaches, since they had transported him bodily into euphoria. Into paradise.

The trees past which he moved burned at him, the bark blistering in his vision and the leaves rattling like gold. He had felt like this before, but he could not remember when. His boots made the path shiver. If he hit hard enough with his heels, he could open a crack all the way to the planet's red, seething core.

Asleep now, Julia reached the opening to the roof and walked out onto baking tar paper that adhered tackily to the soles of her shoes. The sky into which she moved was a flat field of gray striped with vibrating, humming pink. The strange union of colors gripped the pit of her stomach and made her bowels full and watery. Her mouth drummed, lined with a bitter substance like tobacco juice. A pine needle pierced her tongue. She wanted Kate, but Kate was dead. Olivia raged beneath her in the empty house screeching with laughter. Even up on the flat roof, hopelessness pouring into her like salt, she could hear the noise from downstairs: hoarse screams, shouts, loud breakage. It no longer made any difference. She was watching herself as in a mirror. Her skin burned in anticipatory shame.

Lily pushed herself away from the counter and went unsteadily into the living room. She knelt before the telephone and with a shaking hand dialed Julia's number. Now instead of the ringing she expected, she heard only the bottomless space, filled with the echoes of static, which precedes the dial tone. She punched the button and the gray depthless space hung in the receiver. When she struck the button again, the depthless sound mercifully gave way to the dial tone. She tried Julia's number again, and heard the digits slot into connection; then a sound like that of a man falling through deep space, spinning away from life.

Lily banged the receiver down, waited until she felt safe enough to lift it again, made sure of the reassuring, chunky dial tone, and then dialed 100. She gave the operator Julia's number and waited.

"I'm sorry," the operator's twanging voice came back a minute later. "That number appears to be temporarily out of service."

"Why?" asked Lily. "What do you mean, out of service?"

"We are not permitted to offer that information," the operator disdainfully said. "You may speak to the supervisor."

"Yes."

"Hold, please."

Lily licked her lips and waited again. The silence in the telephone was furry and dense, more solid than the other. She listened to it for what seemed entire minutes before she could bear the waiting no more and hung up. Then she paced nervously in her living room, waiting for Magnus to return. She would not go to Ilchester Place alone.

Something flew along the upstairs hall, something infinitely despairing.

Slowly, with merciful intent, the knife in her hand slid into Kate's blocked throat. Her hand, the hand she had dreamed of turning toward herself, gripped the sleek little knife between thumb and finger, blade up. Kate uttered a half-conscious, choking noise and opened her eyes at the instant Julia began to carve into her throat. Kate's eyes were clouds. As in a mirror, the scene glinted at her from where it was happening at the flat edge of the roof, two figures bent together in a clumsy parody of love. She heard the door to her room bang open, and the hot wind gusted about her, making the scene before her and the pink-striped sky mist over, like a mirror. The one who wanted her was with her, and she whirled about on the roof and saw only desolation, dirty tar paper and a ruined sky. A white column of air blew toward her. She could see dust and scraps of paper whirl about inside it, spinning crazily. From somewhere below in the streets or from another side of the bedroom came a chortling sound she knew was the suppressed laughter of a small dark-skinned child whose name she could not remember. Strong arms braced her, and Olivia's smoldering odor invaded her nostrils and the white column of air whirled her into it, caught up with dust and scraps of old newspapers, dust and paper.

November

"You said you'd heard from Mark at last."

"Yes."

"Still in California?"

"Still in California, yes. Los Angeles."

"With that girl?"

"What was her name?"

"Annis."

"Odd sort of name for a girl. Or is it her patronym?"

"I don't know. He said that he was working at last. He'd found a job as maintenance man at something called a free school. Annis apparently has a little money each month."

"Do you think he will marry her?"

"I don't know whether she would marry him."

"I suppose that means you are becoming liberated, Lily."

She sniffed, and returned to her novel. When she was certain that he was not looking at her, she peeked across the room to the Sisley. Magnus had bought it for her in October. It hung in the place of the Stubbs drawing of the horse, although she had actually preferred the Stubbs horse. That had been relegated to the dining room.

"Mark has found his level at last," Magnus was saying. "Maintenance man. That means cleaner. I'm surprised that in the city of the angels the position is not referred to as maintenance engineer."

"He said he is also taking classes at a yoga institute."

"And belongs to the Che-Mao-Lumumba Revolutionary Tactics Chess League, no doubt. Didn't he tell you sometime before the inquest that it was yoga—those damnable exercises—which had finally pushed him over the edge? I should think he'd stay away from that sort of thing."

"You know very well it wasn't that. I don't imagine I need particularize."

"Please don't," said Magnus, sounding rather wounded. "But even he said that it played a part in his crackup."

"Julia played a larger part," Lily said maliciously.

"I think I just said that I did not require reminding. A very nasty shock, finding that my wife spent her last night before committing suicide in another man's bed. Especially that lunatic's bed. And the bloody fool didn't even possess the wit to see what Julia was going through." Magnus stared at his hands, which he had clasped tightly in his lap.

"We can be very grateful she left that—letter," Lily said substituting the last word for "note." "It really did make things much clearer. I did think the coroner was right, don't you? To think that it proved instability of mind and was a clear indication of suicidal intent?"

"It offends me to see any man lead a jury to that extent," Magnus growled. "Coroners have far too much power in this country. Little gods. But yes, Lily, for the thousandth time, yes. I do think the coroner was right. Of course he was bloody right. There's no doubt about it. Any fool looking at the condition of that house and her car would know that her mind was gone. Now do you suppose we might have some tea? Actually, I'd rather have a drink. Would you get me one? No, I'll get it myself." He rose and moved toward the drinks trolley.

"Do have some cheese and biscuits, Magnus. There's a bit of Stilton on the sideboard."

"One cannot get a real Stilton anymore," he said. "Only supermarket rubbish. And have you seen or, heaven forbid, tasted what they have the gall to refer to as Sage Derby? It should be fed to birds. A decent pig wouldn't touch it."

"I just thought you might like a bite of some nice cheese and bikkies," she said, watching him splash whiskey into a tumbler. He took even more than she had expected. "I didn't mean to upset you."

"I . . . am . . . not . . . upset."

"Magnus, you know that I am deeply, truly grateful to you for not being affected by my silliness on that last day Your steadfastness was simply remarkable. I lost my head, I was an utter fool, and you were so strong, you wouldn't be shaken, not in the least, and I am enormously grateful to you for that. I am grateful for your clear head and for your strength."

He glanced at her, and took a long swallow of his drink. "You shouldn't be grateful that I avoided being an ass. That's a negative sort of compliment." But she saw that he was calmer.

"And I shall never cease to be grateful that she wrote that note," she said. "If she hadn't given the game away by naming two of you, well . . ."

"Well," he said. "Tellingly put, Lily." He went back across the room and sat carefully in his chair. Magnus seemed to Lily to be gaining weight with every day. "I should have been in the soup, at least until they tried to 'pin it on' Mark."

"Do you know, I think that I appreciate how she felt. Not about you or even Mark, of course, but how she must have felt about *life,* when I was being so foolish on that day, I experienced the most remarkable sensation of utter hopelessness and despair. It was quite total. I felt utterly gray and washed-out, as though everything bright was long behind me. Julia must have felt something of that kind."

"Julia was not in a rational frame of mind. None of us can know what she thought about anything, much less something so vaporous as *life*." He looked at her sourly. "You didn't see the condition of that house."

"I couldn't go in there," she said. "I just couldn't do it." She switched to a safer topic. "Have you had any luck with the house?"

"Nobody is buying houses now, especially not houses as criminally expensive as that one. That officious twerp at Markham and Reeves told me the market is worse than it's been for fifteen years."

"Have you been to the cemetery yet, Magnus?" She had been earlier in the week, to see to the flowers.

"No, not really. Not since the funeral. I can't abide Hampstead cemetery. It looks like a suburb of Melbourne."

"Julia never liked it either."

"Rot. Utter rot. How can you claim to know such a thing?"

"Because she told me on the day of Kate's funeral. She said that she wished Kate could have been buried in an older cemetery. In Highgate."

"I don't believe that Julia held a firm opinion on a boneyard she saw only once, and then so exhausted she could scarcely stand upright."

Lily shrugged, irritated with him.

"Anyhow, nobody seems to want the damned house," he said. This was an oblique apology to her, and she peeked again at the Sisley painting. He was still talking, of course. "People look at it and they don't like it, for some reason. Did I tell you that that McClintock person wrote wondering if Julia would sell him his furniture back? Said he couldn't find any furniture like it in Barbados. He'd have had a shock if he could have seen his precious furniture."

"That frightens me," she said. "Please don't dwell on it."

"I wasn't about to dwell on anything," he said and

gulped at his drink again. "Anything good on the goggle box tonight?"

"Nothing," she said. "I thought I might try reading one of those books Julia had. I'll be finished with this novel by tonight, and I thought I'd try one of hers. That's an odd coincidence, isn't it? I didn't have time to look at them for ages, and then I didn't want to. But it seems a pity to let them go unread. There's a nice long one about a rainbow. I think I'll begin with that, it looks a lovely read. She did have a lot of books, didn't she?"

"It was because she was friendless," Magnus said flatly.

"How can you, Magnus?" she said, genuinely surprised. "Julia had friends. You and I were certainly her friends. And I suppose Mark was a friend of a sort."

"Bloody Mark. I hope he falls under a bus."

"Mark has suffered a great deal."

Magnus turned away in impatience. "Are you sure there's nothing on the box? I'd like to watch something tonight."

Lily knew that this meant that he wished to spend the evening with her, and that he would fill it by insulting the television and all who watched it. She wished that he would leave—Magnus was in one of his carping moods, which lately annoyed Lily more than they once had. "Nothing you would care for, Magnus. You despise the television, as we both know. But," she added more from habit than desire, "you might stay for dinner. This is one of my vegetarian nights. I'll make a big salad."

Magnus shuddered. "I could get something from a restaurant and bring it back. I don't like these meatless Tuesdays of yours."

As neutrally as possible, she said, "If you wish."

"Right, then."

In exasperation, she thrust down her book and went over to the window on the terrace. Her flowers still bloomed vigorously, and were dazzlingly, violently colored in the damp gray air. To Lily, they looked like little flags of contentment—they said *we, at least, have no problems.*

Behind her, Magnus cleared his throat. "Just out of curiosity, my darling, do you still go to those groups of yours?"

Lily looked into the deep green of the treetops.

"Not as often as before," she said.

"Why is that? Don't you fancy the new swami?"

She let her gaze travel down the rough, pitted bark of the trees. On this cold, cheerless November day few people lingered in the park, and the men and women on the long path rushed by, their hands deep in the pockets of their coats. They looked gray and insubstantial before the great trees, like smoke blown past.

"Oh, Mrs. Venable is acceptable," she said, not paying much attention to what she was saying. "I don't feel the same about the meetings." Now she was watching a child in a blue hooded coat recklessly ride a bicycle down the path, which was forbidden. None of the people on the path seemed to care, as if their opinions were smoke too. "But I don't like to disappoint the others," she said. The child swung off the bicycle and propped it against one of the trees. A girl's bicycle, Lily noticed. "Rosamund Tooth is such an old dear, and Nigel Arkwright can be quite charming when he doesn't babble on so," she said. The child on the path had turned around and was now apparently scrutinizing the ground, her cowl making her look like a dwarfish monk. "But I'm not as interested as I once was," Lily said. "Mrs. Venable's speciality is communing with the departed, through a control named Marcel, and I've always thought that was a shade—you know." Irritatingly, Magnus snorted, lumping her with the class of people who sought information from controls named Marcel. She could now see the pale glimmer of the girl's face. The child was staring straight ahead, as if counting to herself. Then she tilted up her face and looked right at Lily. Her eyes were blue and expressionless. With both hands, still holding Lily's eyes with her own, she swept back the hood and revealed hair the color of white gold.

Lily jumped back from the window, whirled around, and uttered the first sentence to appear in her mind. She said, "We should never have buried Julia in Hampstead cemetery."

Magnus said, "What?"